PRAISE FOR T

"Jerry Mikorenda's first novel for young adults, *The Whaler's Daughter*, ticks all the boxes: a fascinating saga that takes place in a faraway place and time featuring a courageous and ambitious young heroine who aspires to more. Twelve-year-old Savannah Dawson's efforts to earn a place on her father's whaling boat at the turn of the twentieth century in Australia will inspire twenty-first-century readers to hold fast in their quest to attain their dreams. A rollicking good story!"

— Karen Dionne, award-winning bestselling author of *The Wicked Sister*

"In *The Whaler's Daughter*, main character Savannah Dawson's engaging honesty and rollicking energy sweep readers up in this coming-of-age adventure. Jerry Mikorenda's YA novel debut delivers a touching, funny, sometimes gritty, always heartfelt ride."

— A. M. Jenkins, author of the Delacorte Prize-winning novel *Breaking Boxes* and the Printz Honor Book *Repossessed*

"What if *Moby Dick* were turned inside out? *The Whaler's Daughter* brings a girl and a pod of blackfish—orcas—together in a dance of vengeance and takes them to a place of hope. You'll fall in love with Savannah Dawson, a mashup of Scout Finch and Kahu Paikea Apirana, the heroine of *Whale Rider*."

— Elizabeth Gaffney, author of *When the World Was Young* and host of *The 24-Hour Room*

THE WHALER'S DAUGHTER

Jerry Mikorenda

Fitzroy Books

Published by Fitzroy Books
An imprint of
Regal House Publishing, LLC
Raleigh, NC 27612
All rights reserved

https://fitzroybooks.com

Printed in the United States of America

ISBN -13 (paperback): 9781646030705
ISBN -13 (epub): 9781646030958
Library of Congress Control Number: 2020941120

Interior and cover design by Lafayette & Greene
lafayetteandgreene.com
Cover images © by C.B. Royal

Regal House Publishing, LLC
https://regalhousepublishing.com

Printed in the United States of America

For my wife and to Mom,
who began her final journey before seeing this.

"O wild West Wind, thou breath of Autumn's being."

— Percy Shelly, "Ode to the West Wind"

PART I

The Chock Pin

1

There were only two whaleboats on the bay. Neither one of them had room for me.

I began my day as I always did, lugging those dreaded pots to the fire pit to make a bushman's stew. Their big iron bellies slogged through the sand as if they were drunken sailors being dragged to Sunday service. I set them on the coals, dropping my gunnysack of victuals to climb the dunes looking out over the water.

Low tide stretched the sandbars into the bay. I pulled my shawl tight against the breeze and removed my cooking bonnet. The wind lifted my hair across my face. I listened to the familiar sounds of oars locking, feet stomping, and wood slapping water. I gathered in my long billowing tresses from below my waist and held them like an infant in my arms. The crew rowed past without the slightest notion I was there cooking their meal. Lon stood in the nearest boat waving his oar like a cricket bat to belly laughs.

My whole life, I had heard that the Dawson name meant something. That a Dawson's word was trusted and their skills unquestioned.

I cupped my hands around my mouth and yelled out at the boats, "Well, I'm a Dawson!" but the waves licked my words out of the air and everything went quiet.

I glanced over to where the Echo River flowed into Reflect Bay. Dawson Station lay there like a rotting fish in the sand. On the far end sat the tryworks, with its caved-in brick furnace and rusty cauldrons that turned Bible-sized slabs of whale blubber to oil every autumn. The bunkhouses lay a quarter-mile away from our highland castle, Loch Bultarra—a name that made no sense and sounded more important than it was. Beyond the family graves, smoke from the village huts clung to the hills.

It was all dying the slow, painful demise of neglect.

I wasn't sure if I was feeling the sun beating on my head and shoulders or if it was Papa's glare. It was a fine thing for him to be spending his days guarding me as if I were in a gaol yard. He stood watching from the widow's walk atop Loch Bultarra. He liked to observe the crew from a distance, see their weaknesses. Staying in the shadows, I knew he saw everything from up there. The whole empty house sighed with regret whenever he took a step. But he never chose to go in the direction I wanted—we never visited the graves together to make our peace with what lies there.

It had been eight years since my brothers, Eli and Asa, had perished in the bay and since the madness from it had driven Charlie Brennan from harpoons to soup ladles.

"Been six weeks since ya kissed off to the Pelican House, Brennan," I shouted, scattering my cats. "If I'd known you retiring meant me being cook, I would've staked you here by ya beard."

I pulled my hair back from my eyes and looked over at the iron pots. I was shackled to those two iron galoots staring at me with gaping mouths. I slide-stepped back down into the pit and opened the gunnysack filled with whatever fish, meat, or poultry ended up being caught, found, or plucked that day. That's the delight of a bushman's stew. You never know what the next mouthful will bring.

Lugging the sack, I said to myself, *Savannah, you're twelve now, the same age your brothers were, what do you have to show for it?*

I pulled Brennan's heavy cleaver from the wood block and took to hacking at a golden snapper. I threw the good parts to those who deserved them—my cats.

"Of all the chowder-headed jobs," I mumbled, thwacking the tail off. "I ain't no Jack Nasty-Face to trifle with."

"All these gentlemen of three outs," I hollered, tearing the leg of a skinned rabbit from its socket. "I'd like to knock every one of 'em in the head with last season's ship biscuit."

The tails, fish heads, and guts went into those hungry pots for the crew. I did the same with the salt horse. I cut off the dried green parts of meat just like Brennan had showed me, but they were destined for the pots, not the pit. I hacked possum joints, a right large iguana, onions, and spuds into the mixture.

Looking up from my bloody chopping stump, I saw the crew in the first boat catching crabs. Their oars cut too deep into the water and they didn't keep time with the stroke. I laughed as the two guilty dags slipped off their seats onto the hull. Neither vessel had been left in the harbor slings long enough to swell up their planks proper. Those boats would leak before long. Listening to the lads singing agitated me even more. I ripped a still-wiggling eel out of the bag. Its long neck flopped up and down on the chopping block as the crew's hoots and hollers bellowed across the water.

"I ain't no cook. And what's fair is fair!" I shouted, whacking the large round center of the eel and snapping it into a pot with my blade. "It's my birthright to be part of the hunt as much as any of them."

I kicked a bag of duff into one pot and slammed the iron lid down onto the other. I salted the open pot, then plopped down on a dune.

A glint of sun caught Brennan's cleaver, winking at me where it was stuck upright in the chopping block. The boats were off in the distance, out of earshot now, and the curtains were drawn closed inside the widow's walk.

I walked over to the wooden stump and sank to my knees in front of it. I ran a finger along the edge of the cleaver. I brushed off what dried guts remained on the block and placed my face next to the blade. Brushing back my hair, I could see my reflection on the shiny flat steel. Papa had removed all the mirrors in the house years ago. The light shadows on the walls where they had once hung were the only footprints left that showed they'd ever existed.

I studied the reflection of the scars on my right cheek. The deep, bumpy crevasses reminded me of gullies after a storm. I ran my finger down the terrain of my cheek and then along the razor-sharp edge of the blade. I flinched as my blood mixed with all that went into the pots. Then I pried the cleaver loose from the wood with the twisting sound of bone cracking and grabbed a fistful of my hair, laying it across the block.

I lifted the blade as high as I could.

And brought it down. Again and again the blade swung. Left, right, up, down.

Large chunks of my hair fell next to me as I slashed and slashed again. When I couldn't cut any more on the block, I stood and hacked as much as I could pull. It tangled in my hands as if trying to bind me, but I continued to slice and cut and rip until I grabbed for hair and there was nothing but air to hold.

The breath rushed out of me as the cleaver fell to the sand. I felt the coolness of the offshore breeze on the back of my neck, tickling the jagged hay stalks of hair sticking out of my head. All at once I was frightened of what I had done—but free, too. If Papa needed a boy for the boats, I'd meet him halfway.

2

The boats slowed and drifted as the sore shoulders of the lads gave way to fatigue. The whole group was flatter than week-old beer in an open barrel. Papa watched his crew limp in. He bit his lip, trying to swallow his agitation at their sloppy performance.

I tied my cooking bonnet on out of habit and got to serving.

I lifted the pots from the cinders, using a log to set the handles straight up, and dragged them about four feet apart. Next, I grabbed the old yoke Brennan had made with cut-out grooves on the arms for the pot handles to slide into. I squatted in a most unladylike fashion to get the handles aligned before pressing my weight upward. The wooden harness bit into my shoulders and bent to near cracking but held. I must have looked like an ox slowly trudging toward the table.

The pots warbled and belched steam.

My left knee buckled.

I stiffened my right leg and shifted my weight to it, making sure both feet were far enough apart to keep me from toppling. I felt the steady flow of heat rocking on both sides of me as I took baby steps back toward the crew's mess deck, which was never a deck if truth be told. The shortened steps gave me plenty of time between the balancing and shoulder pain to think of what I would say to Papa.

It was a practical thing I did.

Yes, it was, wasn't it? Cutting my hair would make sense to an adult if I made it seem that I had a whole slew of reasons for doing it. At the right moment, I could mention how easy it would be for me to slip into one of the whaleboats with no girlish encumbrances.

Papa was already waiting in the grove of trees near the tables. He had one foot on a stump. The wrinkles on his face drew sail taut as he puffed air out of his cheeks, mumbling to himself. Papa stared out at the bay, his head half-cocked to the left as if he were expecting it to answer him back. His long fingers snapped, pointing me to the big table.

"Set 'em apart on either end so they won't go picking through one pot and trying to grab something else from the other," he barked, looking straight ahead.

"Aye," I mouthed, out of breath as the sand crunched beneath the pots.

Papa continued watching the boats without giving the slightest glance toward me. I was a ghost to him as much as any hiding in the graves across the way.

I wrapped my shawl around the handle of the farthest pot and hop-dragged it to the other end of the table. Still managed to burn my forearm and wrists, not that anyone cared. What was left of the bowls, spoons, and forks from last year sat waiting for the crew. There was hot water enough for them to dip-clean their dishes afterward. I started to angle for Papa's line of sight when the first boat hit the float dock. The second one knocked the first away, followed by a stream of cussing that flowed faster than whale oil down a hot plank.

Lon strutted through the dune grass followed by Warrain, Abe Hobson, and Ned Hanlon. Some of the seasonal blokes had already straggled into camp. The Gretch brothers came up from Victoria; Uri the Mad Russian worked his way down on a steamer from Sydney. Every year, the Arab Bashir appeared as a blur dancing out from the conical wind of a willy-willy before quietly taking his place.

I remained away from the table as they pawed and grumbled over the victuals. I was as invisible as the forks and spoons banging the table. They each got their bit of duff and passed it to the next, complaining all the while that there were no rations of beer with their meal. Papa said the beer would flow when the oil did. He filled a bowl and sat next to Abe, stealing some of his duff to dunk into the gravy. Nodding his approval, Papa looked about. That's when I stepped up and removed my cook's bonnet and stood there with my hands folded as if waiting for Holy Communion.

The crew kept grunting and snorting, tossing fins, fish heads, or bones on the sand or at one another. When I could no longer take the yapping, the farting, the belching, and the laughing—

"I'm here!" I yelled, stomping my feet. "I do exist."

Abe dropped his spoon and looked the part of a boy hearing his mother calling. Lon's jaw dropped the way a man's does when his birthright gets yanked out from under him. The rest of them froze in silence as we all waited for the one man whose opinion mattered to say something.

My arms stretched out to him as he dug deeper into his bowl without looking up.

"Papa," I said softly.

His nose lifted slowly from the bowl as he continued chewing.

"Something wrong with yer head?" he asked.

The unexpected lift in his voice made the whole table laugh. I realized the long shadows of the demons dogging me were, to the crew, just sand gnats brushed away by these lugs. Papa pushed his face back into the bowl.

I started to stomp back toward Loch Bultarra when one of them yelled, "Rapunzel, now you'll never leave your widow's walk," to laughter and whistles. Well, I turned around and gave one of them pots the flat end of my boot sending all those steaming parts flying at the table.

"I can always jump," I said under my breath.

❧

The next morning, I awoke just before dawn even though I wanted to sleep forever or hide under my pillows with my cats without speaking to anyone again. Ever.

Usually I'd stay up late reading or playing tricks on the blokes in the bunkhouses, but no amount of fun could sway my mood. I was alone and that's all there was to it. Still, I snapped straight up in bed. It was as though the demons from the cook's pit chose that moment to pound my brains back to life.

I shooed meowing Descartes and Humphrey off my bed and tiptoed downstairs. I scanned the purple-shrouded water. They called it Reflect Bay because one-half of it looked the same as the other. The only difference was no one ever said they came from the Doddstown side where we lived. Everyone wished they were in Paradise, even if they had no business being there. The just-lit lamps of Paradise twinkled across the water, wrapping the town in anticipation.

I perched quietly on the front porch railing, longing for the waning stars. This was my wondering time when I imagined what the night sky must look like from Canada, South America, and hundreds of other places I would never see.

In their dying glow, I saw my family whole again, with Mum alive and my brothers Eli and Asa back from the sea that had swallowed them. I pictured us putting out for a hunt. Me pulling the bow oar in front with my brothers rowing behind me. Papa stood in the back, tall as a mast, steering the whaleboat. In just that moment, we caught a perfect glimpse of one another. All of us waved to Mum, who yelled from the shore for us to—

"You're up early for such a cool night," I heard Papa rasp from inside the screen door.

I turned, startled from my vivid imaginings to see his gray shadow in the darkened doorway. Pulling my knees to my chest, I covered my arms so he couldn't see my burns.

"I come down here sometimes when it's quiet," I said.

He walked stiffly toward the porch steps and sat down. Papa lit his pipe and crossed his legs. He brought a heaviness to the air. The longer he sat there the more his pipe smoke smothered my dreams. We stayed that way for a long time, as if we were both alone watching the quarter-slice of moon dissolve into blue ink. I didn't mention that I was thinking about our family and he never asked, either.

"What's this all about?" he asked, motioning his free hand around his head. "Ya caused quite a commotion."

"Well," I said, choosing my words carefully, "I figured it was time for a change, considering the future and all. The calamity wasn't all on me."

"The lads," he said and nodded. "You know there are professionals that do that sort of thing. Frieda barbers a lot of the crew; maybe she can even it out a bit."

I wanted to jump up and say, "I'm part of the danged crew!" but I knew that would make Papa nastier than a cornered wombat. No captain wants his authority questioned. Soon enough, he'd see my deed and sacrifice for what it was.

"That puts me in line with everyone else," I said.

"Good," Papa said. "Spotted the killers making their way back today."

Papa was fond of giving those black-finned beasties credit for helping us hunt oil whales on their journey to winter feeding. As a reward, he shared our catch with them. He told me this story every fall, and the older I got, the harder it was to believe. Off in the distance he'd spotted three gloomy top fins sailing on the inlet. They'd jumped and thrashed about like bandogs waiting for their master. Papa said those clicking sounds were from Matong, he knew them that well. *You know more about them killers than you do me*, I thought bitterly.

"Mighty early for them to return," he said, puffing smoke into the warming air. "Bodes well for the season."

Papa seemed so content sitting with his elbows on his knees that I just let my earlier thoughts tiptoe to my mouth.

"Now that they're back, could you use another—?"

"Got crew enough to fill the boats we have," he said, standing to relight his pipe.

The boats we have. They hadn't been full the last season, being two oarsmen short most hunts. All of a sudden, one of the demons in my head broke its leash and raced straight out.

"Aye, you do at that," I said, glancing down at the railing, "and not one of them female."

"We'd be in damned napkins if it came to that," he said, shaking his head.

"Brennan says cook's helper always leads to the boats. It's tradition," I said, jumping off the railing. "I've been doing it two seasons now and this one's looking more like cook than helper."

"Crazy Brennan, he's one to yabber," said Papa, his head bobbing as he leaned on his knees. "Maybe the two of ya should start your own station."

"He might be off his beam, but he sees when fair is fair," I said, folding my arms, "and you promised."

"I promised a little girl we'd fly in a balloon over a volcano, too, but I didn't expect the near adult would hold me to it."

"I'm a Dawson, ain't I?"

"For now, but that'll change too," he said, exhaling. "It's the nature of things." I was close enough to legal marrying age to know what he meant. Close enough, too, to worry whenever Lon Taggart or the likes of him were skulking about. I had two choices to carry as my burden—become the crew cook or a wife, as if there were a difference between them.

"You looking to square me up for a new boat?" I snapped. "Because if ya are, you're selling short."

"Just thought you handled cook pretty well, that's all," Papa said, getting up slowly until we faced each other.

"Did what I had to do," I uttered, understanding the gravity our talk was taking.

I stood eye to eye with Papa these days, but I couldn't look straight at him and lie. "Not wanting regular service with it," I croaked out, as if my mouth were full of sand.

Papa took off his cap and slapped it against his thigh. "No crew would serve in a hen boat if that's what you're thinking," he said, biting the pipe stem as he turned away from me, "and there's no one worth the risking of finding out." He marched off then, leaving me to stand alone on the porch.

The harshness of his voice wilted me. The weight of each word pounded my image of our family into the sand. I realized that I didn't know anything about my brothers or my mother. The whalers whom I've played with—and who taught me everything they knew—never wanted me around. All my dreams about this place were just shadows from my imagination, night fog that disappeared by morning.

I'd never asked Papa for anything before this. Well, once for a bisque doll at a harvest festival and he got me a spyglass instead. Another time I wanted to try perfume, but everything stinks of whale oil anyway so I didn't utter a word. I'd forgotten about those balloon stories. I used to make Papa tell me about faraway places we'd visit. We were going to anchor the balloon to the widow's walk and escape whenever we wanted. We'd be mates drifting over the plains of Africa and the Great Wall of China, and be back in time for brekkie.

All we had left now were the dead embers of those memories. How could things go so wrong between us when all I did was grow into who I am? Somehow we ended up on opposite sides of the Capertee Valley, me just a cook's helper and him barking orders.

It wasn't supposed to be this way in a million years.

I always thought Papa and I saw the world the same way. That we'd come around to agreeing about most anything that came up. Having your dreams trampled by someone who could help you realize them is worse than not having them at all. Papa trusted those blubber dogs in the bay more than me.

I stayed there until the tide let out, and my hopes of whaling with Papa went with it. Before long, the wind rose off the bay and I stomped back up to my room with lathered demons in tow. I slammed down onto the damp aired sheets and felt I was evaporating into them. If I was old enough to be chasing a bludger of a husband down the streets of Paradise, I could surely handle wallowing in a whaleboat. Not worthy of the risking? Given the chance, I'd out-swim and out-row any boy from here to the old Northern Territory. I cut my hair so it wouldn't tangle with the irons or get caught in the lines. Yet the crew looked at me like I was some street yobbo.

I heard the killers starting to thrash and play. How Papa could still look at them after what they had done to my brothers was beyond me. If this was my watch, I'd run the lot of those blackfish out to sea with hot lances. Their flute-like songs mocked the few memories I had of my family. It was as if they were singing that I wasn't good enough to hunt with the likes of them.

But I knew I was.

"I am! I am!" I shouted, pounding my fists into the mattress.

3

I stretched out to ponder the barney I'd had with Papa, and my pending visit to Frieda, but my feet kept dangling off my bunk. It's been that way for a while. I had grown a bit these past months. Papa had had to get the carpenter to saw off the aft end of my bed. He added a section fastened with wood dowels and tar, thinking it wouldn't change anymore. The next thing he knew, in a few months he'd had to add another piece. Three times he'd had to do that, and three times he'd given me the evil eye, as if I'd been growing just to spite him. Next time, he said, he would haul up a stoved whaleboat from the bay and be done with it. Bunking in that might be the only way I get in one.

The whole blasted place was built that way. A piece of driftwood found here, a cabinet that had washed up on shore there. Best as I can remember, Papa said they slap-dashed Loch Bultarra together from three shipwrecks. The main mast from the *Lincolnshire* was smack in the middle of my room; her large brass porthole gave me a view of the inlet. The floors came from the *Rosa Lee*'s afterdeck, and the outside walls were planking pried off the Spanish whaler, *Coracini*.

We lodged in a most curious hovel where all sorts of odd things suddenly appeared and got nailed, tied, or tarred to walls, floors, or ceilings. Reweighing Papa's words, I imagined I might end up as another one of those things fixed to a wall. The best way to hedge that bet was to get my visit to Frieda going.

Stepping onto the front porch, the warm breeze caressed my face like a mother's hand. The bunkhouses were empty and the boats were gone. All that remained from the morning was Papa's cold pipe lying on the rocker. I wanted to toss it into the bay. Instead, I placed it in the porch rafters where he couldn't find it. Strolling to the Hobson's cottage, the emptiness of lost memories returned with darkening clouds.

Frieda poked, pried, and pulled every bristle of sheared hair on my head. I was her plucked chook at a Christmas fair ready for dressing.

"What on earth came over you, Savannah?" she lamented in her heavy Castilian accent.

It wasn't anything on earth, I thought, as I fiddled in my head for an answer. Frieda asked me again with a chop of anger in her voice. "I don't know. I got inspired."

"People get inspired to do great deeds, not to take hatchets to their heads," Frieda added with a hard pull.

"Ow!"

"It would be more than that if you were my daughter," she said, before uttering something in Spanish that made me glad I never learned the language.

"It's only my hair," I offered weakly.

"Your hair was an ocean of honey. It was your door to all the niceties of Paradise," said Frieda, motioning where my phantom locks once covered my scarred cheek and down to my hips. "It was so long and beautiful that Queen Ena could've fashioned it into a wig."

The back of my hand jerked up to shield my pitted face. I kept it there as Frieda tried to even out all the cowlicks and slanted chops I'd made. She slapped my hand away, saying there'd be no hiding from it now. Frieda tried to even out what was left of my hair and that was that.

"You were the first Dawson girl in three generations," said Frieda, admiring her repair work. "Every day, your mum and I would brush each side of your hair fifty times while singing to you. You loved the attention."

"I don't remember any of that," I said, none too happy

with the way this new style felt pinned to my scalp. "No one ever talks about my mum, including you."

"Well, time to get back to my poddies," said Frieda, abruptly stuffing the scissors in her apron and chasing after Benjamin, Etta, and her three other giggling children flying about the room.

I wandered back from the Hobsons' feeling as if Frieda had pulled a rug out from under me again. She's always been like a big sister, but she only goes so far. She dropped hints of what it was like in the old days, told me about certain things that had happened, and abandoned me in a room empty of memories.

I veered off from Loch Bultarra and headed toward the clearing in the woods to pay my respects at the family plot. Humphrey, Mr. Nubbles, and Quilp spotted me there and followed me into the woods, their tails curled in the air like question marks. Moss tears and dampness stained the worn stones of the long dead. Most everyone I'd heard about was there. Pop and Nana were in the back row with some of Papa's uncles and brothers. In the front, where the sunlight broke through the trees, Eli and Asa were close enough to be arm in arm. Mum was next to them with spaces for Papa and me when it came to it.

I looked upon all this grayness and tried to imagine the bone and sinew of those lying beneath. I picked up a long stick in front of Mum's stone and drew in the dirt where the dry grass shrank below the earth. Whenever I did this, it felt as if I were poking the sleeping dog of the past awake to make him do tricks for me. Ever the bad boy, Quilp pawed at my every movement until I chased him away.

After a minute I pictured what Mum looked like. She appeared a little different every time I sketched. Sometimes, I just formed her eyes or lips. Other days, I showed her reading, looking for me, or smiling at plain nothing. Happiness.

I remembered last year Abe Hobson told me Mum had once been a missionary. It was during the final boiling of the season, when the air hung heavy with black smoke and the smell of rancid, smoldering blubber. I started etching her likeness wearing a uniform with her hair under a proper bonnet, just as Abe described her to me. I added a brooch to her jacket like the one I'd found in the attic. I drew Eli and Asa wearing fishing caps and smiling, their lines waiting to drop. I carved Pop Alex with a stern look that was all beard bursting from his face like the wild surf after a storm.

It was as if that drawing stick were my hand reaching down into the loamy darkness and pulling them back to life.

The sun baked the back of my neck as the voices of the crew bellyached off the groves of red ash and sandalwood in front of me. I ran down to the beach and onto the quay where the boats pulled alongside the float dock.

"Only two boats?" I yelled down, catching their lines. "No whale?"

"Was a good chase we gave, but that's all we have," bellowed Papa, tapping his lance on the tub filled with unwound rope.

"Empty barrels and stiff shoulders is our reward this day," said Abe, before ordering oars up as they glided in. "We were done in by leaky boats and men who couldn't hold their water."

Sure enough, our two empty boats were taking on water just as I knew they would. The first sank up to the gunwales. The second leaked from the bow, making neither seaworthy. I turned to Papa, but he gave me a look as though I didn't belong, so I headed back to the family plot.

The wind was already blowing my etchings to smithereens. Crouching by Mum's grave, I noticed two sticks on her stone. They were charcoal drawing pencils. I glanced about the clearing but didn't see anyone. A gentle breeze lifted the tree branches in a heaving sigh. Behind me the men continued to laugh and make light of their blubber-less try pots.

I picked up the pencils and studied them. The point on one was sharp; the other had a flat edge for drawing thick black lines. The hair stood on the back of my neck as I peered into the green gloom in front of me. I wondered who had left them and why those pencils were there.

4

After I found the pencils, I felt someone was watching me everywhere I went. When the pickers left for the orchard the next day, I fetched some eggs. Carrying them up the front porch steps in my apron, I saw another pencil lying on my dreaming spot. This one was green. I dropped all the eggs on the stairs. I ran from one side of the deck to the other but saw nothing and heard nothing.

You'd think with all those well-trained cats to patrol the place one of them might have made a peep. Instead, I had eight silent scallywags not worth the insides of their cat boxes. I picked up the pencil and slipped it into my dress pocket. I paced back to the front door, keeping my eyes on the tree line and ran up the stairs. I placed the green pencil next to the others on the barrel I used for a nightstand. I yanked the pulley rope to remove the canvas covering the porthole. I stared intently, barely breathing, hoping to catch a look-see of something, anything. It was a long time standing for nothing.

I washed the eggs off the porch so Papa wouldn't see them and popped out the back door. Whistling "John Kanaka," I stopped to adjust my garments before marching past the well, coop, and hog pens toward the apple and peach groves. Papa bought all this land when the whale money was good. He owned fifty-something acres filled with lumber, fruit, vegetables, and who knew what else.

The orchard was teeming with activity. Oliver and Noah, the Gretch brothers, drove the second wagon far behind Papa and the first batch of pickers. With one eye on the hard cider, Lon and a couple of dags from the bunkhouses were lifting the heavy wooden crates, filled with apples by the wives and children from the farm village, onto the brother's wagon bed.

I should've come sooner, for there was nothing funnier than watching a whaler try to work a horse and cart as if they were boats on the bay. I told the lads the stern was the part with the tail. The bow was the part with the teeth that bites their sterns if they didn't treat the animal with respect.

Abe was lost without an oar or an iron in his hands. He stumbled up the ladder, unsteady as a cabin boy making his first crow's nest climb. At the top of the tree he shouted out a prayer in Hebrew and started plucking apples. The forbidden fruit dropped into barrels faster than gulls into a garbage heap. They corralled me with the children when I should have been up in the trees. I knew Papa liked me on the ground to reach the 'tween areas that fall below the ladders. Each of us had baskets to fill and turn in for wages. I carried ten lug boxes out to where the Red Delicious and Royal Galas were waiting. When I could, I dropped apples into the wee ones' baskets to keep them in the game.

As the afternoon wore on, the sun tucked under the folds of the Cooa Cooa Mountains draping bands of purple mist across the orchard. Papa let the swaggies who showed up feed before they headed off toward a jumbuck station near Walter's Peak. We walked back in a caravan of silence except for Lon. He and the sandgropers broke into the hard cider when Papa wasn't looking. They sang a sailor ditty that hastened the steps of the proper wives frantically fanning themselves against the heat of the lyrics.

The lavender brush reflected a soft violet sheen on the water. Everything led back to the bay. Lon leaned over the wagon slats.

He yelled out, "You, yeah you, lassie," until he finally got my attention.

"You're an unstayed mast, you are," he giddily quipped, staring at my head, "with no rigging to steer ya right."

"That means you're free," offered little Aiden Parsons, pulling on my sleeve.

Because he walked with a limp, everyone called him Peg except me. I figured he had troubles enough without my adding to them. Besides, I knew a thing or two about being marked.

"I know my sails," I snapped, under my breath, "and I'm anything but that."

Lon was a bit of a larrikin. His infatuation with me had more to do with his love for Papa and whaling. He saw himself as the heir apparent to Dawson Station and me as some of the equipment that goes along with it.

He stood in the wagon about to make another grand proclamation. "I...eh," he said, pointing to the sky as he fell back into a bin of apples. His legs kicked straight up like a boxed boomer in the funnies. I let out a bellow that led to more laughs. Papa turned around from driving the first wagon. He gave me a wink and a nod as he snapped the reins. Did that mean he thought I liked Lon and approved? Did he want me to befriend him?

It was hard to tell.

It was sunset before we finished putting all the picking gear away. Papa said he would get a good price for this lot in Paradise. He placed me in charge of storing the rest. Out on the darkened bay, I heard those blackfish snorting like a bunkhouse full of sleeping whalers. I hoped they'd just up and leave, but they didn't seem about to.

The darkening porch matched my mood as I got madder and madder thinking about what Papa had said to me. At the same time, Papa didn't say "you can never" or "you can't be a whaler," he only mentioned the crew wouldn't serve with a girl who wasn't worthy. I sat on the steps bathed in blue after-light and did some thinking. Maybe I could learn my way into this. If I showed Papa I knew my way around a whaleboat, he'd have to give me a shot. There was one person who could tell me if my plan would work or was even worth trying.

Abraham Hobson.

Since it was Sunday the day after next, there wouldn't be any picking and likely no whaling the way those beasts loafed about the bay. That gave me some free time to visit Abe.

I jumped up from the porch steps to take a good stretch before bunking down. That was when I saw it – a ghastly shadow in the distance moving from the forest edge to the graves. At first it looked like a flying fox or maybe a cassowary, but this was much larger. It was the shape of a person for sure. The apparition wavered slowly through the headstones as though drawn by a breeze. There were ghosts enough around to know this was the real thing. Ebenezer Dodd himself haunts the Doddspoint Lighthouse. During a hunter's moon, the barren couple that hanged themselves in the old stone cottage call for any idle, wasteful children to help them.

As quickly as it appeared, the dark specter vanished like hot breath on glass. Shaken, I danced up the steps and into the parlor. The front door slammed shut with me against it. Papa glanced up over his spectacles. He was reading *Lord Jim* again with a plate of cold meat, biscuits, and a cup of buttermilk to keep him company.

"There's more in the icebox," he offered, looking back down at his book.

"No thanks," I said, striking a match to the hallway candle.

I thumped slowly up the stairs, trying to hold the flame. The light pushed in with a soft amber glow, as if the room were dripping with honey. I lit the big lamp next to my old captain's desk. As I started getting into my night things, I looked on the desktop and there was a fourth pencil. This one was blue. I raced down the stairs half-dressed.

"Has anyone been in my room?" I shouted frantically. "Has anyone come into the house?"

"No one here but us," growled Papa. "Put something decent on, for land sakes."

I ran back up and flung open the porthole again. Outside it was as black as the inside of a stove. As hard as I tried to see, nothing rose from the bleakness. I reached down and grabbed Mr. Nubbles by the scruff of his neck. He meowed sorrowfully, flailing his black and white paws.

"What'd ya see, you mangy oaf?" I said, scratching under his chin. "By jangles, I ought to make mittens out of the lot of ya."

5

The next morning when I began pulling out the apple racks, I found two black bush rats. They tried to scamper out, but I grabbed one by the tail and caught the other under my boot.

The twitchy one I grabbed by the tail yanked this way and that trying to gnaw at me. The other lay quiet under my heel, knowing his days were numbered. I didn't want to prolong the poor vermin's misery, nor take any pleasure in my duties.

Gripping its tail, I whirled him about and whapped his head on Papa's anvil. Sensing impending doom, the other scratched and clawed at the barn floor. It didn't seem a fair or noble fight, so I reached over and dropped a heavy lump hammer on it.

During the rest of my chores, I looked out at the graves. Those twenty gray stones seem so settled, part of the scenery. I tried to imagine that ghost floating around and it made me smile. Perhaps I let my humors or the night vapors get the best of me. I rolled those four pencils around in my pocket to feel where they were. I figured to go over to the graves after hanging the wash.

Passersby who spotted our laundry flapping in the breeze from the exposed mainmast spars atop the roof believed Loch Bultarra was some sort of a rescue station. I always tried to look serious when people asked what type of approaching storm my bloomers and Papa's skivvies were warning them about. With the last sheets snapping in a westerly tacking breeze, our homestead looked like a packet ship at full sail.

On laundry day, I also made a point of spending time in the widow's walk. I pictured Mum up there with my spyglass searching the bay. With no wife to pace its floor longing for the boats to return, the walk remained a glum hollow space haunted by Papa.

After a leftover bean sandwich, I told Papa I was going for my walkabout. He knew I visited the family during them. One day I'm going figure how he can come with me so we can do proper grieving together.

But not this day.

I needed to find out what the devil was stalking me. It wasn't any of the crew playing me because none of them had the patience to drag things out this long.

I made my way over to the wee glen down the gully past Loch Bultarra. I checked grave after grave, but there was no sign of any ghostly presence. Propped against Nana Effie's stone was a shingle-sized piece of wood nearly as thin as cardboard. Behind Nana's grave was another piece of wood and beyond that several more. I picked them up as I walked. The wood slices trailed into the dark green forest.

Dingoes roamed there for sure, along with venomous snakes, water dragons, and deadly funnel spiders. Many a bludger walked in never to walk out. I stood holding my paper-like shingles and wondered what to do. A lone kooka-burra circled overhead, landing high in a boppel tree. It sang a little tune Mum might have hummed to me.

I edged my way into the gully, carefully stepping on the damp rocks.

Phosphorescent moss clung to sun-neglected areas of the forest. The canopy of lush green leaves and column-like trees made it feel as if I were entering a great cathedral rather than a forest. Without much sky to navigate my way, I could easily get lost. I began breaking the wood shingles into strips that I left along the way. Breadcrumbs to help me find my way back.

The ocean of green in front of me was silent and immov-able. I ascended a steep hill as though entering a winding tower. At the top, I rested in the crook of a root to a massive eucalyptus tree that was wider than a whaleboat and as tall as I could see. I felt humbled by its presence and quickly moved along the rim of the hill. I thought of turning back but a yearning to see more drove me down the gully into the tapestry of willowing ferns, flora, and draping moss. I heard a sudden rush of leaves behind me, then one to my left. The wood strips I'd placed to create a trail were gone. It could be playful dingoes…or something else.

"If anyone's there, show yourself!" I shouted.

I sat on a stone outcrop and began sketching the landmarks around me on the shingles I had left to remember where I'd been. I walked further into the thick vegetation, stopping now and again to sketch landmark plants along the way. I pushed aside brush and vines from low-hanging tree limbs. A poisonous tiger snake slinked through the branches above, eyeing me curiously. Now I knew how those rats felt in the apple racks. The ground cover was as high as my waist. As I sketched my location, the pencil point broke.

While I looked in my pocket for another, I heard a great swoosh like a hawk landing.

I snapped up.

Just inches from my nose, the upside-down torso of a bare-chested boy dangled.

Smiling.

His long wavy black hair billowed downward, dancing like a waterspout on the bay. His almond-shaped eyes glowed.

"Might you require this?" he asked, holding a pencil sharpener between his thumb and forefinger.

My mouth opened, but no words came out. I looked up and saw only the empty branch where he'd once hung among a blanket of leaves.

"It came with the set," I heard him say behind me. And there he was standing with his arm extended holding the sharpener in his open palm. He wore a copper inscribed medallion around his neck and white knickers tied with a drawstring. His skin was dark as cocoa.

"You're the one that's been hunting me like I was a wild boar," I shouted, taking a roundhouse swing.

"I assure you I meant no harm," he said, backing away.

"Then who are you?" I asked.

"I am from the village across the inlet."

"I know the crew from there, how's it I've never seen you?"

"I have been training with Uncle for my station in life."

"Well, station this!" I shouted, swinging at him again.

I might as well have been grabbing at wave caps for all the good it did me. He vanished with every swing I took, reappearing just out of arm's reach, with that glint of sunshine smile.

"Your perceptions of my intentions are somewhat askew," he said, effortlessly popping off the base of a tree.

"Only thing wrong with what I'm seeing is you're in the picture," I said, taking a big step as I launched a kick at his gut with my right leg.

As I planted my foot, it slipped on the follow-through.

I was heading to meet whatever crawlers were on the forest floor when a firm grip took hold of my forearm. I could hear tons of critters hovering near my head.

"Please," he said, holding his open hand with the sharpener still in it, "it's meant for you."

"Seeing you got the upper hand, thank you," I croaked.

Before I could say *Free Ned Kelly*, I was back on my feet, dizzy from all that dangling. The blood rushed to my head as he continued to look at me quizzically.

"Are you satisfactory?" he asked.

"Steady as a stockman's hobble," I muttered, unbuttoning my dress pocket and placing the sharpener next to the pencils.

"My name is Calagun," he said, eyeing the landscape.

"I'm Savannah. Savannah Dawson," I replied, offering my hand to shake.

"Indeed, you are related to the master whaler, Caleb," he said, with a firm grip. "I am joining his crew as an oarsman this season. What is your chosen role?"

This fella was full of surprises. My chosen role? How could Papa allow a total stranger into our boats and keep me away? Rolling oakum last season, I did hear some of the girls talking about a young prince. Still, I didn't want to reveal too much about myself.

"Aye, his cook," I answered.

"Cook?" he said. "My observations suggest you are much more than that."

"True," I said, brushing myself off. "I'm also the washer-woman, an apple picker, holystone roller, and whatever else needs to be done that no one wants to do."

"That seems quite odd," the boy said, folding his arms across his chest. "Are you not an heir as Queens Elizabeth and Victoria were?" he asked.

"I am at that, ain't I?" I said, proudly standing up straight. "But Papa rules over me pretty good these days."

"I see," he said.

"The rest of us are over yonder," I said, pointing back toward the glen, "but I guess you know that."

"During my initiation, I wandered through there on occasion," he said, flashing that smile again. "My tossing ceremony was held not far away."

"That's onya!" I said, having overheard the crew talk about the arduous manhood rituals of the villagers. "We don't have anything like that to brag about at Loch Bultarra."

"Loch Bultarra," he said, grazing a hand across his chin. "Scottish for 'lake' and Bultarra meaning the 'joining of two lands' in my tongue. It's a symbol of the bond between our grandfathers who founded the whaling station."

My mouth hung open like a caught cod. It strewth me

through my bones it did. Loch Bultarra had always been a funny name to me. How's it I'd never met this lad before and he knew more about Pop Alex than I did? Why didn't I know more about his family than he did mine?

"Savannah is a very pretty name," he said, changing the subject.

"Anyone who knows me spends time trying to forget it," I said, sheepishly.

"Calagun means 'blue fig' in English," he added. "My mother's Dreaming brought it to her before I was born."

"Calie…" I stumbled, trying to pronounce his name.

"Ca-la-gun," he said, slowly trying to coax me.

"Cal…" I said, trying again. "Would you mind it if I just called you Figgie?"

6

I followed Figgie away from the path I was taking. Anyone picked as an oarsman first time around is worth knowing in my book. For a moment I hesitated, staying a step back as he pushed ahead. The farther we moved away from where we'd met, the more he glided effortlessly through the brush. Like it or not, he was my compass home. I put my trust in him the way Papa did the wind or the stars at sea.

We paced along in silence for a bit when I up and asked, "So why the pencils, mate?"

Figgie didn't answer right away but walked a few steps before stopping. He didn't face me as he talked. "I hope you will use your talent to tell our story to the world," he said, before continuing.

I laughed aloud and asked, "What talent might that be?"

"You are an artist," he said, pausing again.

"You mean that chicken scratch I been doing over by the family plot?"

"Give yourself good measure, Savannah," he said, glancing back. "We both know it's more than that."

"Well, perhaps," I said, feeling the blood rush to my face again, "but I don't know enough about your village to do right by it."

"You're more part of it than you realize," he said, changing direction. "Initially, I did not recognize you with your mane shorn, but I knew only a true artist would be curious enough to follow the trail I made."

"Ah, you've been spending too much time in the woop woop," I said, not liking him putting his stickybeak in my business.

He froze. One leg high in the air, arms outstretched.

I got frightened, wondering if some snake I hadn't heard of had bitten him full of paralysis. "Are you all right?" I asked, looking into his stone face, mouth and eyes wide open. He didn't move or seem to breathe as I approached him. "Say something, dang it."

"Apologize," he said, without moving his lips.

"What?"

"Apologize, for your words have made me stone."

I had a clear shot to slug him right there and walk away from all this nonsense. "So—sorry, mate," I said, stomping my foot.

"There we go," he said, continuing to walk without missing a step. "Cutting hair is a sign of death and mourning in our camp."

"No one's died near the station in a while," I said, leaving it at that.

Figgie led us up a hill to a rocky outcrop. At the top we stood together. Although he was nearly a foot shorter than me, in a way I already looked up to him. Across the ravine, a cliff of red sandstone glowed molten gold in the afternoon sun. "The sand art you practice is sacred to us; it talks to the power from the Great Ancestors of the ground," he said, pointing and speaking to the cliff more than me. "That was once the most sacred place of my people before the miners came."

I heard the pain in his voice and saw the blight upon this place. I imagined the mountain face pristine again and tried to hold on to its beauty, but a sadness flowed over me, washing the image away.

"There is a bond between my village, our ancestors, and the Earth. The miners destroyed it. Now we can no longer connect with who we are."

"Can't you start over?" I asked. "Papa says in Scotland we always did that, it makes the faith grow stronger."

We sat down on the big rock and he told me about the Dreaming. It was an odd conversation to have with someone I'd just met, but I was starting to feel as if I had known Figgie for a long time. His people didn't have places of worship the way we did. In the beginning, he told me, the spirit ancestors created the Earth. When they finished, they became the land, sea, and sky.

"We don't own the earth, the earth owns us," he said, picking up a handful of soil. "This is where we began; this is where our spirits return to be reborn as a rock, bird, or fig tree."

All objects were alive and part of the ancestors' spirit world. The Dreaming was the way Figgie and his people stayed in touch with these spirits. It was something that he was born with and it stayed with him all the time. Through the Dreaming, the laws and the rules for living pass from the ancestors to the next generation.

Listening to Figgie yearn for what his people lost made me think my own problems weren't so desperate after all.

"I'm honored you shared this with me," I said, standing again. "How can I help?"

"Your artwork can show our culture in a way that will help the world understand us," he said. "Please, come in-country and visit our camp. After, we shall return to your station."

We ambled down the ridge toward a sand spit that dripped out the side of the river mouth like tobacco juice from an old sailor's lips. I wore thick leather brogans and Figgie was in his bare feet. I asked if the sharp rocks and thorns bothered him much. He said no because the pain reminded him of what the plants are feeling from my heavy boots. So I took them off.

"That was unnecessary," he said.

"Yet you're glad I did it, aren't you?" I said, wincing with every step.

"Indeed, I am," he added, with a slight look back.

Smoke from the cooking fires mixed with a salty breeze as we approached the encampment. The dark brown wattle-board huts looked like tortoise shells strewn about the bone-white sand. We crossed to the river mouth on a bed of onyx nearly covered by the rising tide. From a distance, villagers said, we appeared to walk on the water. Figgie reached down into the soft wet sand and pulled up several oysters. He pried one open with a pocketknife and offered it to me.

"You must be hungry," he said.

I devoured the cool plump flesh with the briny liquid in one gulp.

The tide dragged at the hem of my skirt as we stood there eating. A crowd of wee ones came to greet us. Figgie tossed the empty shells to them as if they were gold coins. I towered over the whole group as our procession headed into the village. Figgie guided us to a lodge in the center of the camp. He called it the Tjungu. It looked like a meeting hall.

Inside, coals from a circular fire pit glowed orange and green. An occasional flame grabbed toward the sky, spitting gold embers harmlessly toward a hole in the roof. A lone figure sat in a rattan fan chair. He wore a colorful kimono and dark knickers. His hair and beard were as white as mountain snow. Sitting cross-legged, he motioned us to him.

Figgie approached, greeting the old fella warmly in his own tongue. They nodded in agreement as the old bloke waved for me to sit next to him. "This is Uncle," said Figgie, respectfully. "He is a cure man. Please…" Figgie motioned me to move closer to the old man. "He can no longer see with his eyes, but his mind remembers you."

Well, fancy that. I knelt next to him so he could touch my face. He talked to Figgie in rapid sentences. The tips of his fingers felt like croc skin.

"He says you have high cheekbones and a slender nose," said Figgie, embarrassed by the observations, "but wants to know why your hair is so short."

"So I can work the whaleboats someday," I said, crossing my arms.

Figgie looked surprised as one might be catching the scent of something awful that passed.

Uncle nodded his head repeatedly and wanted to know if I had green eyes. "She does," Figgie said, matter-of-factly in their tongue and in English. The old man nodded in recognition as he rubbed the back of his hand on my right cheek where the pockmarks gullied my skin. I looked away, ashamed of my disfigurement.

"Uncle thinks your Dreaming is very strong," Figgie said.

Before I could say anything, Uncle clapped his hands. A group of men entered the Tjungu. Two of them carried a sea tortoise shell and placed it upside down on the coals. They shoved heated rocks into the neck hole and tuffed grasses in the other openings so it cooked in its own juices. We sat in a circle and listened as Figgie translated Uncle's tales of Prince Jimmy and the ancestors. With each spoken word another coal glowed until the whole fire pit flickered blue.

The simmering sweetness escaping the shell made me hungry. Uncle shouted and two older women entered the hut. They quietly scoffed at me as they cut blocks of the chalk-white meat and strips of bright green fat from the shell. One of them slapped my hand away as the steaming coolamon passed my way. Figgie grabbed the long, flat plate and held it before me. Uncle chastised the women. They knew I didn't belong with the men, yet where was my place? Where were my table and ancestors? We drank kava tea as the afternoon sun drifted toward the mountains. Everyone seemed so content and relaxed.

I had to ask.

"Does Uncle know any stories about my family?"

Figgie looked at Uncle, who sat motionless absorbing what Figgie translated. He threw his hands in the air. I wondered if he was reacting to the whispering among the other men. Uncle held a shaky finger aloft as if he were about to proclaim something and slumped into his chair.

"Uncle grows tired," said Figgie. "He must rest now."

"What was he going to say?" I asked Figgie, rising to my knees.

All the loud chatter in the room dribbled to a stop. Figgie looked confused by my question so I asked it again. "We must go," he said. "It has been a long day."

Uncle reached for help to stand. I stretched across the fire pit, grabbing his hand before any of the others did. The heat seared my arm as I solicited him again. I squeezed his palm as hard as I could, but his grip lashed my fingers, crushing them together.

"He knows what you want, Savannah," said Figgie. "The question is, do you know what you are asking for?"

"I just want to learn something about my life," I said, looking at Uncle's weathered face.

"But not today," said Figgie, looking at Uncle. "I'm sorry, Savannah."

Figgie walked me back along the shore in silence. Soon we reached the river mouth. I'd never realized how close his village was to Loch Bultarra. I heard the men in the bunk-houses singing and carousing as their oil lamps flickered in the dusk. Farther away, Abe's settlement was finishing a day of worship while a few Arab whalers prayed facing northwest. The next morning, church bells would ring. We stopped at a grove of trees. Papa angered if I didn't return before dark. I felt most peculiar that day. Yet I wanted to see this perplexing boy again.

"Might you be coming about from time to time?" I asked.

"Unquestionably," Figgie said, disappearing into the trees.

I glanced at the darkening cemetery. There were no ghosts. Although I could barely see, I knew that from now on everything would look different.

I rolled the pencils over again in my pocket to make sure

they all made it through the journey. These woods and graves aren't so silent after all. At least now I knew there were some secrets buried about my past. Yet I couldn't let them deter me.

I had much to do if I ever expected to draw wages on a whaleboat. It all started with Abraham Hobson.

7

We didn't waste any time getting the boats refitted.

Papa, Abe, Warrain, and Lon did a top-to-bottom inspection of the whaleboats. For good measure, they pawed over the tryworks, too. One of the boats wasn't seaworthy and needed the hull planking removed down to the ribbing because of woodworms. The other three had to be repacked, sealed, and painted. If you added in the one that went missing after the storm last season, we were down two boats. They also found split oars, two ripped sails, and broken thwarts. Frayed ropes, rusty irons, bent lances, and missing buckets were among the other things that needed fixing.

The tryworks had its problems, too. Three courses of brick holding the pots broke loose. It seemed to agitate Papa more than any brick should. He kicked the loose ones off with his boot and started pawing at the cracked mortar with his hands.

The history of Reflect Bay was holed up in those layers, Papa earbashed to anyone listening. I'd never paid his talk any mind before. But now that I knew that Figgie's and my grandpops, Prince Jimmy and Pop Alex, were partners, the story took on a whole new meaning. Papa said they both dragged the lower stones for the tryworks here when whaling was just a side business for them. They made lime for the mortar by burning oyster shells. Convicts shipped here on the *Castle Forbes* made all the bricks with the arrows on them. The next five rows of brick had come from abandoned buildings in Doddstown.

"This place isn't worth whale scat," Papa said to no one in

particular as he smacked two bricks together. "Well, there's
no time for wallowing, work's to be done after the Sabbath."

Sometimes the best way to get a history lesson is to witness it.

Everyone at the station was set with chores to put the
place in Bristol fashion. I was to seal and paint the boats
with the children from the village while Papa and the crew
prepared to do the heavy lifting. I held my breath as he went
down the list, praying he wouldn't bring up cooking. I let out
a deep sigh as Papa headed back toward the house.

"Don't forget we have meals to plan, Savannah!" he yelled,
without turning around.

Well, that made it as good a time as any to go visit Abe. His
cottage was just down the hill from the bunkhouses where
the orchard began. Eight other Jewish families had settled
there along with a blacksmith and a tanner. Abe had been
Papa's first mate for as long as I could remember. If you
talked to Abe, it was as good as gamming with Papa himself.

Abe and Frieda lived in a whitewashed wattle-and-daub
house with their five smiling poddies. I gave a heavy knock to
their dark blue door so they'd know I meant business. Inside
I could see the stringybark beams holding up the thatched
roof.

"Oh, Savannah, it's you. Come sit at the table and let me
look at you," Abe boomed from the fireplace.

He invited me to an afternoon repast of damper bread,
mutton stew, and a pot of sassafras tea. Frieda rolled her eyes
and shook her head with a smile as she set another plate.

"Can she get any taller or prettier, Frieda?" Abe asked,
without expecting an answer.

Abe smothered me in compliments the way Frieda
smothered the mutton with onions. In both cases, I found
the recipes to my liking. He mentioned he'd seen three killers
moving up the inlet that morning. I wanted to say, *If we relied
on me instead of those blackfish, we wouldn't need their blood money*

and my brothers could rest easy. Before the words came, Abe mentioned how tasty the stew had been the previous day.

It was a mistake right away.

"I ain't meant to be no cook, Mr. Hobson," I said, pounding the table.

Abe knew full well that I'd wanted to be a whaler ever since I could walk. He'd imagined I would outgrow my fancy for it, but I hadn't.

I wouldn't.

"I am no cook," I told him again. "I got a right to choose what I do as much as the next person."

Abe laughed, then muttered something in Hebrew as he looked skyward. "What under Yahweh's vaulted blue sky does this have to do with me?" he asked as he offered more bread.

I threw myself on his mercy. "All I want is a chance to prove myself, no better no worse," I said, grabbing his rough hands. Abe asked me what I had in mind. "Tub oarsman would be the first step," I added, knowing that everyone started at the bottom. I already knew how to wrap rope in the boat tub. All I had to do was wet the line once the whale was harpooned so it wouldn't burn while being pulled out.

"Hmm," he added, stroking his beard as if he were trying to see the sense of it. "Those lines are fickle," he said. "Doubtless there'd be broken fingers, burns, and worse. You've not chosen an easy path for yourself."

"I know the ropes from lugging, storing, and rewinding the tubs every spring," I said.

"You know it's not rope I'm talking of," said Abe. "A crew's a superstitious lot; they'll blame you for every misery and mistake they make."

"A wee bit of sailor wind won't get the best of me," I declared, thumping my chest.

"Well, if that don't stone the crows. You're a Dawson if there ever was one," he said, laughing. "There's no lack of starch in you. Your papa and me were near your age when we took our first whale. There's danger to it, for sure," he said, "but there's danger in plain living, too."

"Think you might be answering your own question," I said.

Abe nodded and agreed to have a gam with Papa on my behalf. I jumped out of my chair and bear-hugged him with a forehead kiss. Frieda and the wee ones laughed at their pa's red face as I smoothed myself out proper and sat again. With the meal ending, we sang the Birkat in Hebrew as Abe had taught me when I was younger.

And so, I set to practicing a tub oarsman's ways.

Over the next few days, I took a tub of old rope and a bucket of water out behind the bunkhouses and sat down next to it as if I were in a whaleboat. I grabbed Quilp and tied him to the open end of the rope. This didn't mean much to that lounging cat until I whistled for Ulysses, the sand-gropers' border collie. He came running and Quilp took off like a whale during a hunt. I practiced wetting the line so it didn't burn or break. I did this until Ulysses and Quilp were too tired to chase each other and just lay there with tongues wagging. I rewarded them with water and bones. By the time we were finished, neither of those animals wanted to come near me.

Bringing the line and buckets back to the storage barn, I heard muffled voices. I didn't recognize them until they were right on top of me. It was Papa and Abe. I could stroll by with a nice friendly greeting, but instinctively, I ducked behind the half-stable door to the tool room. Holding my knees to my chest, I sat there quietly.

Abe reminisced about how his family had come to Paradise some sixty years earlier. His father's whaler, the *Coracini*, had been caught on the rocks off the Camel Spit. I never knew that or any of what had transpired. Pop Alex had offered his father, Solomon Ben Hobson, food and shelter while Prince Jimmy and the villagers repaired the hull. It got so that Sol loved Reflect Bay so much that he and twelve of his crew decided to stay. The try pots, whaleboats, and all the salvageable parts from the *Coracini* had launched the whaling station. I'd always wondered where those big iron pots had come from.

"That day a partnership was formed between three peoples," Abe said softly. "A bond I trust that will never be broken."

"Sounds serious, Abe," said Papa. "What's eating you?"

"Not me, Caleb, you," said Abe.

"Well," said Papa. I heard the two men moving about crates to sit down. During a long stretch of silence, I didn't dare take a breath. "You're not gonna lecture me on the orchards again, are ya?" asked Papa.

"No, no," said Abe. "It's about Savannah."

"I see," said Papa as the bracing on one of the crates creaked.

"I believe no man has the right to interfere with another's family," said Abe. "So I say this as a member of our station family."

"Say yer piece, Abraham. You always do," Papa said in his firm voice.

"You should consider her for the boats," Abe said. "On merit alone, she deserves it. She's got the gift."

"Maybe so," answered Papa, "but there's more to whaling than wanting."

"Did we have much more than that when we were her age, casting about in that old rowboat when the crews went on without us?" Abe asked.

"Different time, mate," said Papa with salt in his voice.

"Not so different in these matters," said Abe.

"There's three hundred fathoms of line sizzling through that loggerhead," said Papa, raising his voice, "and the limbs and lives of six crew that go with it."

"Caleb, the lads aren't coming back to whaling the way they used to," said Abe, his voice weary. "They're off to the clean new factories in Sydney and Melbourne."

"She's a girl, blast it all," snapped Papa, slapping his hands together.

"In clothing only," said Abe. "In her heart, she's more whaler than the both of us."

"Let her on board and it's Rafferty's Rules," said Papa as a crate thumped flat.

"Listen, Caleb," added Abe, again lowering his voice. "I know what you've lost and what you're afraid of losing. But if you deny her a chance to be something she really wants, it will eat away at the both of you as surely as those worms ate the innards out of those whaleboats."

"You're a good man, Abraham Hobson, and a better friend," said Papa.

"And another thing," added Abe. "The men can't take much more of this diarrhea from the cooking. We'll both end up in the pots over that."

I heard the two of them laughing and slapping shoulders in a steely hug.

"Join me for a smoke-o on the porch?" asked Papa.

When their voices trailed into vapor, I stood up and dusted myself off. It was hard hearing yourself talked up like a sheep going for shearing. It was even harder trying to figure which way the wind would take this. I was indignant about Abe slighting my cooking. It was one thing not to want to be a cook; it was quite another to hear you were unfit for the task.

One thing was for sure. Quilp wasn't a whale and I wasn't a whaler—yet.

Maybe there *was* more to whaling than the wanting. The wanting had always been about Papa and me doing something together that mattered. Mattered to him. Only I couldn't say I knew what mattered to Papa anymore, outside of counting barrels of oil and keeping those black beasties happy. There were others in the boats too—Abe, Warrain, Lonny, the Gretch brothers, and now Figgie. We'd all be relying on each other.

As Abe said, I'd thrust a heavy load upon myself. All the stories from the last two days buzzed around me like mosquitoes. Figgie, Abe, Papa, and Uncle were telling me about the past and how the present got to be. It was a lot for my bloated brain to digest. And I hoped to handle it far better than the crew did my last supper.

On Sunday nights, Papa invited the crew over for draughts tournaments. Bring your own boards, pieces, and spirits if need be. Papa had a fancy board made of mahogany and oak that Pop Alex had given him when he was my age. He polished it with oil and kept the black and red pieces in a velvet-lined box. Before the lads arrived, Papa always took out his big tin of tobacco and box of matches and put them on the fireplace mantle.

He gave me fair warning. "Be scarce. Gambling and girls don't mix."

It was no different that night.

To entertain myself, I often snuck behind the bunks where the lads ran a shebeen. Once they dipped their tins into the homebrew, I'd blow a walloper's whistle and watched them cursing and flopping about looking for blue uniforms. The next day, when I knew the druth was chasing them, I'd swap their water bucket for an old leaky one and watched the thirsty crew snipe the day away.

I had done that twice already and couldn't chance getting caught at it.

I resigned myself to sitting in my room with those eight scruffy cats jumping on me. Since I'd gotten the pencils, if I couldn't make sense of something, I sketched to calm my brain fever. With no paper around, I looked for anything to scribble on. Above my bunk a picture of the good Lord hung. I took it off the wall and, sure enough, the back had some nice white illustrating room. I removed the frame and started drawing, unsure of where it was taking me.

Slowly, the figures from my feast in the village with Figgie took shape. I rubbed yellow and blue together for the fire pit and used red for the faces of the sneering women. I sketched myself all pale and out of sorts with oyster shell eyes. I was inspecting the drawing when I heard Lon, Warrain, and a bunch of the other crew barge through the front door like cattle after corn.

Sneaking to the top of the stairs, I saw them rumbling about, arranging chairs and putting their boards on barrel heads. Those meowing cats nearly got me skinned alive, so I backed up to the hallway as the tourney commenced.

"Bay's as smooth as these boards," said one.

"The weather's holding and the glass is set fair," I recognized Papa saying.

"Right whale weather," said another as draughts began tapping on boards.

"If you believe the *Hook & Harpoon*, the bay isn't big enough for whaling and fishing anymore," added Lon, knowing how to get Papa riled up.

I heard Papa's special chair creak and I peeked down as he got up. He kicked his boot heel back against the hearth whenever he got all riled.

"'Sharing our bay's bounty' is what that newspaper barks," said Papa, relighting his pipe, "but it stands with the trawlers every time."

He went on about how whaling had put Paradise on the map. Whalers, settling the bay, had given people a reason to live there. The old Doddstown harbor was testament to that, I thought. Now it was just a bunch of rotting pilings.

"Was a time when Doddstown stood toe to toe with Sydney and was a good bet to be the territorial capital," added Abe.

I could tell Papa was worried about something by the way he kept adding those hiccup laughs after he spoke.

"Not the past I'm thinking about," said Papa. "Sam Hopkins sent word Jacob Bittermen bought out the rest of the Paradise fishing fleet. That means trouble."

"You know, whenever that Yank buys something he loses interest in it and starts looking for a new toy," said Lon, knocking something over to much laughter.

"Still, it's best to be ready," said Papa, sipping his grog. "Before we lift a hammer to the boats, I want to take the temperature of our syndicate in Paradise."

Suddenly, draughts were on the back burner and Papa was talking business again. They were leaving with the morning tide. I smelled the uncertainty in the room. I grew tired of eavesdropping and floated back to my room on a lingering cloud of pipe and cigar smoke.

Twitching with anxiety, I fell asleep on Mr. Nubble's warm, bulbous belly, worrying about the day to come.

8

I awoke to Papa saying he was shanghaiing me. I was to grab my jumper and meet him down at the float dock. I was going to Paradise with him and the others on a barter mission. If that wasn't enough of a shock, I saw Figgie hoisting the main sail as I boarded. *Fancy that, a junior Jack Tar raising sails on Papa's shad.* Figgie gave me a glance and nod as we prepared to shove off. I wasn't sure how to act, so I followed his lead.

Papa handled the shad so smoothly all he had to do was think of a command and the boat obeyed. He did this while jawing with Abe and reminding me every five minutes to hold their fancy walking-around-town hats.

Papa told us that this time of year whale oil was liquid gold and he intended to leverage every drop of it. Each of us had a job to do. I had to get a dress for school, along with some cooking staples; Papa and Abe had to secure collateral from our syndicate and find out more about Bittermen's intentions. Warrain and Figgie were to stock up on rope, oakum, and tar to repair the boats. Little Aiden Parsons needed to let the doc examine his bum leg. Sensing an opportunity, I wrapped the forest sketches I'd made on Figgie's shingles in my jumper, hoping to show them to the lithography shop.

Deep down all of us felt this was a fun day for dressing up and feeling like townspeople. Before long, a school of speckled porpoises tagged along our port side. Their acrobatics had us laughing; even Papa let out a hoot. With the mood light and the wind to our backs, Warrain stood up and began singing "*Old Polina.*"

"The noble fleet of whalers went sailing from Dundee," he bellowed.

Warrain was the size of an ox, with a neck as wide as a ship's cannon. Papa often said he was going to save the lances and let Warrain wrestle the whales into submission. His deep voice echoed off the sails and when he stomped his feet the whole deck shook.

"Sing," demanded Warrain, raising his arms high. "Everyone join in!"

We clapped and thumped our feet. Halfway through the song, Papa handed the wheel to Lon and sang a chorus while doing a little jig-step with Warrain to much laughter.

"It happened on a Tuesday three days out of Dundee. The gale took off her quarter boat and a couple of men you see..."

Before we knew it, the shad was waiting for the harbormaster to let us dock. I started to follow Warrain and Figgie, but Papa called for me to go with him. He took off his sailing cap and gently placed the bowler on his head with a slant over his right eye. Abe adjusted his kippah tightly to his forehead, and on dry land the two of them looked like city gents.

We walked a short distance over to Studsberry Street where we'd left Aiden with the doctor. Papa and Abe stopped to say, "G'day" to a few of the shopkeepers in the village square. As they lumbered about, I sat on a barrel between the woodturning shop and Zeb's leather goods store. I liked the way the smells of the two mixed. The ball peen hammers in each workshop harmonized with the precision of Swiss clocks counting the minutes. A couple of cockies from the fields came onto the footpath, talking loudly.

"Did you see those dags dancing into town from Doddspoint?" squawked the taller one with a high-pitched voice as he slapped his mate on the shoulder.

I pulled my knees to my chest and yanked my head inside my jumper.

"It's that Dawson bunch," his friend replied.

"Whalers," the other laughed, "using blackfish to bring in their catch."

"Damn shame what happened to those boys. Only the crazy or the criminal would work with that lot," the shorter one preened.

"Or worse, darkies."

A third man called them across the street and I ducked down an alley. I was in no mood to be earbashed about my brothers. What happened was my retribution to bring. I made my way toward the town center where Papa and Abe were meeting Sam Hopkins. His Hooks, Lines & Sinks Dry Goods was the tallest stone structure in Paradise. All sorts of pulleys and winches hauled goods in and out of there. The three of them were already gamming as I approached the loading dock.

"Savannah, good to see you," exclaimed Sam, trying not to stare at my missing locks. Hopkins took the supply order from Papa and squinted at the contents.

"A few hours at most," he said, waving the list with confidence. "Come in. You too, Savannah, come. Come quickly."

Hopkins swayed and lurched as he hobbled into the warehouse. My head was still swirling from what I had heard in the street. Nervously, Hopkins spied his workers as we made our way to his back office. Papa and Abe rushed through the door with Hopkins pushing me in behind them. He peered out through the narrowing space until the door clicked shut. Standing there in the dark, I felt the suspense raising an itch on the back of my neck. Hopkins lit a match and raised the flame on two oil lamps.

"There now," he said, reaching for a book on his desk. "Savannah, this is the latest from our very own Henry Handel Richardson. Why don't you take it over there?"

I knew when they wanted me to be scarce. I read the title aloud, *"The Getting of Wisdom"* to approving "Ahs."

"Hmm," said Papa, showing the book to Abe as if they

might read it one day. I took it back from Papa and headed to the far corner of the room like one of my cats. The spine cracked as I opened it. Knowing that if I appeared uninterested enough in what they were saying they would start talking in front of me, I thumbed through the pages.

"To my unnamed little collaborator," read the book's dedication. The words on the page intrigued me as much as the conversations across the room. Sam Hopkins was head of the syndicate that provided our whaling supplies in exchange for shares of the profits on the whale oil. Best as I could hear, he was telling Papa that the syndicate demanded bigger shares. They wanted to start using the new government money instead of barter.

"That money is just paper with fancy pictures," Papa said. "You might as well have the loose kangas in the Pelican House printing it."

Sam said he still would honor his handshake on barrels of oil for supplies this season, but it was getting harder to give goods for services. People wanted wealth these days.

"Those are the types who'd rather toss about money in town on nonsense than take home the grain they need to live," added Abe.

"Whatever it is, there's too much of it for my blood," said Sam, shaking his head. "Just walk down Cornwallis Street and you'll see what I mean."

"Cornwallis Street?" Papa and Abe asked.

"Bittermen's idea. He didn't like Whaler's Walk," said Sam. "Everything is changing and not for the better in my opinion."

I saw my presence was distracting Papa and Abe so I told them I was heading over to Dilly's Dresses as they lit out to see McMahon at the ship works. Out of sight, I slipped down to the ropewalk where I knew Figgie and Warrain were loitering. Well, I figured Figgie would be there, and Warrain was likely visiting one of the women he was sweet on. The hemp dust from the walk made me sneeze. Startled, Figgie whirled about with a serious look on his face before that smile of his lit up the damp room like a second sun.

"Savannah, so good of you to join me," he said. "What's that you have?"

"A book Sam Hopkins gave me," I said, "and a darn good one at that."

It didn't take long to see Figgie didn't care much for books because he couldn't read. He had no need to. The villagers memorized their song stories and repeated them to one another. I told Figgie reading was something he should learn so he could deal with the government authorities.

"I'll teach you to read if you tell me about your village," I said.

"That sounds like an ideal exchange of services," Figgie said, spitting into his palm and offering it to me.

We shook on it. Figgie's flowing locks tumbled in the breeze as we tested each other's grip. With the deal sealed, we headed back toward town with a promise from the master ropemaker that he would deliver dockside in three hours.

We walked along the brightly painted row houses on Bay Avenue to the archway that led back into the village square. Years ago, someone whitewashed the wrought-iron bars and they've been called the Pearly Gates ever since. The sign above them used to say Village of Paradise, but they painted over that too, and now it read City of Paradise.

Fancy that.

Figgie was unfamiliar with this part of town so I showed him the opera house that heard more mooing during cattle auctions than bellowing from baritones. Best I could count, there were now five hotels, three boarding houses, and six churches in this city. On weekdays the old Charyn House served as a finishing school, where I would be heading soon. On weekends, it doubled as a place where young men and women with certain relaxed liberalities met. When school began, I planned to restrict all my learning to Monday through Friday.

Figgie asked about the new bridge going up over Bitter Ditch. Since we were close enough to smell it, I figured we might as well see it, too. I knew a shortcut between two houses. We slipped through the first yard, but on the side lot of the second we stopped dead in our tracks. A white stallion quietly grazed on salt grass, paying us no mind, with no bridle or rope to hold it. As we came closer, the horse trotted away with a sideways gait.

"Is that the Town Horse I've read about?" I asked aloud.

Figgie cupped his hands around his mouth and made an odd bird-like sound. The horse stopped, waited for Figgie to pet it, then reared up on its hind legs.

"You certainly have a way with horses," I said.

"I learned to ride before I could swim," he said, as the horse loped onto the street like a boat with a broken rudder.

We continued to follow the stench down to the thirty-foot-wide river of green sludge, penned in on both sides by yellow brick. It was supposed to be a three-kilometer long canal connecting the Cow Bright meadows at Snuggler's Cove to Horse Head Bay, but everyone called it the Bitter Ditch. The sound of hammers and saws gave away the construction of new homes on the other side of the ditch. At the end of a crushed-gravel road, a man sat in an open tent behind a large table piled high with rolled maps and drawings. Figgie walked up to a surveyor's tripod and peeked into the brass scope.

"Do you know what that is, young fella?" the man asked, without looking up.

"Some sort of measuring device," said Figgie, still staring into the scope.

"That's right," said the man, walking toward us. "It's called a theodolite. We use it to measure elevations and property lines. The crew that operates it is off on their noonday."

"I see," replied Figgie. "Why doesn't this waterway fill up?"

The man pushed his hat back on his forehead. He explained that most canals need a series of locks to keep the water flowing from one end to the other. This one misjudged the laws of gravity and the flow of water.

"When will you begin construction?" asked Figgie.

"I was hoping next week, but my draftsman is still stuck in Port Phillip, and I need to send preliminary drawings to Sydney on tomorrow's packet ship."

"If you need drawings, Savannah here is a fine artist with a steady hand," added Figgie, making me blush yet again.

"How do you do," I said, offering my hand to the stranger. "Savannah Dawson."

"Wallace Brown," he said, shaking both our hands.

I showed Mr. Brown my wood landscape renderings. The engineer seemed genuinely interested, but I told him I didn't have my drawing materials. He put me at a portable drafting table with ink pens, pencils, and fancy onionskin paper. My drawings, he said, were as good as photos. With his measurements, he said, we could get this done right away.

"Can she have that portable board, case, and the suitable drawing implements in exchange for her services?" suggested Figgie.

"Mate, if you two do right by me, you can have any supplies you want," said Mr. Brown, slapping Figgie on his shoulder.

"What do you say, Miss Dawson?" Mr. Brown asked.

"I'm game as Ned Kelly," I said, bouncing on my toes.

I bartered out my skills with another handshake. Mr. Brown wanted me to render the section of the ditch where the new bridge would connect both sides of the road. He wanted a cutaway showing how far the bricks went down and where the cement pilings would enter the bottom of the canal bed. I jotted down all the numbers Mr. Brown had calculated. He was impressed with my ability to draw a straight line with no ruler.

"This bridge must be strong enough to withstand heavy automobiles and trucks," he said, trying to impress me.

"Can't say that I've ever seen any of those things around here," I added.

As I finished inking the pages, Mr. Brown asked if I would swap renderings for art supplies when needed. We shook hands again as his surveyors returned from their meal. One of them used the scope to show Figgie the dandy new mansion on Resurrection Hill where they used to hang recaptured convicts. He called me over to take a gander while Mr. Brown and his men reviewed my handiwork. The mansion had a three-story turret with terra-cotta roofs, white plaster walls, and Moorish arches. It looked like a painting out of a boy's pirate novel.

"Who lives there?" I asked.

"Why that's the estate of our benefactor, Jacob Bittermen," Mr. Brown said.

"Well, if that ain't a rippa, I don't know what is," I said, looking up at it again.

By the time we reached the shad, Papa was inspecting the just-delivered rope. The harbormaster's pointy moustache twitched with delight—he hoped to charge us a demurrage for delayed loading. My stomach turned raw when the pulley lowered sacks of the cook's flour onto the shad as Papa patted my back and gave me a wink. I hid my traveling artist's kit from his prying eyes. I didn't want him to learn about the renderings I did for Mr. Brown until long after that packet ship left for Sydney.

I moved as far away from the cooking supplies as I could. Aiden explained that the doctor reckoned that swimming exercises would cure his limp. Papa jokingly threatened to leave Warrain behind for causing a ruckus with his lady friend and drawing the ire of the constables. All the time the harbormaster kept us under a watchful eye. Knowing it was teatime, Papa slowly let out the mainsail. Not wanting to miss his tea, the harbormaster glared, waiting for us to leave.

We all laughed when he shook his fist over his head. Papa trimmed the sails and we set a course back home. We watched the bridge construction off in the distance. The last thing we saw was that white horse cantering lopsidedly along the shoreline, shaking his mane. Figgie and I looked at each other with raised eyebrows. No one else seemed to notice the Town Horse.

"Imagine that," said Papa, tossing his fancy derby back to me, "kicked out of Paradise."

9.

Repairing the boats got underway after brekkie the next morning.

While Papa pawed over the spot prices for whale oil in the *Hook & Harpoon* in the kitchen, I lugged the toolboxes onto the beach where we would be working on the boats. My eight cats followed me in a line like camels crossing the Sahara. Pip, Scud, Descartes, Humphrey, Mr. Nubbles, Quilp, and Barnaby, all led by wee Emma. I kept a steady eye on the bay for the hunter-green sail from McMahon's repair hoy tacking east. The wind was stiff and the waves snapped at the air. There was no sign of the killers since Abe had last seen them sneaking up the inlet. It was as if the whole bay was laughing at what we were doing.

The bell rang, calling everyone to the station.

The boats lay there belly up on sawhorses like corpses in a morgue. It was our job to bring them back to life. I scraped paint off the hull, paying extra attention to cleaning between the planks. Large leaves of white paint pulled off the cedar boards. The seams came clean as I tapped out what was left of the old red putty with a chisel and wooden mallet.

Between the tapping, I heard the village children squawk as they approached. Figgie was with a group of boys, bringing up the rear like jackaroos pushing sheep. A fair amount of horseplay preceded them.

I recognized some of the girls from last fall. A few had grown and a few others carried their own babies. Corowa helped me arrange the group in small circles around the older girls who remembered the way we did this in past years. Figgie and the boys took over my work with the mallet. I was none too happy about that, but the job had to be finished with the folks we had to do it.

So I swallowed hard and bit my lip.

There was no fun in spinning out oakum. You roll it, stretch it, and ease it into thin lines to stuff between the boat planks to seal them. I showed our group how to pull the stringy hemp over their legs. They say the oakum picked in Australian prisons kept the British Navy afloat for a hundred years. I didn't doubt it one bit. I tried to make a game of it by getting the group to sing "The Dying Stockman." Each new chorus reminded us it was time to stretch and ease out the oakum again. We sang an old bush tune, "Click Go the Shears," and a shanty, "The Female Rambling Sailor," along with some chants and songs from the village.

All the time I kept my eyes on those lads smirking at us, our thighs and fingers rubbed raw from the burred hemp. Their mallets stopped as one of the fellas shouted. He saw the green sail on the horizon.

Everyone knew McMahon had a standing pledge to let the first swimmer who reached his deck steer the hoy to the pier. The four boys and Figgie rushed toward the shoreline, followed by two red-haired lads. I stood watching them laughing and running carefree from their posts.

None of them looked back at us.

"These boys always find a way to leave us for their adventures," said Corowa, tossing her pile of oakum into the sand with disgust.

I watched the giggling pack dive into the surf. Figgie charged into the water without any concern for the rest of us. I grabbed Corowa by the shoulders and shook her.

"I've watched you swim," I said. "Let's show those blokes a thing or two."

"I can't. I must stay and watch the young ones," she said, turning away.

"They'll be fine for a—"

"You race," she said, with a sad look, "for all of us."

As the boys swam past the breakers, I could no longer hear their squeals and laughter. "Hold this," I shouted, pulling off my jumper and handing it to her.

I bounded toward the breakers. At first, I just wanted to yell something clever to give the girls a laugh, but instead I jackknifed into the water. I was four lengths behind the last swimmer and six behind Figgie.

I was just about to give up when those demons started nipping at the back of my neck. With their anger coursing through me, I laid into it, passing two boys bobbing in the waves. Pulling even with the next one, I hit the crest of a whitecap. When I came down on the other side, I could see Figgie smiling as he sliced through the broiling swell. In another minute, he'd be on board. McMahon ordered a rope ladder tossed off the side with a hearty laugh.

"Ease up or you'll both pass me," he chuckled from behind the wheel.

I summoned one final surge. As I thrust through the waves, my hand slapped against the hull. My fingers slid along the planks to the rope ladder. Grabbing it, I felt the rope tug away from me.

"I'd say we have a draw," yelled Figgie with a wide grin. "I slowed down quite a bit."

"Nor was I really trying to break stride either," I shouted, pulling back on the ladder.

The two of us dipped up and down in the sea like a couple of tea bags as the hoy lurched and rip-sawed its way portside. We decided to jump on deck at the same time.

"Welcome aboard, Calagun," called McMahon waving to us. "Savannah, I didn't know you could swim like that. For a moment, Connor here imagined a mermaid was approaching."

McMahon's other apprentice reported that we were in a close and proper fetch to pull in. Along the way we scarfed up the four bobbing heads, who eyed us suspiciously from the aft deck.

"No need to worry," said Figgie, taking the wheel. "I'll observe all caution."

"In a pig's eye," I shouted, grabbing one of the wheel handles.

"A two-headed captain is harder to handle than steering between rocks in a crosswind," said McMahon.

"Savannah, this isn't the place," said Figgie, pulling the wheel starboard. "I will show you another time."

"My place is where I am, and I'll learn as we go."

Figgie glanced at McMahon for support, but he just laughed. "Can't help you. Yer on your own, laddie."

"I'm in charge, but I will allow you to help," Figgie said, with a glint of anger in his eyes.

"Allow me?" I growled. "Why don't I take over, and you can go be the figurehead on the prow of the ship?"

"Best decide before we drift off course," said McMahon, his hands clasped behind his back.

Figgie gripped the handles harder as I did the same. The two of us tugged at the wheel while Figgie looked at his mates shivering behind us.

"Very well, we shall share the task," he said.

"Equal."

"Equal," he said, loosening his grip.

"See, didn't hurt that much," I said, with a wide grin breaking across my face.

"Says who?" Figgie remarked glumly.

I told him to pay his friends no mind as McMahon and his crew coached us on the finer points of bringing a ship dockside. Figgie didn't fight for the wheel when I pulled on it. He released his grip as I turned the wheel half-portside to feather the sails. Figgie pointed off the starboard bow. On the horizon, five black top fins drifted lazily by as if amused by our squabbling.

"Steady as she goes," said McMahon. "You're doing just fine."

Across the way, I saw Papa perched on a piling like a pelican waiting to grab a fish at low tide, his face as rigid as a mountainside. I held the wheel with one hand and meekly waved with the other. Abe nodded, stroking his beard as he mumbled and looked skyward. McMahon ordered his crew to toss the hawsers onto the quay. A couple of whalers grabbed the heavy ropes and secured us. Once we docked, McMahon blew his boatswain's pipe and his crew assembled the rails. As we disembarked, they gave us a nice Jack Tar salute, tugging their forelocks with tipped caps and huzzahs.

McMahon told Papa it would be best to bring the boats on board for the repairs. That's when I noticed the deck was set up for surgery like a city hospital room. *If only people repaired as easily as these boats*, I thought.

Figgie thrust his hand out as we disembarked. "Perhaps one day we'll have a real race with a more definitive outcome and I shall steer alone."

"Alone is easy to arrange," I replied with a firm grip. "I'll miss having you by my side."

"Well, there it is," he said. "Tomorrow we paint."

I veered off the path home toward my still-cheering group of girls. Corowa hugged me around the neck and whispered in my ear. I nodded in agreement when a commotion behind the whaleboats startled us. A gaggle of brightly dressed village women carrying baskets of fruit and iron pots on poles pushed toward the bunkhouses.

"I cook for my son, no other," a woman shouted, chasing a young man with a long stick to much laughter.

"Okay, momma-girl," the lad yelled. "You're camp cook, no other."

She came up to me and stabbed the stick in the ground, as if she were Captain Cook claiming the land for the king himself.

"You get no argument from me," I said, hoping against hope this passed muster with Papa.

She marked her territory with the stick and began creating her own kitchen far away from my ash pit. "I cook," she proclaimed one last time, as all those within striking distance agreed.

❧

The next morning, just as the sun caught sky, I shot out of bed. The bay was as flat as last night's pea soup curdled in the kettle. Out the porthole and down the tree, I snuck over to the float dock. I rowed slowly through the lagoon toward the location that Corowa had whispered to me the day before. Two salties looked like lost luggage tucked in the tall grass. Their heads bobbed up and down like logs as they crawled onto the beach to sun themselves.

That was when the remembering began.

The snouts of two killers bobbed and thrashed while my brother's hands reached for me on shore. The screams grew louder, chasing me as I ran for help. Help that never came.

The blood drained from my head and my arms felt too weak to paddle. I drifted past the marshes trying to get my bearings.

Soon I heard other voices, happy ones, beyond the dunes. I landed, shaking and wobbly-kneed, and walked unsteadily to the top of a sand hill. On the other side my oakum-rolling chums were doing the wash. Tathra, one of the younger ones, saw me standing there and ran for her sister Kabam, who shouted something I didn't understand. Before I knew it, fifteen cheering girls surrounded me.

"Savannah, we are so proud of you beating those wet puppy boys," said Merinda, who lived up to her name, beautiful woman. "We want to be your—"

"You're already my cobbers," I said. "There's no reason we can't be mates just like the boys."

I glanced back over my shoulder at the marsh and beach.

All was quiet. We dragged the logs and driftwood to a small clearing where we sat in a circle, grinning and giggling.

"What can we be mates about?" asked Corowa, kneeling as she ran her fingers through my stubbled scalp.

"Whatever we want," I said. "What's wrong with losing control? After all, they reward young men for acting up all the time."

Why should we have to fit in a mold? Maybe the point of being mates was to have no point at all but to know deep inside that each of us will be there for one another. We just needed free time to do what we wanted.

"We like to dance," Ghera said, standing to burp her baby boy.

She was stout and broad-shouldered, like momma-girl but with a wide grin that made you want to smile too. She was bound to a man almost Papa's age because her older sister had died in Canberra while in domestic service. To honor her family, Ghera took her sister's place. Now she had returned with her own brood.

"Well, let's give it a burl," I said.

We all crushed together in a circle, not sure what to do. So, we mussed up each other's hair and jumped up and down. Tathra taught me a little step-dance she was learning, which evoked fond memories among the older girls. Soon we were all clapping, chanting, and dancing together. I tried to imitate their moves without stumbling. The girls didn't mind. They enjoyed sharing something that was important to them. We raised quite a bit of dust.

When we finished dancing, Corowa took me for a stroll. She told me the government planned to take ten more girls from their village and place them in missions far away. She cried, saying Tathra might be among them. We watched the wee girl running about, happily unaware. I wondered what she needed saving from.

"Men wearing black robes have visited us," said Corowa

sadly. "They say we need protection from our own country and people. I do not think this is so."

I didn't know what to say. Walking back to the group, we heard screaming and the pounding of horse hooves in the sand. We ran to the top of the dunes. Five men in blue uniforms charged through the salt marsh on horseback. I recognized them as the native police from the Chief Protector of Aborigines. They began chasing the girls the way rustlers round up cattle. The girls screamed and ran into one another, clutching together in a small circle.

Corowa sprinted over to them, afraid the wee ones might run under the hooves of charging horses. "Don't move," she shouted.

I stood on the dune, trying to figure out what these men were up to. Finally, a fella wearing gold epaulettes rode across the marsh and stopped to speak with me. "Explain yourself. Why are you here?" he asked, pulling up his horse in front of me.

"We saw smoke and came to investigate."

As he advanced closer, there was something familiar about him. I didn't pinpoint it until he removed his shako to wipe his brow.

"Bardin, is that you?" I asked, squinting.

"Haven't been called that in years," he said. "I'm Borbo Wilkins now and you are?"

"Savannah Dawson," I said, shielding my eyes from the sun. "Surely you remember me from Dawson Station?"

"My word, you've grown and then some," he said, scratching his head.

"You were boatsteerer for Charlie Brennan's crew," I said.

"Old Charlie," he nodded, fluffing the plume on his helmet. "The crustiest salt took on the youngest crew."

"I don't remember that," I said.

"I was sixteen when I was made harpooner," he said. "Your brother Eli was to take my oarsman seat, but—"

"My brother was working the boats?"

"Both were set to," said Bardin, circling with his horse to avoid my stare. "The accident changed many things. Made me realize that bay will always deceive you."

Corowa charged back up the dune until she was standing between us.

"Why are big men on horses attacking little girls?" she barked angrily.

"We're here for your protection," Bardin said, pivoting his horse toward the sobbing girls. "You best be careful about your actions. Females shouldn't display such boldness in public. I say this as a friend in country."

"A friend?" said Corowa, moving closer to Bardin. "You're a traitor to your country. Your mother and uncles are ashamed of you for taking such a silly name."

"Come!" Bardin shouted angrily to his men. "There's nothing here."

"Miss Dawson, perhaps you can explain proper Abo behavior to her," he added, pulling on his chinstrap and visor, "and stick with your own people, for everyone's sake."

"These are my people, Bardin," I replied, "and always will be."

As they trotted off, the horsemen's circling motions reminded me of the killers and my family's uneasy reliance on them. My memory of the killers' gnawing snouts still horrified me. I helped the girls gather their laundry and digging sticks. I picked up Tathra and carried her across the onyx stream toward the village.

"I'm so happy we found ourselves to be mates, Savannah," said Corowa, taking the girl.

Rowing back to Loch Bultarra, I watched my new mates file home in silence, the songs of their youth stolen from their voices.

10

I knew it was in the nature of young men to want to eye me as if I were a salted cod at the market. Others would try to corral me like the walers galloping across Lorimar's Ridge. Lonny figured things that way. Being six years older than me, he hoped to talk Papa into giving me up by showing he could rein me in proper. He had a Buckley's chance thinking I'd put a quid on that horse.

Figgie was another thing, a peculiar thing at that. I had known him only about a week, so it wasn't a lot to go on. But he was as dinky di as they came. Figgie just didn't seem so bunched up with the goings-on in the world as most lads were. Yet it irked me how cocksure he was about everything that had to do with the bay.

The next morning, I stomped to where the boats lay stripped to the shallow like flensed whales. They weren't boats so much as waiting to be boats again. Figgie and his swimming partners were already mashing red lead into the caulk. Nearby there were cans of white, blue, and yellow paint. Papa had already cleared the two boats McMahon had repaired for painting. I began cutting the burlap used to keep the oarlocks quiet during the hunt as I watched Figgie.

His eyes and hands darted across the hulls as he caressed the planks to make sure the wood was dry. Figgie said he'd spent his last two summers working for McMahon in his boatyard.

"They're ready as ready can be," I said, finishing my pin wrapping.

"You must always check," said Figgie, without looking up.

"The late summer air is heavy with moisture from the bay."

"I reckon you would know, this being about the bay and all," I said, sloshing two cans of white paint into the sand between his feet.

"Savannah," said Figgie, taking a can of white paint to the other side of the whaleboat, "you understand a great deal about the bay—the shifting winds, the tides, and where every snug, cove, and sand spit is located."

My head cocked to the left as I dipped my brush in the white paint. I said, "I've picked up a few things over the years."

"They're important things to know, but they aren't what the bay is about," said Figgie, brushing the seams first. "It's more than water, currents, and fish."

"Upon my word, you're more confusing than a needle-less compass," I said, shaking my head.

Now Figgie was the one who looked like he'd just taken an oar to the head. He paused his painting for a moment and added, "Perhaps I should explain."

He told me that among his people there were many sacred stories about the bay. Some of these tales were only for the ears of a few; others were for the rest of the villagers and even outsiders to hear. What he was about to tell was a story for all to hear. I signaled for Corowa, Ghera, and the other girls to come over too.

Figgie began his saga while we painted.

"Many thousands of years ago in European time," he said, "the ancient peoples of the bay lost their Dreaming. The plenty provided them by their ancestors made the people sad with abundance. So much was available; no one cared what the village needed. Instead, they listened to false dreams about the plenty they had been given. They weren't wise or humble anymore. They placed themselves and their shadow stories of wealth above the ancestors' words.

"Their wise and powerful leader, whose sacred name is not spoken, had an orca totem. The orca promised to warn the leader when the bond with the ancestors was broken. One day the leader saw the orca breach and heard it call out the danger to him. Alarmed, the king tried to warn his people, but they were deaf from the loudness their shadow stories had created and did not hear him. The leader left the bay with the orcas as the people danced and forgot the ancestors' ways. As the years passed, the echo from the ancestors fell silent, forgotten," said Figgie.

His story made me think of all the silence that surrounded my kin and me.

"The bay became devoid of life," Figgie continued. "The bounty it and the land provided disappeared. The people grew hungry as great deserts engulfed the land. A small group of villagers, who kept the ancestors' stories alive in their Dreaming, saw visions of their leader returning."

Figgie had the attention of all his mates, who had put down their paintbrushes and gathered around him. Everyone stopped working.

"One day the villagers felt a powerful storm blowing from the west. The people were afraid that the bay would swallow them. They waited in fear as the sun fled from the sky and the west wind—the orca Jungay—arrived. The spirit of our great leader returned with him. Jungay summoned the spirits of all the village ancestors with him to live in the orcas. They showed the villagers how to live in harmony. Jungay taught our people the Law of the Bay," Figgie explained.

"What's that, mate?" asked one of the town boys.

"We take only what the bay gives to us, what we need to live," continued Figgie. "Above all, we honor the spirits of all things. Every fall, this pact is reborn when the orca ancestor spirits return. They guide sick and dying whales to the inlet for us to hunt. The large whales accept this, knowing they are nourishing the bay that fed them life. It is the natural way of things. We, in turn, share our catch with the orcas. Every creature—man and animal—gets a fair share."

I knew those beasts helped with the hunt. I figured at

best they were pointer dogs, at worst a nuisance, like seagulls hovering over a school of fish. Now Figgie gave us this to chew on. His story was a rippa, but I couldn't see any good coming from relying on those killers.

Somehow, Figgie made river stones seem like diamonds.

"Savannah, our grandfathers shared Jungay's gift with both our people," Figgie added, looking at me as his voice strengthened, "and vowed to always uphold the Law of the Bay—Jungay's Law. His return one day will deepen our sacred bond with the bay, but it will bear a warning too."

"About what?" I asked.

"I do not know yet," said Figgie, starting to paint again.

We finished painting in silence—white hull planking and blue gunwales trimmed with a yellow stripe underneath. Figgie revealed what the colors of the boats meant. I knew the blue and white were the Scottish colors of St. Andrew and a symbol of hope for Zionists. The yellow trim stood for the villagers. All united in one vessel, just as Abe had said to Papa. Those colors were as good a mark of ownership on the bay as signing a land deed was in town. Now I knew they meant even more than that.

Figgie said the spirits of many of the old whalers had gone on to join the pod. His grandfather's spirit was in Burnum, the great warrior.

Seemed those blackfish were behind all my agitations. They kept popping up in my life, haunting me. By rights I had a score to settle with them. Bay or no bay, those killers hadn't protected my brothers none. It was high time I found out what made them tick.

Figgie's storytelling got me thinking that our folks had some special things to share with the world, too. After we finished painting, I planned to show him.

In just a few days Figgie had darn near learned his ABCs and could pronounce a few words I fingered. I wondered at times if he had been pulling my leg about not knowing how to read because it came so naturally. To show him what was in store once he could read, I invited Figgie to my secret space.

Papa never went up to the attic, so I'd made it into my private area. We lit a candle and crawled through a narrow passage toward my space. Along the way, we saw old dolls and toys from my younger years and the two lockers containing Ezra and Asa's things.

"This is what I like about you, Savannah," said Figgie, finally able to stand. "You're full of surprises."

As I lit a few more candle nubs, Figgie rummaged through things propped against the wall.

"A bit small, but well made," he said, retrieving a fishing pole and snapping it with a surf caster's wrist. "I would do fine with this."

"Don't be touching that. It was Asa's fishing pole," I barked, grabbing it from him. "There are some things that need to be let be."

"A new sketch," said Figgie jumping across the room.

"Must you touch everything," I said, rolling my eyes but glad he found it.

"That is a fine drawing," he said.

"Thank you. It's my family as I figured we'd look," I said, proudly holding it up.

In the drawing, we were all there. I was sitting at my wondering spot on the railing. Asa sat on a lower step with his legs crossed, wearing shorts and long socks. Eli crouched on the top step, elbows on his knees the way Papa sometimes did. Mum leaned forward in Papa's chair, knitting. Papa stood behind her, his hands on the chair, smiling, his face bright and unwrinkled. Two cats were slinking around behind us because that was what they did.

"You have long hair and appear the same age as your brothers?"

"Artists are allowed to do that sort of thing."

"How do you know what your mum looked like?"

"I don't really," I said, placing the drawing back on Papa's old locker. "This is all I had to use."

I led him to where Mum's things were in the far corner by the chimney so they wouldn't get musty from the dank air. Her cedar chest was half-open like a clamshell on its side. I'd put shelves made from scrap wood and loose nails inside it to hold her books. I proudly pointed out the highlights of the collection. There were six Dickens novels, two Jane Austens, and a few philosophy books, along with many others.

Figgie didn't wear the expression of astonishment I'd expected.

"You're lucky I'm the one teaching you," I said. "I had to learn from Brennan by reading *The Boy's Manual of Seamanship and Gunnery.*"

I told Figgie that I'd named my cats after many of the characters I read about in these books.

"That's the great thing about reading," I added. "After hearing the words in your mind, you kind of own what they say too. They stay with you the way your ancestors do."

Inside the concave lid of the chest, I showed him the few mementos of Mum's that I'd pinned to the cloth. I had her nurse's hat, silver mission pin, and a gold brooch with a rose that sprang open. Inside it, I'd found a sealed note that she had written to me. Figgie asked what the note said, but I couldn't tell him since I was still afraid to read it.

"This isn't a library, Savannah," he said, touching the chest. "It's a shrine to your mum, the way the landscape is to my people."

"You see, we both have things worth sharing," I said.

Yet there were secrets that the world still withheld from me. For all the bounty it brought forth, the bay remained an exacting master offering nothing freely. It would be up to me to decide if the levy was worth the sacrifice.

11

The glen behind Loch Bultarra was mowed only twice a year—once in early spring and again at the end of the summer—to create a cricket field for the annual fishermen versus whalers trophy match.

It was quite an ordeal for us working females. We not only had to put up with weeks of listening to male bluster and gamesmanship, but were expected to remove the grease, grime, and grass stains from their uniforms after each practice. Just before the whaling season, the tryworks turned into a giant laundry. The iron pots filled with lye as we spent an entire day boiling away last season's memories.

Everyone dressed to the nines for the whalers trophy. I had to wear the one white dress that fit me, though it ripped under the arms every time I moved my shoulders. Frieda still bemoaned my missing locks, combing what little hair I had straight back and stiffening it with Abe's scalp tonic. This made my forehead look like a giant bulbous growth. Frieda slathered some cream on my face as if she were painting a whaleboat.

"Stop fidgeting," she said, grabbing my chin. "You ought to get used to making such sacrifices if you want to attract young men with serious intentions."

"Well, even a show horse draws plenty of unwanted flies," I half-sassed back.

Frieda threw back her head, laughing and grabbing both my cheeks.

"Oh, my chica bonita, such sweetness of youth," she said, standing me up. "But you understand nothing of becoming a woman." She laughed again, turned me around, gave my hindquarters one good smack, and told me to get on with it.

I borrowed one of Frieda's floppy straw bonnets to hide my hideously painted face. The field looked particularly lush, making the long rectangular cricket pitch of bare earth stand out even more. The umpires set the bails upon the wickets as they went about inspecting the pitch and creases in the box. Papa, Lon, and Abe stood for our crew while lads from seven other stations made up the Whalers Club.

I went to grab a bat and hit a few practice balls to our fielders, as I always did, when two of the wives escorted me back to the food table. One of them said it would be proper if I wanted to bring a plate to Lon during the lunch interval. I replied that he'd be waiting longer than a Federation drought for that meal.

As I skedaddled away from the women, the fishermen arrived in a white-painted wagon with a canvas awning drawn by two horses. Exiting the cart, they held aloft one of the most prized possessions of Reflect Bay—the Dodd's Plug. It was only a brass scupper plug from Ebenezer Dodd's ship, but for the past fifty-three years, the trophy gave the winners of this match bragging rights across New South Wales. We hadn't won since I'd worn my first smock dress. Bowlegged, the fishermen strode onto our grounds in their pure white uniforms with red bow ties and red-and-white-ringed caps. A garish red *B* appeared on their shirts, which Papa said was contrary to match rules established at the *Hook & Harpoon* office in 1857. Our lads wore dignified light blue trousers and matching caps with plain white open-collared shirts.

Papa readied himself to bowl. As the umpire yelled, "Play, play," our eleven took their places. I settled down far away from the sitting area with my new book. As much as I enjoyed smacking the ball around, I didn't care much for watching cricket. All the finery and the men worrying about leg kicks and falling wickets gave me a good laugh. Most of the afternoon I kept to reading about poor Laura Rambotham and her classmates in *The Getting of Wisdom*. I wouldn't think any boarding school could be that terrible, especially after living in Dawson Station. Occasionally I looked up from the goings-on in my Melbourne book to applaud a good play or an innings change.

The foul barks from the fishermen's fans interrupted my reading. Looking for a new area to sit, I glanced toward the far end of the field. Lon snatched the red ball out of midair, stopping the white-suited runner in his tracks. While others clapped politely, one man stood, shook an angry fist at the sky, and bellowed at the clouds.

"Savannah, Savannah, over here!" I didn't turn to acknowledge Lon's shrill calls and whistles. "Help us give it back to these bottom feeders!"

I pulled Frieda's bonnet down to my eyebrows and made a beeline away from the crowd. Now Lon was hunting me. I moved through the food area, avoiding eye contact with the mothers and wives who wanted to pair us off. Lon's cries chased me as the teams switched places. With all the milling about, I slipped across the field behind the wickets to the footpath that forked down a gully and back toward Loch Bultarra. The last thing I expected was a blood-red carriage rumbling through such a narrow lane. The driver had whipped his horses into a gallop so they cut the turn where I was standing. The driver yanked the reins as I jumped out of the way and hid behind a tree.

"Hold on there!" he shouted in a strange accent. "Did you see someone?"

"It's too hot to pay attention to such things," came a female voice from behind the canopy.

The man leaped out of the carriage. He wore an old-fashioned cream-colored frock and matching Panama hat. He had a face like a dropped pie with dark beady eyes, and he craned his neck as he surveyed the area like a snake about to bite.

"Whatever it was, it's gone," he said, climbing the buckboard.

"Spoken like a true Bittermen," added the female voice from the seat. "Must we really watch insects?"

"Cricket is a game you ought to learn," he said, snapping the reins and charging off.

I ducked into the forest and followed the ridge of yellow gorse down to the graves. I hid in front of Pop's large tombstone. So that was Jacob Bittermen, the bloke Papa had talked about over draughts. He seemed an odd fellow and hardly the sort to cause a sensation.

When the match and the cheering began again, I headed toward the beach. I wanted to visit Figgie's village, but he'd told me he was part of a tossing ceremony for one of his friends. Instead I walked along the river mouth, gawking at the vessels from across the bay that invaded our shore. One of the ship-to-shore rowboats had gotten loose from its moorings and bobbed helplessly against the sand. Pulling my dress up to my knees, I pushed the bow free with my thigh and hopped on for a spin. I saw a young boy anxiously splashing between the float dock and an anchored boat.

"How am I doing, Savannah?" he shouted, continuing his lap toward me.

"Is that you, Aiden, swimming so well on your own?" I hollered, clapping loudly.

"It sure is," yelled the boy, struggling to keep his head above water. "Soon I'll be able to race you with the others, see."

Aiden lifted his deformed leg above the side of the rowboat for me to examine. I pinched the misshapen muscles and congratulated him on his progress. Satisfied with his success, he headed to shore to catch the rest of the match.

Paddling my way around these floating neighborhoods, I saw every facet of life from Paradise tethered to our pylons. I wanted to cut each anchored line and let the whole town float away, taking those cocky gents I'd overheard in Paradise with them.

The bluff loomed over the inlet as a final marker before I hit open water. I didn't know what to do. I couldn't go any farther in the small dinghy, and I had no plan or destination in mind. In some ways, I realized, I was as chained to this place as much any of those boats.

I drifted in circles for a bit, the late afternoon sun casting shadows on the dipping waves. As I was rowing in, the torches and campfires were already glowing, and singing and fiddle-playing drifted from the bunkhouses. The roar of the crowd rose over the trees, flooding the inlet with noise. I tied up the boat close to where I figured it should be as people streamed down from the meadow.

"Is it over?" I asked a passing stranger with his wife.

"Over?" said the man, annoyed. "It never started. Those whalers gave us a throttling we won't soon forget, especially that Logan fella."

"You mean Lonny?" I said, scarcely believing my ears.

"That's him," the man said. "Mark my words, he'll be playing for the test team one day. Well, it's done with."

I wanted to ask another question, but the approaching throng distracted me. The heaviness of their footsteps made the rickety boards of the quay shake. Atop the shoulders of the team were Papa and Lon. Papa held the brass scupper plug over his head, laughing in a joyous way that I had never witnessed. The lads, and those following behind, were singing the victory song.

> Beneath the Southern Cross I stand
> A sprig of wattle in my hand
> A product of my native land
> A voice within me cries aloud
> Australia you...

Lon yelled that I was his good luck charm as the entire team ran toward the end of the dock where I stood. Abe whisked me off my feet, and we all cannonballed into the drink. Floating and singing with the team, I knew this white dress would never fit again.

I didn't see much of Papa or the crew the rest of the evening. Just as well. They expanded their shebeen into momma-girl's outpost kitchen. It seemed every ounce of potent beverage in New South Wales flowed through there that night.

When things quieted down a bit, I took my fancy white dress and tossed it on the still raging bonfire at midfield. It had a dampening effect that I hoped would extend to Lon's intentions toward me. He howled my name in a wounded dingo growl as he prowled from campfire to campfire, trying to sniff me out. Well, I tied my door shut and pushed my locker up against it just to be on the safe side. I fell into an uneasy sleep with a belaying pin under my pillow as I intended to be the only one lying there come sun-up.

The next morning I had the run of the place. It would've served them all right if three sperm whales had come waltzing into the bay while they were dragging the whips and jingles about. When Papa appeared on the porch, all bent up with his shirttails out, I used my book to cover the ear-to-ear grin I was growing.

"What are you looking at?" he said, patting himself down for matches. "Where's my pipe?"

"You sure those are your pants you're wearing?" I said, continuing to look at my book.

"Ah, be done with ya," he said, waving me off. "I need to find my old army locker."

Papa fumbled about some before he flopped back inside. When a man's mind is hovering somewhere above where it ought to be, there are two ways things can go. Agreement with anything you ask for because he never had any stake in what you wanted anyway, or two, he'll snap at you the way a wild animal does when suddenly trapped.

I drew a good cold bucket from the well, went inside, and set a glass beside him on the table.

"That fella from the *Hook & Harpoon* said the punts were paying top fluc against us," I added, pouring water into the glass. "It was the biggest upset he'd ever witnessed, he said."

"They'll know better than to take us lightly the next time," laughed Papa as he downed the glass straight up.

"I'd still like to be part of that next time myself," I said, refilling his glass.

"If things go between you and Lon the way they're look-ing—mind, you still got some growing up to do," he said, pointing a finger at me. "You'll have your place among all the other wives, right next to Frieda."

"That's not what I'm asking, Papa, and you know it," I said, slamming the pitcher down hard enough to slosh water across the table.

"Then you'll know what I'm going to say. They'll be no girl in the boats as long as I can grip a lance."

"It's not fair, Papa," I cried.

"This isn't trying on dresses at Dilly's," he said, his eyes glaring like a bird of prey. "Men, good lads, get killed out there."

"How can someone who takes down sixty-ton beasts be afraid of a hundred-pound girl?" I said, starting to shake with a fury from within.

"Listen, Savannah," said Papa, leaning toward me with his palms flat on the table, "this is about keeping you safe."

"Safe?" I cried. "Do you really think I'd be safe with the likes of Lonny? I know what happened on the bay, Papa. I know all about what those whales you love so much did. Everyone knows. They still talk about it."

"Talk is cheap. That claptrap is no reflection on us."

"Is that why we have no mirrors? Are you ashamed of me?"

"There's no shame in protecting your own and keeping food on the table," Papa growled.

"All's we have to show for being a Dawson is blood money from the very creatures that killed my brothers."

"Disrespecting me won't put you any closer to those boats. Nothing will."

"I hate this rotting station! Every day I wish, I wish—that I had been in that boat with Eli and Asa so I wouldn't have to be here!"

"You're hysterical!" shouted Papa. "You didn't want to be cook so now you're not the cook. What more do ya want?"

"I'm not hysterical, Papa," I said, gasping for air. "I'm dying, can't you see? You're…"

If I'd stayed there a moment longer, I would've passed out. I ran for the front door as Papa yelled at me to come back. I kept running past the bunkhouses, the empty trypots, and the smoldering remains of victory to the quay and float dock.

When my head stopped spinning, I was alone and disoriented on the open water, gripping two oars with only one thing left to do.

12

I took long, sweeping strokes, trying to put as much distance as I could between Loch Bultarra and me. I glided past the point of my meanderings the day before and approached the intimidating bluff that had claimed my hair and stopped me from leaving many times. The barrier bar already reached across the inlet, choking it from the bay.

If there was one thing I had learned about sandbars, it was that they wrecked people as much as boats. This bay gave no quarter, stirring up all sorts of things once long buried. No one went near the bar during a bore tide, which made me lay in for it even more. Within minutes I'd be hitting those swirling waters.

Screaming, I rowed with wild abandon, pulling harder and faster.

The first bump knocked an oar out of its lock; the second turned the skiff back toward the inlet. "Dratted rip currents!" I shouted, rowing with increased force toward the bar. The skiff suddenly lifted off the water, as if tossed sideways. I grabbed hold of the gunwales as the hull roiled high on the port side, nearly capsizing.

The boat bounced violently up and down. As I stared into the shadows of the azure waves, one of them coalesced into an apparition and a killer floating up to me. It gave a sideways glance and nodded its head back toward the inlet, as though it wanted me to follow.

"You're the last thing I want to see today!" I yelled, stabbing at it with my oar. The killer jerked the oar down, knocking me to my knees, but I wouldn't loosen my grip. "Let go, you blubber head!" I shouted as it pulled me back a half-mile toward the shore.

I wanted to let go, but trying to row a skiff with one oar was a useless enterprise. I held on as we cut through the breakers.

Finally the killer released its bite and I pulled the oar back into the skiff. As I tried to get my bearings, a large black fin sliced into the air behind the boat and propelled me as if motorized. I picked up the oar to whack the top fin. When I saw the coffee-can-sized dents in the wood from its teeth, I slumped down into the hull, resigned to an unwanted ride.

About a hundred feet from shore, the fin lowered and a tail wider than the boat emerged. With one mighty smack the skiff hit the beach. The killer wagged a side fin and blew a puff of spray in the air as it slipped below the water. As easily as they could redirect a skiff, I realized, they could have sunk Eli and Asa.

I wasn't far from Figgie's camp, so I pulled the skiff ashore and made my way toward it. My head was still swirling from the morning's events. There was no sign of Corowa and the girls, or Figgie for that matter. The village was desolate except for a few old women and dingoes. I headed straight to the Tjungu—the only place I knew.

The thatched walls whispered with the occasional sea breeze; otherwise, it too was empty, silent. I didn't venture beyond the darkened entrance.

"Savannah?"

I couldn't tell if I heard my name or if the wind had picked up, so I didn't answer.

"Is that you?"

I strained to see into the darkened hut. The voice sounded like Figgie's, but I wasn't sure.

"Yes," I said, turning to leave. "I'm sorry for disturbing you."

All went quiet again. Then a murmuring of many tongues.

"Why have you come in country?"

"I took a skiff here and was wondering if I might stay a bit."

I recognized Uncle's soft rasp, followed by a shuffling of feet and flashes of light.

"Savannah, please join us," said Figgie.

I broke into the darkness and felt displaced and uncomfortable. Moving forward, I grasped for their shadows and sat down next to Figgie and Uncle on the warm earth.

"You're shivering and wet," said Figgie, lighting the fire.

His smile was like a sliver of moon on a dark night and made me nearly forget what had happened in the bay. I wrapped myself in the blanket he handed me.

"What ails you?" asked Figgie.

"Well," I said, pulling the blanket tighter, "a killer just attacked me on the way here."

"I do not believe it," said Figgie, sitting straight up.

He spoke in a rapid high-pitched tone to Uncle, a tone that reminded me of the killer's chatter.

"Uncle and I think you're mistaken," said Figgie.

"You weren't there, were you?" I said, trying to convince myself as well. "That black beast knocked me around like I was a bone in a dog yard."

"You seem undamaged," Figgie said.

"That skiff is mighty dinged up, with teeth marks on everything; I'm lucky to be alive."

"I see," Figgie said, folding his hands.

"It wasn't any sandbar I hit," I said, rising to my feet. "That monster...there's just no reasoning with it. Does what he wants and doesn't care what I think."

"Are we still talking about the orca?" Figgie asked.

"We're talking about my life, which doesn't seem to matter to anyone."

"Are you not your own person, a Dawson?"

"No, I'm not, Figgie. You just don't see...understand,

that…I'm just a gawky girl with a scarred face who can't even…run away because stupid whales prevent me."

"Again," he said, "I do not think the orcas are holding you back from anything, Savannah."

"Of course they are, who else could it be…?"

I explained as best I could about Papa and me grinding axes all the time. I just wanted some say over myself. I hoped Figgie and Uncle would understand my side of the story, if it even mattered. Then I sat between them again, pulling the blanket tighter around my shoulders.

"I've had my say," I added, ducking into the blanket like a turtle into its shell.

Out of the corner of my eyes, I saw them making hand and face gestures. Their mouths made tiny popping suction-cup sounds that were soothing in a way. Figgie explained that Uncle thought the killer was trying to protect me.

"From what?" I said, annoyed.

"Yourself no doubt," said Figgie, without any prompting from Uncle. "Your impetuousness is your greatest strength and your greatest weakness."

"Thanks for that, mate," I said. "I just wish they'd leave me alone."

Uncle grew animated, waving his arms and murmuring.

"Uncle says orcas are the guardians of mother earth. They protect her wisdom and are the keepers of all history. They know more about us than we know about them." All I could muster was a roll of my eyes. "You have a connection with the orcas, Savannah," said Figgie, "that you might not be aware of."

I wasn't sure I wanted to hear what they had to say. Every time I came close to getting answers, I ended up with more questions. Men can fog the shoreline with facts, leaving us adrift with nothing to toss an anchor on. I rose to leave when Uncle's hands grabbed mine, imploring me back. As I sat down, he released my fingers and the blood rushed back into my arms. We all clasped hands.

With Figgie as his voice, Uncle explained that when I was young a plague that came from two ships had beset Paradise. He promised my mum to use all the powers of the ancestors to save me. Some saw my skin turning blue and believed me dead. The disease disfigured my tiny face. Figgie explained that, in response to my mum's entreaties, Uncle had performed a ceremony too sacred for him to ever repeat.

Uncle waited for a sign.

At dawn the next morning, it came. A dead killer whale washed up on the beach near the village. Numbly, I listened as Uncle described how he had sliced open the animal and lowered me inside, leaving only my face uncovered to breathe in the ritual smoke. He placed me in the whale's intense heat many times that day until my sickness finally broke.

"Starve the flaming lizards," I said, breaking our bonds. "How'd I end up in a killer?"

"Some might call it providence," said Figgie, "or part of our Dreaming."

"Providence? I might call it…" I said. "I don't know what to call it."

"Uncle says you should just call it life," said Figgie.

I didn't want to seem ungrateful all these years later, but the idea left me cold. We sat there in silence for a long time, listening to the crackle of the fire. Uncle looked about with his blank eyes as if he were reliving the whole episode. Finally, he spoke again to Figgie, who seemed as exhausted as me. "Uncle thinks it is time for you to return to Loch Bultarra," he said, "and I do too."

I didn't want to be part of anything that had to do with the bay, especially those killers. Uncle stood and rubbed my face with his hands before kissing my forehead. He said something Figgie didn't translate and left.

"Let me escort you home," Figgie said. "You don't look like you can fight the currents."

"I got plenty of fight, just not wanting to go back," I said, as we left the Tjungu.

"Not wanting or afraid?" he asked.

"When did you get so blasted smart?"

"I have a good teacher. You ought to meet her sometime," he said, flashing his gleaming Figgie smile.

∾

We got in the canoe with my skiff in tow. The bay had played me once again. As we began paddling, I realized Bardin was right. It deceives and mocks anyone wishing to know it.

"What are you thinking, Savannah?" Figgie asked, as we began rowing.

"Uncle buried me in a dead whale," I said, still horrified by the idea.

"The whale gave you life," said Figgie, "as your mother wished."

"Now I have to live with this revulsion," I added.

"Your mum learned to trust in our ways," said Figgie. "You should too."

I could tell he was disappointed by my reaction. I knew some part of me was off beam with it too. But how can you trust something you can't talk to or understand?

Since those blasted whales arrived, they'd been nothing but trouble for me. I knew if I let it, this agitation between Figgie and me could fester into an open wound.

"Stay with me, mate," I said, turning back toward him as we skimmed along. "This is gonna take some digesting."

"Not all meals are eaten in a single bite," said Figgie. "These events are already part of your Dreaming, who you are. Nothing has changed."

"No, it hasn't," I said, looking up at Loch Bultarra in the distance. "Everything is exactly the same."

"Not everything, I suspect," said Figgie.

"Please, do tell, what has changed?"

"You have," he said, steering us to the inlet. "Because you know who you are now."

I laughed. I didn't understand much more than before. My

life was still a leaky skiff I was trying to bail out using a boot with a hole in it.

It was near dark when we glided up to the float dock. As I tied off the skiff, I could see the house was in total darkness. Somewhere inside, Papa lurked. Eventually we'd have to face each other. I wondered what I would say to Papa about that morning and what I'd learned in the afternoon. I knew one thing for sure. There were no simple answers anymore.

Whatever fate awaited me inside, I was ready to own up to it.

13

I didn't see Papa in his chair by the cold fireplace or in the kitchen reading the paper spread out on the table.

I changed into my night skivvies and opened the porthole to let the cool air draw out the stuffiness. The forest sounds tried to lull me to sleep, but dreams were my enemy this day. I lay awake trying not to think of anything, when the floorboards creaked in a familiar pattern. I could feel Papa standing at my door. His hand squeezed the knob as if he were trying to sense if I was there. I pulled the sheets tightly around me and heard his grip release.

At sunrise, I heard a mournful cry in my sleep. It pulled at me like a piece of thread through a jumper. High-pitched, the shrill sound seemed squeezed, as though a great weight was pushing on someone's chest. I knelt up in bed, looking out the open porthole. What I saw stabbed me in the eyes. I blinked several times. I ran down the stairs onto the porch and gazed out at the bay. There lay a creature longer than a whaleboat and taller than me.

It looked like a mound of coal in the rising sunlight.

In the distance I saw a motorized boat, its engine belching black smoke as it sped away. I walked on the wet sand as the sea bled away with the low tide. I approached carefully. The killer's labored breathing kept pace with my steps as I made my way toward it. Served it right for playing so close to the shore. Moving toward its head, I was careful not to go near those immense teeth. The black and white snout waggled, as if it were trying to sit up to look at me. Its fins and fluke flailed helplessly as the beast accepted its fate. For a moment

I wondered if this was the killer that had attacked me, but it seemed much larger.

I couldn't imagine myself buried in the corpse of such a creature. I knew it was alone, seeking companionship in these final hours, but I didn't want to provide it comfort. I fought the urge to touch it, reaching down before pulling away. Yet the void between us carried its own pain, so I thrust my hands onto its skin. At first it felt like a circus balloon, rough and rubbery.

As my fingers relaxed, I could feel the pulsing power underneath. It breathed.

Not like a dog or my cats, but the way a person does when you happen upon them after a cricket loss or a missed opportunity. Heavy, sad breaths.

"Help us," a presence in my mind begged.

That was the last thing I wanted. Yet revenge against a defenseless animal was no more satisfying than killing bush rats in apple bins. "Now you know how my brothers felt," I shouted, leaning in to mock the creature.

I moved even closer, bending over when the whale looked at me. My angry gaze locked on its brown eye. A large dark mirror draining all light. Drawing me into it in a way that was both frightening and soothing. I felt myself dissolving into a great rushing flow that would always exist, would always welcome me to join it.

We stared at each other for a long time.

The whale's breathing grew shallower as its eye slowly closed.

I sank to my knees, keeping my hands on it. I stayed there transfixed.

Jumping to my feet, I dashed wildly up the beach and stairs to my room. I tore the sheets from my bed. On the way back, I grabbed the largest water bucket I could find. I tossed the sheets over the huge mass and drenched it with water. Bucket after bucket seized from the retreating sea emptied upon the poor creature to keep its skin from blistering. I did this several times as the blazing sun rose.

As I lay exhausted in the lapping water, I saw six black sails cutting swiftly across the sapphire bay. Its pod mates had come to console. They formed a line and pushed water up to the shore, trying to float their friend. I moved the sheet from the eye so it could see its own kind. I returned to filling my bucket when a dark cloud passed. A chill came over me.

Glancing skyward, I saw the largest killer whale I had ever set eyes upon airborne, blocking the sun. As it crashed into the surf, I heard the roar of villagers running up the shore.

"It's Jungay!" they shouted, running along the beach. "He has returned to us!"

The crew streamed out of the bunkhouses, shirtless, suspenders flapping. Papa stood on the porch, leaning against a post. The two groups converged and began digging a trench in front of the forlorn whale with shovels and hands.

Pawing away with my bucket, I listened to the excited throng as they labored.

"Ha, Jungay. Could that old story be true?" said one of the crew.

"His call summoned us," yelled a villager. "The same call described by my ancestors."

"I saw the jagged scar on his dorsal fin."

"And that diamond-shaped saddle patch. No other killer has one."

"As legend has it, that would be him, all right," confirmed a whaler.

With the trench finished, everyone got behind the beached killer and pushed. The whale cried as it rocked and fell back into place. Wiping sweat from his brow, Abe suggested we all take a running start before one final push. Screaming like banshees, we ran into the whale, sliding in the sand as the black mass slowly moved. I saw Papa get in the line and pat the whale's head, as if to say everything would be all right.

We pushed, pushed, and pushed again.

Harpoons used to kill dug into the sand to increase our life saving leverage. Suddenly, the great beast tipped and tumbled into the water. The throng hooted and cheered as we watched the other killers pull their stranded friend free. The Arab and Hebrew whalers hugged villagers as the westies and sandgropers congratulated the croweaters. Papa told Abe that outside of a hunt this was the most time any of these groups had spent together.

"Whaling season is upon us, lads," Papa shouted to the entire group. "Time to look lively and be ready."

I saw Figgie off to the side and waved as he approached.

"He was a goner for sure," I said.

"He?" said Figgie amused. "Derain—the mountain—is female, she's expecting a calf in another week or so."

"A female?" I questioned.

Figgie said the bond between Derain and her pod mates lasts a lifetime. Female killer whales are the leaders of the group. He added that Uncle had known that Jungay would return, which reminded Figgie that my totem had come to Uncle in his Dreaming.

"Your totem is the west wind," said Figgie. "Uncle revealed something else you should know, Savannah," he added, before I could say anything. "The ancestors are Dreaming about your moth—"

"Mum? What...what about her?"

"Your charity today was well-placed," he said. "Your mother's spirit is in Derain's calf."

All I could remember hearing in my mind was "Help us." Figgie waved goodbye as the villagers headed back to celebrate Jungay's return. Everyone believed these were good omens for the hunting season, for all seasons. I couldn't imagine a crueler twist of fate than Mum's spirit in a baby blackfish. Papa started to walk toward me. I turned to say something as he drifted to the bunkhouses with the men.

I wanted to tell him this was a chance for us to start over. Papa was fond of saying, "Know thine enemy." Meeting this killer on the beach made me realize I still don't know anything about them.

I ate supper alone because Papa was out at the bunks. I figured it was as good a time as any to test that signal system Figgie and I had worked out. I went up into the widow's walk and lit a single candle, which meant "Stop by when you can." Two candles spelled trouble and three—well, three candles signified an all-out emergency. I left one candle lit and waited.

From the widow's walk, I could see the twinkling lamps of Paradise, the few pit fires of the village, and the window lights from Abe's settlement. The graves had shrunk back into their gray pallor. In the darkness it seemed I could run across the bay. The steady glow from the Doddspoint Lighthouse was a comfort. Far off to the south, a ship's horn moaned. It churned away billowing smoke I couldn't see as it headed in a direction that I didn't know. All those lives aboard her were full of hopes, dreams, and steadfast confidence in what they wanted to do.

It seemed everyone was on a journey to somewhere except me.

Back in my room, I opened the porthole and glanced out, but there was no sign of Figgie. A heavy fog nuzzled in so I went to close my porthole against the damp air when those gleaming eyes popped down on me.

I jumped back, hand on my heart.

"You ought not to be doing that to people," I said, breathlessly.

"Sorry," he said. "What's the candle for?"

"I was hoping you could help me find those black whalies."

"You mean the orcas?" he asked.

"Aye," I said. "Rescuing that one made me want to know them better."

"You don't find the orcas, they find you," he said, leaning

inside the porthole. "They can sense ill will, and they know whom to trust."

We agreed to meet the next day at three o'clock, behind the bend in the spit.

"I can't promise you'll see anything," Figgie said, "but we'll make a good go of it."

❦

Papa nodded without looking at me when I told him I was going for a walkabout. I wondered how much longer either of us could go without talking. I also didn't mention my stroll was in a canoe with a boy my age.

Now, ideas about this sort of thing enter everyone's mind, and I admit the thought occurred to me too. Figgie was a right smart-looking fella, with a fair bit of wit and charm about him. But the way I saw it, he and I were on opposite sides of a compass needle. I was thinking about all this as I ran through the brush to the spit. I found Figgie sitting on driftwood, throwing pebbles into a hole.

"What are we waiting for?" I asked, grabbing a paddle out of the sand.

We slid his canoe into the surf and rowed out past the breakers. Figgie said his great-grandfather had carved the canoe out of a sycamore tree with an iron axe from Ebenezer Dodd's ship. With a heavy wind to our backs, I couldn't see Loch Bultarra anymore. Figgie stood looking at the horizon, shielding his eyes from the sun. He wanted to go out farther. I wondered aloud if our stamina would hold up when the late afternoon crosswinds put us in irons.

"There ain't much to see this far out except more waves," I barked.

As if they'd heard me, four stingrays launched ten feet into the air, their fins flapping with the ease of hawk wings as they floated airborne. Gray kites drifting on the horizon. I stood up on my knees; my jaw hung open, mesmerized by this sight.

"I see our escorts have arrived," said Figgie, adjusting course.

I didn't answer for the longest time so Figgie began paddling on his own. We were following our guide's rhythmic bursts of flight when I finally asked, "Why are these killers so special?"

Figgie didn't pass judgment or get angry. He made it sound as if I'd asked a smart question. He said the orca pod could sense when his canoe was nearby, the same way a dog could sniff someone out. Figgie had seen the killers do many things that made them seem human. They floated upside down when playing, or hid their top fins under kelp or beneath the skin of another sea creature while approaching prey. Once he'd seen a killer flip a full-grown seal twenty feet in the air. At other times he'd seen orcas playing with them. They followed the Law of the Bay, he told me, and they kill only when they're hungry.

Distracted by our storytelling and by the acrobatics of our stingray guides, we didn't notice that the canoe had drifted far beyond the Doddspoint Lighthouse. Paddling hard, our best hope was to put ashore and to drag the canoe over land back to the inlet. A hard bump knocked the hull of the canoe, and then another that lifted my end out of the water.

"I know what that means," I said, dropping my paddle and grabbing the bow gunwales. If we hit rocks, I knew, we were goners. A heavy wave washed over us, propelling the canoe forward. Figgie steered into a current that pulled us into the bay with a flourish.

When we came to a stop, I stood and gave Figgie a Jack Tar salute.

"I lay down my oars," I said, in respect to his seamanship.

When I turned around, the heads of three killers were spyhopping out of the water, bobbing like mates staring back at me. Three mouths full of savage four-inch-long teeth that waited feeding. Two black top fins rose out of the water on each side of us. I grabbed the gunwales of the canoe again just as the whales opened their blowholes, covering us in a warm, slimy mist.

"I might have known you'd pull this kind of a stunt!" I shrieked as Figgie convulsed with laughter.

"This is your baptism, Savannah," Figgie yelped, wiping his face on his arm. "Welcome to the family."

The three orcas stared at me as they glided to our starboard side, nodding their heads like schoolboys who'd gotten away with a prank. A wee killer rolled over on its side and cut between them, slapping its small belly fin on the surface and soaking me good.

"That's Kayle," Figgie said. "She is a boomerang, always returning with more mischief."

Out further, another orca breached. "During our grandfather's time," Figgie said, "there were fifty orcas in this pod. Now there are only eighteen." It reminded me of Papa and the Dawson clan.

"They really are a family," I murmured to myself. "Not just a bunch of creatures feeding and breeding together."

As we turned to the wind, the acidic smell of heavy engine oil hit my nose. The long bellow from a ship's horn blared behind us. A tail of black smoke from a Paradise fleet trawler whipped at the blue sky. Hard as we paddled, the rusting iron vessel was upon us. The canoe slapped against the black hull. As we spun away, a whitewashed section with the words Bittermen Fleet stenciled in black appeared.

In a moment, the orcas were gone.

"You're in my lane!" a gruff unshaven man wearing a knit cap shouted down at us. I recognized him as Captain Speedwell. "What are you doing out here with her?" he yelled at Figgie. Then, at me: "You ought to know better, young lady."

Another man spit overboard and badmouthed our canoe. He called it floating whale scat. I shouted back that it was an ancient relic from a noble king, which caused much laughter.

Soon the whole crew was leaning over the railing, the tooth-less lot of them uglier than a box of blowflies.

"Just shootin' through, mate," said Figgie, with a friendly hand wave.

"You yabbos heading back to the woop woop?" I sassed.

"You're lucky we don't drop him in the drink and keel-haul ya all the way to Tasmania!" yelled Captain Speedwell to more laughter. "Now back off. It'd serve you right to get dragged under."

I couldn't have felt any smaller if they'd shrunk us to an eyelet on a nipper's shoe. I fought against saying something I knew I'd regret.

"Steady," said Figgie, quietly. "There's twenty of them and your father at home."

As we paddled away from the ship, the crew chummed the waters. A stream of fish parts and guts spewed off the aft deck and rained down on us as the smoke-belching trawler groaned toward open water.

I didn't turn to look at Figgie and I knew he didn't want to see me either.

14

I knew I was up a gum tree with Papa. Three days after our berko and we still weren't talking. He spoke more with momma-girl. It got me thinking that maybe the only reason we talked was my cook duties. Either he was coming up with a humdinger or we were settling into a new way of doing things.

Every day I ran to the dunes to watch as new fellas tried out for the crew. They sat outside the bunks, waiting for a call inside. Each time I could see their hearts weren't in it and mine broke even more. One morning I woke up long after the echo of the oars left Loch Bultarra. Momma-girl was stoking the cooking fires, anticipating a hungry and successful return.

Everything in the station sat quiet, aching for use.

Watching a whaling station come alive is like seeing spring erupt during winter's death. Everyone's busy flensing, blood and guts everywhere. The try pots are all aglow while the quay becomes a forest of bones and baleen stacked to the edges. I called them the crying bones because the oil seeping out of them reminded me of tears.

I sat on the porch near my wondering spot, eating Sunny Jim flakes out of the box. I eyed the bay for a bit before making my way to the dunny. Upon my return I saw the boats coming in.

They were moving fast in silence.

Quick boats meant there was no whale to lug back, and a quiet crew was one of missed opportunities. Each one of them was questioning their fortitude. Momma-girl wouldn't have anything to do with an empty-handed crew. Something was off about the killers, I heard Abe say. The whales seemed distracted, almost anxious this season. They were acting like spoiled children not getting their way.

Later on, I saw Figgie rewinding rope in the tubs, making sure each boat had its proper equipment. His whaling without me was becoming a burr under my saddle. Like all boys, he never questioned his place in the world or had to answer for it. I never asked for his opinion about my place in the boats, nor did I plan to.

"Need a hand with that?" I offered, shielding my eyes from the blowing sand.

"Not so much now," he said, continuing to wind rope without looking up. "Later I imagine we'll be pulling these up on shore. A southeaster's coming."

I told Figgie what Abe had said about the whales acting like children, and I could see it upset him. I felt bad about it because I was trying to get his dander up over something that had nothing to do with him. I promised myself not to do that again, but knew, too, it was one I was unlikely to keep. Some people are like empty bowls we can pour all our problems into and Figgie was that way for me. So, even at that moment I imagined that at some point I'd give into temptation again.

Figgie kept defending those black whalies. He said they followed the natural order of things and we ought to pay attention. I had my own business with those beasts that made me more confused every day.

"The Law of the Bay isn't stored away on a shelf in one of your books," he said, tossing the irons out of the boat. "Our stories must be lived or my people, this place, will no longer exist. The orcas do not appear because barrels of oil are needed to pay for cricket uniforms."

His anger hit me like a bucket of water during a nap. Part of me understood Abe's point, but another part of me wondered if I had ever really listened to what Figgie was telling me. My own ignorance of the world embarrassed me. Rather than admit it, I stuck my nose in the air and choofed off toward Loch Bultarra. Figgie called after me, trying to apologize when I knew all along it was me who'd made a mess of things.

Figgie was right about the weather changing. Around lunchtime, one red pennant fluttered over the Doddspoint Lighthouse. By midafternoon, two flags were snapping in the breeze. When Abe got the horses to pull the boats onto the beach, two red flags with black boxes flew stiff as boards. Papa told the crew if they ever saw a pair of Warrain's massive skivvies flapping over the lighthouse we ought to all run north. He winked at the big man, thanking him for the laughter that made the storm feel smaller.

We all worked until suppertime, dragging the boats onshore and tying the canvas over them. Figgie helped move the shad to the shallows for protection. Whatever storm was coming, it was a whopper. Abe felt it in his shoulder, Papa in his back, and Bashir in his twice-broke foot. A derecho was on the way.

"They'll be no calling us out tonight," Papa said, slapping a few of the lads on their backs as everyone headed home. I veered off the path for a moment.

"Figgie," I called, sheepishly holding out several Arnott biscuits, "would you like some?"

He took several from my hand, looked at the storm clouds, and thanked me. His toothy grin reassured me that everything was square between us.

Later a light rain fell. Momma-girl left a pot of mutton stew simmering on the stove. I saw Papa take a generous portion, so I scooped some into a bowl and started for the back steps.

"Why don't you take a seat?" he said, kicking out a chair leg so I might slide in. His voice sounded like rolling thunder. The dining room, darkened by the storm, seemed empty. I clutched my bowl and peered around the doorway. Papa looked like a statue in the swollen storm light.

"Thank you, Papa," I said, holding my bowl.

"Right tasty," he said, quietly.

"I'm sure it's delicious," I added, my stomach filled with jitters.

We sat in the ebbing light, picking at our meals, the clink of porcelain our only conversation. I reflected on many things to say, but the words choked in my throat before my mouth could open. I barely made out Papa's silhouette when his chair scraped across the floorboards. He rose slowly and took something from the top drawer of Mum's buffet sideboard.

"I was looking for my army locker in the attic when I came across this," he said, turning up the light on an oil lamp.

I recognized Mr. Brown's fancy drafting paper carefully rolled and tied with a string. I swallowed hard as Papa smoothed it out on the table, placing a teacup and saucer on one end, his knife and spoon on the other. It was the sketch of the family I had showed Figgie—which meant that he had also seen my library shrine and all the other unguarded things I'd left up there. I couldn't tell if he was pleased with my rendering or not. We sat there for a while as he examined it. Papa's gaunt, leathery face hung above my artwork like a dark sun, sucking in all light. His wide fingers pawed across the paper, searching.

"You close your eyes and try to remember what a person looked like," he said, staring up as the wind howled, "but their likeness is gone as soon as you open your eyes Your mum didn't wear her hair all frothy and in a bun," he said, pointing at the drawing. "She kept it plain and cut at the shoulder. Her eyes and mouth were smaller," he added, stroking his chin. "It was her heart that was bigger if there's a way to show it. The boys, I can't recollect as much," he continued in a soft whisper, "because we never spent the time together, we should've. I—I was always too busy for it."

"Papa," I said, moving my chair closer to him, "what happened to Eli and Asa?"

"I ask myself that every day when the tide lets out. Was it retribution from the sea? Or—"

"Those killers, Papa," I blurted out, my stout conviction shaken by that whale's haunting eye. "I remember things I saw—"

Papa nodded his head in agreement. "You were there, Savannah, and I was too."

He pulled an envelope from his back pocket and placed it on the table, pushing it to me.

"When I heard you yelling at that beached killer the other morning, I knew it was time for you to read this," he said. "It has been in the top drawer of my desk since your mum died."

I glanced down at it. *Should My Boat Not Return* appeared in his own hand on the envelope. I froze, unsure of what to do next.

"It's meant for you," he said. "There are no others."

I opened the sealed envelope and unfolded the tightly creased pages, lowering them to the light.

My Dearest Daughter,

If you are reading this, the sea has laid claim to me and I have taken my place with your blessed mother, my parents, and your brothers. Have mercy on my soul and those who perished with me.

My Last Will is registered with the Paradise Magistrate Shamus Wimbley. Abe will look after you. In the event we are both done in, the magistrate will appoint Frieda your guardian. Though Irish, Wimbley is a fair and rightful man.

No doubt, you have heard many things about our family that I ain't fully explained to you. It wasn't for lack of wanting, or any desire to hide the truth. When the time came, I figured I'd find a way to explain why things are the way they are.

It isn't the right of no man to be passing judgments about my family, or what's left of it. I cared for those boys more than anyone will know and I grieved, too, though not enough to the liking of those in town who don't got nothing to do but comment on the misery of others.

My boys were good oarsmen for their years.

They knew how these waters flowed better than the blood in their veins, knew how to use the channels and winds of the bay. If you gave them a log and sheet, they could figure a way to beat a steamer across the bay.

Eli was the older of the two, but they might as well have been twins for all the differences between them. He was the more patient and the better swimmer. I say that because he was the one who took the time to teach you to swim. I didn't see the point to it. Having a girl learn all that for nothing, but he said it was in your nature and you took to it proper.

I stopped reading and looked over at Papa, his head sunk low and his hands clasped together as if he was in church.

Asa was a year younger and followed his older brother around the way a piglet shadows its mum. He was more playful than Eli, a trait he got from my da who he reminded me of greatly even at his young age. Pop knew Eli was on the way when he passed. He said it would be a boy and he died believing another Dawson would lead the station.

Nothing stands out on the day it happened.

Charlie Brennan and Bardin had stoved an eighty-foot Right a few days before. With the killers already getting their share, the tryworks were smelting all day and night. Whenever the works were singing with hot oil whistling in the iron pots, your mum closed all the windows and shutters to our home. She'd stuff towels under the sills and doors to block out the greasy air and smell. Then me, Abe, and Brennan would come tramping in and stink up the place anyway. "You married a whaler, my dear," I'd say grabbing her about the waist, "and that stench is the smell of money."

The air was bad for the children, your mum said, so she told the boys not to be dawdling near the works. They'd be there full time soon enough. That put them to thinking that they could take the sail dinghy and come back with some skipjack so they didn't have to eat whale meat again. It took 'em a while to leave, with you aching to go too, but you were too young no matter how good you swam and for that I'm grateful.

"Oh, Papa," I said, tears welling in my eyes. "I just wanted to be with you, with all of you."

The last time I saw them they took the dinghy for a sweep by the tryworks when me and Abe were counting barrels for Sam Hopkins. I heard them yelling, "Pa! Pa!" They sounded like cawing crows. I looked up and waved my hat over my head.

Then they let out the sail, heading due east toward the fishing grounds off the Doddspoint Lighthouse.

And they were gone.

It was already dark and the pots glowed the boiling red of fevered blood when Mum came into the works. She had never done this before so I knew the seriousness of it. The boys had yet to return. There was still enough nautical light and the tide needed to let in for them to cross the bar into the inlet. So we decided to wait an hour as the tide settled, but before half of it had passed, Mum was grabbing a rowboat saying she would go alone if need be.

I grabbed Brennan, young Warrain, and Ned and

launched two whaleboats with lanterns. I sent the
Gretch brothers on horseback to check the shoreline
all the way to the Doddspoint Lighthouse. As the
cloud cover lifted, a full moon beamed down. I knew
our luck would change when Prince Jimmy and Uncle
put out every canoe the village had.

It was light enough that night to read the Bible, but
I shot every distress flare we had. It was after dawn
when I sent the boats back for fresh crews. The tryworks were just smoldering ash as we returned. Your
mum stood on the beach, glaring as if her stare could
boil away the sea to reveal her boys. You sat next to
her, holding the tiny fishing pole Asa made for ya. You
were waiting for them to take you for a spin around
the lagoon that afternoon like they'd promised.

"That was mine?" I mumbled.

Then, I remembered holding the pole as Asa rubbed lin-
seed oil along the length of it. *See, this is your whale pole until
you're old enough to join us*, he'd told me. *We'll all be in the boats
together helping Papa.*

I smiled as tears ran down my face.

It was the longest day of my life.

We checked every swamp, backwater, and inch of
the shore. Ned shot three salties and cut open their
leathery bellies with me too afraid to look at what
tumbled out. The harbormaster from Paradise inves-
tigated, took descriptions, and aided with patrol boats.
We dredged up what we could. As the days mounted,
our nets came up empty, drenched only in tears.

It was the not knowing that gnawed at me.

On the third day after they went missing, I took
you for a walk to give your mum a rest. We paced the
shore, you none the wiser of what was going on, playing with seaweed on a stick. Off to my left, I caught

the shadow of a top fin crossing my eye. Three killers were making their way toward me sounding low soulful moans. "No hunting today," I shouted at them, but they kept moving steadily toward me so we stopped and moved closer to the water.

One come up as if he planned to walk up on the beach.

Then another.

A third pushed between them.

That's when I saw the two bodies gently nudged toward me. I sank to my knees in the water, unable to speak. You asked me why your brothers were sleeping, and I let out a cry that would crack doom. Frightened, you ran to the house as I pulled my boys from the sea. The killers found them and brought the lads back to us, of that I'm sure. There were no marks to say otherwise and sixty years of history with them that spoke to it.

I wiped the tears from my cheeks. It seemed that everything I tried turned out wrong. I had been so sure of what I had seen and knew that I'd never bothered to try to see things with a clear mind.

We buried our dead in the sea that took them, as we had done with my da and three of my brothers. We placed a proper stone for each of them in the burial ground back of the small glen. A week later, the harbormaster found my da's cap that Eli had worn inside their dinghy that had washed up on the shore. I ripped that boat apart with my bare hands.

I burned every piece of it, hoping the flames would consume my grief.

But the ashes remained.

I imagine as you read this they still do.

For all the respect I showed the sea, it didn't grant

me no peace. As much as I tried to protect you from what happened, I knew the day of telling would come. My hope is now you can live with no debt to the past. It's done with me.

Take care and bless you,

I folded the pages and put them back in the envelope.

The rain on the roof sounded like nails pounding onto a coffin. Papa didn't move or look up as I reached across the table and took his hand in mine. It was heavy and calloused and felt like an animal's paw just freed from a trap.

"What are those marks on your arms?" he asked, as if seeing me for the first time.

"They're from hot cooking ash," I said, trying to cover them.

"Do they hurt?"

"It only stung for a moment," I said, still absorbing the contents of his letter. "It's the pain from the sour looks others give that lingers."

"The other day you asked about the mirrors missing from the house," Papa said, gripping each side of the table as he looked at me.

"It wasn't anything, Papa," I said, pulling my sleeves down to cover my forearms.

"It had nothing to do with you or the scars you bear," he said. "It was me. I couldn't bear to look at myself after what happened. All the grief that came our way, and the burden it put on you. I thought it would help heal things, but it didn't."

We listened to the din of the lighthouse warning bell in the crosswind. He looked down at my sketch again and kept rubbing each of the figures, as if it might restore them to life.

"Savannah, I don't ever want to forget your face or have any barriers between us," Papa said. "I'm fearful in saying it, but I need you in the boats with me if you'll still have it."

After all the years of waiting and trying, I didn't know

what to say or do. It seemed like I sat there forever, feeling the house sigh and heave with every hard gust.

My neck hairs were dancing out of their roots.

"Swear to me ya won't look when nature calls on the crew," Papa said, with mock sternness.

"I'd just as soon jump in the bay and hide underwater until it was over," I said, aghast, hands over my mouth.

His hearty laugh made me forget about the storm.

"Thank you, Papa," I croaked. "I'll try my hardest. I won't disappoint you. Honest."

"I know you won't," he said, looking down as if he'd just realized what he had done. "You been around the boats enough to know it's hard, dangerous work. One distraction can kill a man; two can kill a boatful. I won't give the sea another."

"I'm sorry, Papa," I said.

"For what?" he asked.

"For not realizing that rough seas affect everyone in a boat."

"You did your job, now I got to do mine," he said, reaching inside his shirt pocket. He pulled out a chock pin carved from whalebone.

"Pop gave me this pin before my first hunt," he said, looking for a place to stick it on my blouse. "It was from his whaleboat, and now it belongs to you."

It was an old tradition among harpooners to wear a chock pin from their whaleboat. Now Papa was letting me do it. I unbuttoned the top of my collar and he slid the pin into the hole. I ran to the parlor to see it in the darkened window glass.

"There's still the matter of the crew," Papa said, as I preened at my reflection. "They get to vote who goes on the boats and your wage scale. That's the way we've always done it; I see no need to change. We'll call a crew meeting to discuss it."

"That'll make me about as popular as a tiger snake hiding in a lucky dip bag," I said, heavily.

Papa laughed heartily, slapping his knee. "That may be so," he said. Then he explained the way the voting worked. Each crew member got two voting stones—one black and the other white. Black meant they passed you over; white, you stayed for the season.

I gulped hard. "You think I got Buckley's chance?" I asked.

"Buckley had none so maybe more, if a captain's word still means anything."

"Well, I'm willing if you are," I said.

"That's a good lassie," said Papa, patting my shoulder.

Then we turned to silence, only this time it wasn't the quiet of distance and mistrust but the solitude of two people sharing their thoughts without saying them. Though a storm was upon us, it felt as if every window in the house had opened to let a fresh spring breeze flow through. I lay in front of the fire reading *The Getting of Wisdom* until I eventually dozed off, the book splayed across my chest. Scud and Quilp kept walking over me and waking me by wrapping their tails around my nose. It was after midnight when Papa finally woke me. The storm had passed with only a glancing blow to the inlet. Preparation had its own luck, he said.

We stood on the dripping porch, watching the moonlit sky clear out. I reached for my collar just to make sure the chock pin was still there. With Papa on my side, I now faced the uncertainty of the crew.

Storm waves were still thrashing about and I was right in the middle of them, wondering what they would churn up from the bottom of the bay.

15

Papa was more chipper than usual the next morning, whistling a little tune as he bounded down the stairs from the widow's walk. He'd just spotted the red and white flags of a semaphore message from the Doddspoint Lighthouse. The New South Wales government was willing to pay work crews double wages to remove downed trees from telegraph lines, roads, and railways.

"Just the shot in the arm we need while these whales get themselves straightened out," Papa said, slapping his hands together. I couldn't tell if he was happy for the money or for postponing my sponsoring. "I know what you're thinking," he said, grabbing my chin like the old days. "It's best to hold a vote after a crew has house money in their pockets."

Papa planned to call a meeting with the crew to announce the government's offer and to sponsor me. He said all he needed to do was follow parliamentary procedure. One crew member would put forth my name and another would second his motion.

"A done deal to that point," he said.

"To that point?"

Papa explained that allowing the crew to vote helped avoid round robins. I'd heard the term used in a jovial manner and had thought it all a fun affair. Now, I learned, it was not. When a crew submits a round robin, they were one step away from mutiny. It allowed them to voice their displeasure without blaming one leader.

"Everyone signs their name in a circle," Papa said, "so they're all equally part of the grievance."

In sixty years, Dawson Station had never had a round robin; other stations that had done so had since closed for good.

"Papa," I gulped, "I never—"

"Pay it no mind," he said. "We aren't like those other stations."

Papa and Abe were leaving to get an early bid in on the cleanup. They planned to return before billy tea. That left me with enough time to find Figgie and my mates to share the big news. Figgie was busy getting the boats in order and hitching the wagons for the storm crew.

"Ahoy there," I called, waiting for the others to clear out around us.

"Savannah, I see you're unscathed by the storm," he said, rolling canvas.

"Notice anything?" I said, bouncing on my toes.

"Your hair has grown?" he guessed.

I frowned and stomped my foot, then pulled up my collar while arching my neck toward him.

"You have a chock pin," he said, touching my collar.

"Not just any chock pin," I added. "It's a whalebone pin from Pop Alex's first boat. Papa gave it to me."

"That means—"

"I'll be joining the hunts," I said, with a big smile.

"Congratulations are in order," he said, offering me a handshake. "You have claimed your birthright."

"I have—I mean, I will. Once the crew votes me in."

"You can count on me, Savannah, although I cannot vote yet," said Figgie. "A crew member must work at the station for three years to earn that privilege."

Figgie was too busy to be dawdling about with me so I left and slipped down to the float dock. I couldn't wait to show Corowa and the rest that I was practically a Dawson Station whaler. After eons of nothing happening, everything was changing. When I heard the girls at their washing rocks, I realized there were other things worth fighting for too.

Tathra clapped her hands loudly and ran at me full force, jumping into my arms. Within moments, the rest of my mates swarmed around me.

"What an elegant surprise," said Merinda, hugging my neck.

"Tell us of all your exciting adventures," Corowa begged.

"Tell us," Ghera said louder, laughing as she pushed her dribbling baby in my face.

"Well, there might be this one little thing worth mentioning," I said, leaning over the crowd and pulling my collar out for all to see. "I got this from Papa last night during the storm."

"Should we know this thing?" said Kabam, putting her fingers to her lips worriedly.

"It's a chock pin from Pop's boat," I said obligingly. "It's like a badge or a totem."

"Does that mean you will hunt with Calagun and Warrain?" someone asked.

"What's Calagun like? He's a large bag of mystery to us," said Corowa.

"He's a right fine fella," I told her, trying not to blush, "but a bit full of himself at times."

"Did you uncork his balloon?" asked Merinda.

I couldn't deny the girls their laughs so I told them a funny story that involved him. A few days before, I'd put bootblack on the eyepiece of my spyglass and asked Figgie to look at a whale I'd spotted, only Abe, Lon, and Ned grabbed it before he did. Everyone at the station was afraid to tell them. They walked around all day with black eyes until momma-girl yelled out how silly they looked.

The story caused much laughter and imitating of the characters.

"We ought not to waste our precious time talking about the lads," I told them. "We should just do the things that we want to do."

"I want to learn how to kiss boys," said Kabam, smacking her lips together. She turned her back to us and pretended she was in the arms of an amorous partner. I must say that from my vantage point, it was hard to tell if she was alone, or in a fervid embrace. Her hands moved with a mind of their own—a mind not focused on friendship.

Upon my return, the station seemed unusually quiet. Figgie was gone, along with the others who worked the boats. All that remained was an agitated momma-girl patrolling her kitchen and two teams of hitched horses. Neither group appeared ready to answer my questions. I made my way to the storage barn to see if anyone was congregating there.

I stood for a moment in the outer room where Papa and Abe had their gam. The crates they sat on were against the wall. There was no echo of their words. Someone had taken the leftover boat paint and whitewashed the back wall. It looked so fancy and bright. And empty.

I rolled Figgie's pencils around in my pocket. With time to kill, I grabbed a stepladder and began drawing. The dark line trailed rocket-like across the white board. My mind didn't know what my hand was creating until the line fell straight. Why do this? I asked myself as I drew a fluke curled underneath a large body. The top fin and side flippers took shape as I left its gaping mouth open. It was Derain.

I added that mournful, penetrating eye—an eye I will never forget, its stare holding sway over me yet. It was as though that eye, somehow, now orchestrated my rendering. All the distinctive markings—gray cape, cloud patches, and white eye patch—burned from my memory to the wall. I shaded my three-foot-long whale darker on top and lighter toward the bottom, taking care in drawing her large belly as I knew now what it contained.

As I penciled the last strokes, I still couldn't believe I had ever been inside one of those dead beasts. I hopped off the ladder to inspect the ferocious monster of my imaginings. Instead, I saw a creature lovingly drawn as if it were one of my cats. I wanted to paint over it and start again when the stable half-door swung open.

"Thought we heard something gnawing about in here," said one of Figgie's mates.

"This is a surprise," said Figgie, glancing in. "We painted the wall to play darts and handball, but you have trumped our need with your portrait." I offered to return their wall, but the lads would have none of it. "The crew is meeting with your father in the sandgropers' bunkhouse," Figgie said, swinging on the half-door.

"We'd better head over there then," I said, making a move for the door.

"I wouldn't advise it," said Figgie. "It would look foolish and embarrass our captain."

"He's my da," I protested.

"When you step off your porch, he is Caleb, the master whaler, our Captain Dawson," said Figgie.

"Aye, you're right," I said, pulling the pencils from my pocket. "I guess I'll go sharpen these."

Walking back to Loch Bultarra, I spotted the glow inside the sandgropers' bunk. A wee look-see couldn't hurt, could it? I wondered. I couldn't see inside from the ground, but I could perch in the tree next to the back window. A spot on the main branch would allow me to hear everything that was going on inside.

Not that I had ever done that before.

When I was sure no one was about, I hiked up my skirt and started climbing, until I was straddling a limb halfway up the trunk.

"If we're serving with a Jonah it had better be worth our while."

"There's no room for padding the scales, vote as you must," Papa said.

"She can swim better than any of you and might pull one of ya from the drink someday," shot off Abe.

"Boss knows how to keep orcas happy," boomed Warrain. "Happy orcas mean full pockets."

"And a full dance card for you, ya scallywag," someone hooted to general laughter.

Papa pounded his fist on the table to restore order. They decided on full and equal shares for the fifteen most senior men to go tree cutting. The rest, like Figgie, had to stay behind and wait for a whale.

"We're agreed," Papa said. "The next two days, we're working along the new Harbor View Road straight to the Boyd rescue station. We'll reconvene the vote on the other matter when we get back."

I fought off sneezing and coughing from all the cheroots lighted under me. The crowd moved away as I inched out along the tree branch to fresher air.

Crack.

The branch splintered beneath me, sending me hurtling downward. Hanging on to the broken limb, I dangled in front of Papa and Abe as they exited the bunk.

"Just looking for some gum nuts to roast," I said breathlessly as they passed in silence.

The next morning after I dropped in on Papa and Abe leaving the sandgropers' bunk, rumors about what had happened at the meeting drifted through the station on cigar and camp smoke. I heard one of the gropers say we'd do better with fewer boats and a more experienced crew. Warrain and the villagers swore allegiance to Papa. The rest of them were hard to figure. I suspiciously watched a good deal of note-passing back and forth among the brekkie tables.

"As you might suspect, there is trouble," Figgie whispered as we waved to the departing wagons. "Someone high up started a round robin that has many signatures already."

"Who would do that," I asked, getting jittery. "What have you heard?"

"I prefer not to say," Figgie replied. I didn't say a word. I just dropped my chin and, with raised eyebrows. I gave him the look.

"Very well then," he blurted out. "Your father."

"Papa?" I said, stunned.

"I do not believe it, and you must not either."

I wasn't sure which was worse, thinking Papa might do such a thing or believing one of the crew would lie about it. Were the troubles between us that deep? Trust was an oddity to dole out, I knew. It demanded that you retain as much of it as you gave away. Suddenly every glance my way seemed part of a larger sinister plot. I was uncomfortable speaking to Figgie within earshot of anyone else.

"Why don't we go for a boat ride over to the salt marsh?" I said, quietly. "Think I left my drawing kit there."

"Those pencils are getting quite a vigorous workout to-day," said Figgie.

"Ah, be done with ya," I said, gesturing for him to go in one direction while I left in another.

While Figgie got his canoe, I headed down to the beach and waited. Finally, he came paddling around the bend. "A body could putrefy waiting for you," I said, jumping into the canoe.

"It takes time to plot your demise on such short notice," he replied.

"Ain't you one to be bringing the lollies," I said.

We sculled for a while, hugging the shore in conversation and location. I asked Figgie about all the scuttlebutt he was hearing.

"How would you vote?" I asked him finally.

"I told you, I support your cause," Figgie said, cutting his paddle to slow us down.

"Is that my birthright cause, or my-being-a-girl cause?" I pushed further.

"I didn't know they were separated," he said.

"Maybe they are. What if I wasn't a Dawson, just some sheila looking for a job?"

"But you are a Dawson."

"And you're a Prince."

"Indeed. We have met before, have we not?"

"Sometimes I wonder, because to the girls of your village you're a big bag of mystery."

"Why such a concern about village affairs?"

"Because I'm starting to see the world differently, I guess, and if you're going to be a leader you have to lead for everyone's benefit."

"I intend to, with my ancestors' help."

"It seems to me if we're all one big crew, you'd want to put your trust in the best amongst you for rowing, or the best eyes for lookout, whether they're male or female."

"Does that trust extend to other beings?" asked Figgie, as he stopped paddling and looked back at me. "Would you put your trust in the eye of an orca, or are they excluded from your ship?"

"Animals aren't people."

"And yet our treatment of them defines who we are."

We held our paddles as we drifted, the lapping water the only sound. Figgie tried to reassure me that the vote would go my way in the end. "Above all, whalers want to catch whales," he said. "If they think a blind pelican can help them, it will be part of the crew."

Papa and the wagons came in late and left early. When they returned, their pockets filled with new Federation tender, it was a happy sight indeed. We got enough firewood to last the winter and enough lumber to build a new root cellar. Even with the morbs lifted from the crew, I fully expected to see a scroll of a paper nailed to the door, sinking my candidacy.

I noticed a new lad taking up in the bunks. Figgie said he

was a drifter looking for a boat slot. I watched from my wondering spot as each man walked in one side of the gropers' bunk to vote and out the other. Soon enough the doorway was empty and momma-girl's shebeen was full.

Some time passed before Papa's voice from the kitchen startled me.

"Savannah!" he shouted.

"Coming, Papa," I croaked, jumping onto the porch.

I pushed through the damp fall air as if it were bales of stacked hay. When I reached Papa, he was sitting much as he had the first night we'd talked. Glumness hung over him, and I could tell by the expression on his face that things had not gone well. I fought back tears when he took the black rock from his shirt pocket and slid it toward me.

"Oh, Papa, I'm sorry I put you through this," I blubbered.

"I only show ya this so you'd know how I voted," he said. "Seems everyone else voted the same way too."

"You mean—?"

"I mean, you best be ready to hunt when those killers come calling," he said, with a bit of laughter in his voice. "But you still got schooling to do."

I wanted to scream and shout, but I held myself back. I gave Papa a peck on the cheek. We went into the parlor and I sat next to him on the arm of his chair. He said my family rendering would look fine above the fireplace mantel where Dodd's Scudder Plug held pride of place.

Trust does have quizzical side effects.

16

I had the yips.
Every splash from a fish or wave breaking caused me to fumble, stumble, or fall. Figgie amused himself by tossing stones in the water and watching me become discombobulated.

My mind was on the bay, not what I was doing.

"Don't fret," Figgie consoled, "your chance will come soon enough."

I agreed, to a point. With school bells aching to ring, my window of opportunity to go whaling was shrinking every day. The shares voted for the drifter and me weren't worth mentioning. They staked me to a one-three-hundredth share of the catch while the bludger got one-two-hundred-and-seventy-fifth share, just because he was a lad.

I had other problems too.

There was no shaking Lon. He was as determined as a land-grant-seeking-railroad man, even if the mining couldn't start right away.

"Savannah, why do you refuse to acknowledge my fondness for you?" Lon pushed when he returned from the clean-up detail. "We could start a life together and I could get you away from all this."

I should've ended it right there, but I decided to run the line out and see if he tired. "I've read abstinence makes the heart grow fonder," I said, hurrying into the high grass between the bunkhouses. "We should try it."

Lon stood scratching his head as I climbed the tree to my bedroom, flipped open the porthole, and swung inside.

That night I dreamed I was alone in Figgie's canoe. The water shimmered bright cups of sunlight ready for sipping with my eyes. I rowed out and kept rowing. After a while, I pulled up my paddle and glided, breathing in the crisp sea air. Over the port side, I saw two alabaster figures floating below the surface. Their eyes were red and their mouths open as they reached up for me. I dove into the water and stretched to meet them. Farther and farther I sank into the darkness, until I realized I was swimming in blood. I tried to escape but kept slipping downward.

My lungs seemed ready to burst as I sat up in bed, sweating. I felt as if I had just jumped off a merry-go-round mid-ride. I grabbed my pillow, waiting for the room to stop spinning. Humphrey nuzzled me with the back of his neck. I poured a glass of water from the pitcher on my nightstand and popped open my brass window. The glistening bay stretched to the horizon, placid and self-assured, taunting me to reveal its secrets. My brothers still cried for justice, but the answer had grown denser than winter fog.

The next day the sky was low and the air damp. We set upon the rocks, searching for kelp tangles. Old women wore layers of léine shirts, dirndl dresses, and woolen mantles against the raw winds. They looked more like rags blown about the jetties than people, as they scurried over the surf pulling their drags. Mounds of the long, leafy seaweed washed up on beaches after a storm. As surely as the white, pungent smoke from the kelp kilns was a sign of summer rains, gathering the rockweed was a signal that winter was nearing.

Abe asked me to come along to help haul the tangles to their drying place near the old kiln outside Doddstown. People say the fire there made its way from hell and will burn for eternity. Some claim the near-blind furnace keeper, Shadrick Drundel, skulks through those flames without a cinder scorching him or his long beard. Abe warned me to steer away from the sackclothed figure lurking in the shadows.

"He was captain of those plague ships holed up in Purgatory Bay," he said. "Best be mindful."

Our return trip was considerably lighter, with an empty wagon and a brighter mood.

"Is that what I think it is?" Abe asked, pointing to my chock pin.

"It is at that," I said, with a hand on my collar, "and thanks for everything."

"It was nothing," Abe said, jangling the reins.

"It was something because it led to Papa showing me his Last Will."

Abe stopped the wagon and put down the reins with a worried look his face.

"I'm fine," I said. "The letter had some hard words to chew, but now we have an understanding."

"And I brought you here to show you this," Abe said, handing me a folded paper.

"What is it?"

"It's the round robin," he said. "Calagun told me it was bedeviling you."

"Who started it?" I asked, looking at the crude penmanship.

"Does it matter?" Abe asked.

"No," I said, shaking my head.

There were a few scribbled demands about serving with a girl but not a signature on it.

"Look, but you won't find one name," said Abe, picking up the reins again.

"Why?"

"Your father," said Abe. "He gave the crew a little talk right out on Harbor Road before we started cutting storm wood. He said being a good captain isn't always about an iron grip and a set course. It's knowing when to adjust, change direction, and try new ways, just as our fathers did befriending the killers fifty years ago."

❧

I finished putting the drags away as the moon rose in the late afternoon sky. I could see my breath while walking to the porch. I took Mum's old knit quilt from my locker to keep warm. It still had her lilac smell on it.

I closed my eyes.

The hard, flat snapping sound of flags in the wind awoke me. I looked up.

Papa stood in my doorway, wearing his long red nightshirt. "They've come for us," he said, his face glowing.

I jumped off my bunk and looked out the porthole. The moon was set high, beaming down. I could see four black silhouettes lobtailing, their flukes slapping waves of water in our direction. The clicks and chatter of the killers echoed off the walls and through my very bones. The lanterns in the bunkhouses and down the gully, where Abe's crew lived, yawned with light. I ran up to the widow's walk to get a better look. A trail of light snaked its way from the village toward us.

I had to hurry. I could hear the crews getting closer now. I went into the attic and saw the boys' lockers lying there as gaunt as coffins. They never got to make this trip.

Until now.

I threw open the lids. Inside, Pop's Greek fishing cap that Eli had worn lay atop all his things, right where Papa had placed it. I held it to my cheek, smelling the dried salt water and sweat. I remembered those swimming lessons and the way Eli had held me afloat.

"I'll never let you sink, Savannah," he had said.

I was safe and the world was a small, warm place.

I tied Eli's long flannel shirt in a knot at my waist and looped the chock pin to his collar. Asa's pants were too tight on my calves so I used a jackknife to cut a V in each bottom cuff. I hurriedly laced my boots, afraid the boats would leave without me.

Running down the porch steps, I pulled Eli's cap on backward so it wouldn't fly off. Shadows of men and boys darted in and out of the cloud-cloaked moonlight. In the confusion I felt Papa's hand on my shoulder, pointing me straight ahead.

"We're in the center boat," he said.

I put my shoulder to the hull with the rest. My heart thumped like a drum going into battle. Figgie nodded at me as he pushed the far boat with Warrain and the villagers. We moved arrow-like toward a target. Someone yelled it was bad luck to bring a hen along, but no other voice joined his. I could feel the heaviness of the cedar planks scraping along the sand. As we became buoyant, everyone slipped into their positions.

Except me. I tumbled, banging my knees on the hull and my head on the thwart in front of me where the oarsmen sat. Ned, our boatsteerer, said Pop Alex's hat was a might big for wearing on my first hunt. I wanted to say that it was Eli's cap, but I kept that to myself as I shoved the rope hatchet into my belt. Papa was too busy barking orders and steering the rudder to pay us any mind.

"Give way all!" Papa yelled at his oarsmen to gain speed. "Lay into it!"

I filled my bucket with water and grabbed the loose oar next to me. Lon shouted from the starboard boat that the whale had gone "Up flukes." It would stay under twenty minutes or so before it surfaced again. The boats spread out a quarter mile apart with one not willing to yield palm to another. We rowed in determined competition; each oar rose and fell, slicing effortlessly through the dark satin water. The oars shone bone white like the claws of some giant creature.

An onyx topsail surfaced between our boat and Abe's. When the killer lay on its side as if to look up at us, the white patch over the eye showed it to be Matong. His mouth gaped open as Papa swung a lasso rope to him. Each of the other three boats did the same, tossing ropes to the other killers. I had seen much with these beasts, but never had I seen anything like that. Matong pulled our whaleboat to our prey faster than we could row. Four other killers chased ahead after the whale.

As we sliced across the silver cove, the crew pointed at sharks following us. The whole bay seemed alive to our quest with a stake in its outcome. Matong's teeth gleamed with each rise and dive. The killers dropped their ropes and we glided. We were now beyond the bay, with light from the Doddspoint Lighthouse the only source to pin us to shore. We waited in silence until a whaler from Figgie's boat stood on the bow, crying,

"Akama!"

An immense blackness erupted from the sea, rising twelve feet above us. Two killers thrust out of the surf across the whale's head, trying to smother its blowhole. As it ascended again, Warrain's harpoon found its mark with a whistling thud in the whale's flank. Ned's harpoon landed near the dorsal fin, like a flagpole planted on a hillcrest. I was so entranced by these efforts that I forgot my place.

"Tub oarsman, look alive at your station!" shouted Papa, over the din of the hunt.

I emptied a piggin full of water onto the smoking line as it tore out of the tub at ferocious speed. The line made a hissing sound as it yanked the whaleboat around, to the hoots and hollers of the crew. I reached overboard to fill the bucket again and nearly fell out of the boat as the lads all lowered their heads and held on to the gunwales. Papa grabbed his lance and made his way to the bow as the boat bounced and danced on the tops of waves. He switched places with Ned, who took over steering the boat.

Ned was almost next to me when the bowsprit chock pin holding the sizzling line snapped. If the rope ripped upward, it would tear Ned's arm from its socket.

I grabbed my oar and swung it down on the line as I might an axe. The crew all looked up. Their jaws slacked open as I used all my strength to hold the oar down on the sizzling rope. Ned staggered but was unharmed as the rope burned a groove in the oar's throat.

"You saved my neck this day!" shouted Ned, slapping my back as if I were one of the lads.

"Three cheers for the tub oarsman," came a shout from the bow.

"Huzzah, huzzah, huzzah!" they all shouted, thumping their oars on the hull as the whale sped us along the line still snapping across the gunwale of the boat.

Papa nodded at me with a wink and tapped his lance on top of the gunwales.

"Steady, lads. Hove up!" Papa shouted, raising the lance over his head. "Stern all! Stern all!"

Every oar hit the water, backing us off the mark where the whale would surface.

At that moment, a blaze of light broke through the clouds. The bow of the boat rose as if being lifted by a cresting wave. We kept rising higher and higher, until all the loose items inside the boat were raining down on Ned and me.

Papa fell without thrusting his lance. The bottom of the hull splintered, tossing us in all directions as fragments of wood and metal tumbled around us. The whale's vast dark fluke stirred the cauldron of the sea like Poseidon's trident, smashing what was left of our boat into indistinguishable pieces.

Stunned, I sank below the surface, unable to move. I saw Lon, Warrain, and Figgie jump into the bay and swim toward us. Unperturbed by our efforts, the whale continued on its ancient journey. I heard my name but couldn't respond. Debris, rope, and tools dating back to Pop's time drifted downward. It was as if the past were trying to ensnare me. The brightness of the light allowed me to see the others thrashing

onto the boats as I sank lower and lower. The dream I had
was coming true. The coldness of the deeper water shocked
me to my senses, and I swam toward the white bottom of a
boat.

My lungs burned for air.

As I angled for the surface, I realized the "boat" was a
white pointer, whipped into a frenzy by whale blood. It spotted me flailing with its flesh-stained teeth stretched across
wide extended jaws. Paralyzed with fear, I couldn't move. My
heart pounded heavily in my chest.

As the shark lunged at me, a shadow darted between us. I
felt a hard edge catch under my arms and pull me toward the
surface. As water rushed over my eyes, I saw ghostly white
patches rising with me.

Was it my brothers' angered spirits come for revenge?

Suddenly, I surfaced and slid onto a killer's head. The creature floated motionless, its massive top fin stabbing into the
inky sky. I felt the hatchet in my belt as I lay there. I'd been
waiting for this moment all these years. By some twisted luck,
I ended up on this beast. Despite Papa's letter, the moment
to complete my vengeance had arrived. I could avenge Eli
and Asa with just a few whacks to its blowhole.

I slowly drew the hatchet out by its neck.

Hesitation tormented me. What little I had learned about
the mammal under me suggested my rescue had been no
accident. Was this some sort of trick? Was the beast resting
before finishing me off or was I chasing a dark dream? There
was no way to find an answer before I had to swing that axe.
I thought of Figgie's Law of the Bay and how simple yet
resolute it was.

The hatchet slipped from my grip and slid across the
whale's glistening head. The killer shifted its weight beneath
me, as though trying to keep the axe within my grasp. The
waves lapped at us as the hatchet lay halfway between its
blowhole and top fin, challenging me to action. As I reached

for the handle again, the events of the past few weeks washed over me. The alabaster figures of my brothers from a dream, Papa's letter, my sandbar rescue, and Derain's hypnotizing eye all numbed my reaching muscles.

Eli's words echoed through my mind again as he taught me to swim and I felt upheld by them. With one solid thrust, I shoved the axe into the dark water. My body shuddered as the hatchet sank, dragging all my sadness and vengefulness to the bottom of the bay.

Exhausted, I rolled on my back. The warm steam from the killer's breathing covered me like a blanket. I felt its heart throbbing below me, a giant pulsing engine. My heart slowed until both of ours matched drumbeat for drumbeat.

In the distance I heard the boats pull in upended crew while the men shouted that Lon had just killed the white pointer with his lance. Calling for me, Papa sounded as mournful as I'd ever heard him. I was too weak to answer. Slowly the killer turned so I could see the boats. I stood wobbly on its back, holding the top fin like a wind sail.

Still catching my breath, the blackfish propelled itself cautiously in the direction of the boats and circled from a distance, as if trying to attract attention.

"Papa, Papa!" I shouted. "I'm over here!"

Warrain was the first to spot me. He stood, raising his arms over his head, and broke into a song in his natural tongue. Figgie and the rest of the villagers joined him.

"Savannah, great saints, are you hurt?" yelled Papa, grabbing an oar to move toward me.

"I'm fine, Papa! Don't worry!" I yelled back, waving.

The village crew pointed at the sky while singing. I looked up to behold a frightening yet spectacular sight—a large glowing disk with a white tail. A mysterious comet had appeared out of nowhere.

As the killer approached the boats, I moved my hands along its top fin and felt the deep gullied scar the whalers and villagers had marveled about seeing during Derain's rescue after being beached.

Under a glowing comet, my vantage point from this behemoth gave me a different view of the bay. I could clearly see the figures of Figgie, Lon, Papa, and Abe, and more importantly, I was beginning to understand where I stood in relation to them. Looking at the ocean and the stars, the bay didn't seem quite so confining any longer.

For I knew deep in my bones that this killer whale was Jungay, the spirit king of the orcas. Suddenly, my possibilities seemed endless.

Yet still unanswered was the fate of my brothers.

PART II

Jungay's Journey

17

I remained motionless, afraid that if I moved or let go of Jungay's top fin, he might roll over or flip me twenty feet in the air. Inside I wanted to shout to the world, "I'm standing on a spirit whale!" But the brute enormousness of his presence and the advantage he held over me tempered my joy of discovery.

"Savannah, stay put, we're on our way!" Papa shouted off my starboard side.

"Wait, no. I don't know. What should I do?" I yelled, wanting to stay and jump at the same time.

"Over here, it's dangerous!" shouted Lon, waving me in the direction of his boat. "Come to me, I'll protect you—"

"Listen!" Figgie shouted. "Hear what she has to say."

The bay was as soundless as it had ever been. Even the stillness of the water seemed to await my reply. Whenever I grew fearful, old Charlie Brennan used to tell me, "Explain the situation to yourself as if you were telling a friend. The fearing parts seem less scary that way and you can move on."

I wobbled on Jungay's slippery back, thinking that just minutes before I'd wanted to kill him. Without having moved, it was already a long journey for me.

Before I could reply to the crew, Jungay dipped his head and descended into the water until my boot tops were submerged. I hugged his top fin as we moved swiftly toward the remaining boats. He rocked slightly and let out a burst of air mist. The water droplets reflected the comet-lighted sky with Roman candle glitter. My feet slipped, my knees buckled, and I fell with every jerk and turn he made.

As we passed the bow of Lon's boat, the behemoth lifted his head out of the water, revealing gaping rows of jagged ripsaw teeth. With one quick shrug, Jungay gently tossed me into the water right near the gunwales where Papa stood.

The lads started cheering and shouting, "All present and accounted for!"

Those first oar pulls back to Loch Bultarra drew a void into me. I felt inexplicably desolate and hollow, with each stroke toward home stretching the umbilical cord of some new life near to snapping.

That night I didn't sleep much. My bunk seemed to float on water, more raft than bed. I lay awake, the events of the day looping through my mind—Figgie and Lon butting heads, my oar on the burning rope saving Ned Hanlon, and that hatchet sinking into the depths.

It all flipped by in kinetoscope fashion.

Now that we had returned again without a whale in tow, I worried Papa would end my whaling days once and for all. I worried even more that I might never get a chance to see Jungay again. Every thought I had lying there, no matter how distant from Loch Bultarra, ended in the same place—me standing on Jungay holding his black sail.

As awkward as I had felt on his back, and as frightened as I was, I needed to find him.

I had to ride with Jungay again.

The next day I heard Papa banging around, getting ready to leave for his army reunion. By the time I hobbled down the stairs on cramped legs, he was bent over his ledger at the chopping table.

"Some red oats?" I asked, offering him a biscuit.

"We can't afford it," he muttered to himself. "I'll have to go back to Sam and the syndicate, or make do with the boats we have."

"They won't like it none," I said, glancing at the ledger. I picked up his boots and started dubbining them for a shine. Papa rose wearily to his feet.

"Just bad timing with me lighting out for a few days, nothing Abe can't handle," he said, giving my shoulder a squeeze. "We'll get by, we always do."

"You're not gonna stop me from whaling now, are you?" I asked, buffing his boots.

Papa turned to leave, the ledger tucked under one arm.

"You're crew now so there's no need to ask," he said. "Seeing you sink below was my worst nightmare, but we survived and the killers done their part looking out for you."

With his swag packed, Papa seemed yipped up the same way I had been before the hunt. It's been twenty-five years between handshakes with the lads of the NSW Contingent Infantry. He said his shirt and uniform still fit and his Martini-Henry still fired.

"My unit never made it to the Sudan, but I met your mum in Sydney getting ready to set off on a mission," he said, smiling widely. "Now there's a fair exchange..." Papa's voice trailed off as he opened the front door. "Don't pay no mind to the bull's wool out there," he added, waving his hand.

I went outside to see what he was talking about. It was hard to ignore. The comet glared down in broad daylight, the angry brother of the sun. It hung in the sky, a glowing wafer demanding our recognition. A crowd had gathered by the bunks where a horse-drawn wagon, which looked like an Amscol ice cream truck with Comet Hunter painted on its side, was parked. A man wearing an old top hat and red suspenders sold pills to prevent poisoning by gases from the comet tail. Most of the crowd was content to look up. Others cautiously observed through bottles or colored glass, afraid the light from distant shores might blind them. By the time Figgie arrived for his reading lesson, the villagers had weighed in too. They said the comet looked like a bundle of spears or a headdress. Uncle lamented its sudden appearance.

It foretold of a great battle with evil, he said, one that even the sun couldn't subdue.

"It's a vaporous omen that will drain all life from the bay with its long tail," said Figgie, holding one of my old Dumpy books on the front porch. "But I am not afraid, because Jungay has returned to protect us."

"So, you really think it was Jungay I rode on?" I asked.

"Without a doubt," he said. "The question is, what do *you* think?"

I wanted to explain to Figgie what had happened with Jungay, but how could I explain something I didn't understand? I had wanted to destroy a being that I now considered part of me. To be wrong all those years, and to spend that time hoping for the wrong thing to happen, made for quite a quizzical feeling. Yet Jungay accepted me for who I was, knew what I wanted to do, even if it had taken me some time to figure it out.

"I felt like I ought to have stayed with him, but why'd he pick me, mate? You know those whales better than anyone."

"Precisely," Figgie said, jumping on my wondering spot. "His scar is our symbol for a journey. You have to decide whether to begin one."

As part of Figgie's lesson, we read chapter twelve from *The Getting of Wisdom*. I could tell he was bored hearing about a girl's elocution lessons. He needed a more direct line to his education and chose to spend the afternoon with a fishing net off Doddspoint.

Papa bounded onto the rickety boards of the quay. He and Abe were taking the shad back over to Paradise where Papa was shipping up to Sydney. Abe wouldn't be back until tomorrow, with all the syndicate business he had to take care of. I asked him to drop off some drawings for Mr. Brown and to pick up my list of art supplies. A subdued Lon hitched a ride with them on his way to Adelaide for another cricket tourney he was playing in. I was supposed to have dinner with Frieda and spend the night with her. I accompanied them down to the float dock wearing Frieda's fancy bonnet she'd lent me from the Dodd's Plug match.

"Help Mrs. Hobson best you can," said Papa, tossing his biddle on deck. "Do me a favor."

"Anything, Papa," I said, clasping my hands behind my back.

"Stay away from the killers while I'm gone."

"Papa," I said, placing a finger to my cheek. "They're orcas."

"Savannah…" he said, waiting for an answer, "I don't need to be worrying."

"Aye, I promise," I said, crossing my hands over my heart.

Abe had already trimmed the mainsails, making Papa run and jump into the shad as it left the dock. Lon looked down at the deck without saying a word.

Abstinence had won the day.

But I couldn't resist.

Even hearing the voices of Papa, Abe, and Figgie making wee whispers in the back of my mind, I still had to. As hard as I tried, and despite putting a mite bit of thought into it, I still wanted to, needed to—

Find Jungay.

I sat down on the float dock, dangling my feet in the bay, and waited till the shad had disappeared. I splashed about like a seal and jumped up and down on the dock, causing wobbly waves. I threw big rocks into the water, hoping to clunk something wagging by. Before I could hear Papa's voice warning me again, or imagine that last picture of him setting sail, I slipped off my house dress and into the water. I kept my bathing things on underneath, just in case.

Breaking the surface of the bay, my anxieties evaporated. I moved effortlessly as though supported by cupped hands. I knifed through the bay with an inner grace that was far from the gawky gait I exhibited on land. Underwater, my mind was unfettered from the snares of everyday living. I felt protected. There were no boundaries in this sapphire expanse. Surfacing for air, I felt a presence.

Two orcas flanked my sides.

"Ah," I said, taking a deep breath, "out for your walk-about?"

The orcas lowered their top fins as they sank into a horizontal position on either side of me. I wasn't sure why as I continued scissor-kicking my legs to stay afloat. In a flash, those large snouts pushed up at me. Both noses slid under the palms of my hands. I locked my elbows, like a trapeze artist on the rings, as the two orcas breached out of the water shooting me fifteen feet in the air. For a moment, I saw Loch Bultarra and the whaling station laid out before me. I squeezed the memory hard, as if it were paper on a printing press. The three of us dropped straight into the water.

"Do it again. Do it again!" I shouted, gleeful as a nipper.

We rose from the water three times until exhaustion set in. Up close I could see, from the gray saddle marks behind their top fins, that I was playing with Towrang, the shield, and Yindi, the sun. I didn't attempt to ride them, nor did they offer to take me.

I knew only Jungay was for me.

Resting, I sat on Towrang's wide fluke. He unceremoniously flipped me in the air whenever he grew tired of me sitting there. Each time he did that, the orcas made clicking noises that sounded like laughter.

Soon other top fins appeared nearby, like schoolyard children waiting for an invitation to play. They followed me as I swam back to the float dock. I recognized the sounds Matong made and the markings on Burnum. Derain with her bulging girth lumbered about, protected by the other orcas. She left as though on an inspection tour.

The head of a smaller orca, with a large tongue hanging

out of its mouth, popped out of the water next to me. "You again," I said in mock anger, shaking my finger at her. "I haven't forgotten what you did."

I told them all to wait while I ran back to my room and got the art box Mr. Brown had given me. Sitting on a nearby piling, I set up the table on the dock, sketching what I could remember about each orca I had seen that morning.

"Later, Kayle," I said, pulling Frieda's hat over my eyes. The wee whale kept nudging up against the float dock. "I'm drawing all of your pictures on the tool room wall so I can remember you after school begins."

One by one they paraded past me, showing their unique features. I noted notches on top fins and flukes, missing teeth, saddle marks, and white patches. Before long the orcas grew bored with my sketching. I packed up my art box and went back down to the lower float dock to figure out what they wanted to do.

Kayle rolled over and splashed me with a side flipper. I ducked as several orcas blew streams of mist into the air at me. "You missed," I said, triumphantly, only to feel the slimy green kiss from kelp leaves as the sodden mass hit me in the face.

"You're a very naughty whalie," I said, with a laugh, pulling the seaweed off.

Kayle waited for me to toss the kelp back at her, as if she had rolled me a ball. I dropped the heavy wet leaves onto the dock only to pick them up when the wee one wasn't looking and throw them at her.

I laughed heartily at my own prank until I turned to see that another orca had made off with Frieda's floppy hat. Three of them moved far into the cove, tossing it about between themselves like a cricket ball. I leapt in the dinghy and rowed toward them, demanding the hat back. It didn't take me long to see that I was the monkey in the middle of this game.

With the sun dipping below the mountains, the top fins of two large blackfish appeared far out on the bay. The adult presence meant an end to the day's playfulness. The remaining orcas solemnly made their way out to sea. I rowed to the remains of Frieda's hat. When I reached out to grab it, a wave kicked up, knocking me overboard.

I'll swear to my last days that little Kayle tipped my dinghy over.

I was by myself in the calm cove, but I didn't feel alone. I felt connected to Figgie, off fishing in the deep waters, and to my new girlfriends preparing dinner in the nearby village. I finally had a place, but it wouldn't be complete until I found Jungay again.

Frieda called me from the top of the dunes. My search would have to wait. I could only hope that Jungay wanted finding as much as I needed to find him. He wouldn't wait forever, and with Papa's trip ending in a few days and school right around the corner, my clock was ticking.

18

For the next two days, I was stuck in dry dock. The sudsy water from Frieda's dish bucket served as the only reminder of the roiling surf I wasn't able to enjoy.

The orcas were calling.

I heard their clicks in my sleep and saw them parading up the river the way Abe had always described it. Frieda wanted me to try on her old clothes to see what might fit me for school. She was going to make a proper lady of me yet, she said. *Gulp.* Her good intentions threatened to ruin what was left of my summer if I couldn't find Jungay in the next three days—before Papa returned and school started.

I decided to make a break for it on the third morning of my exile from the sea. I excused myself to go to the dunny after brekkie and snuck around the back. I crawled on my belly through the salt grass so Frieda couldn't see me and slid down a dune to the shore. I walked for a while before spotting an abandoned skiff. Hiding my fancy outer garments inside a hollow log, I commandeered the skiff.

I wrote *Your boat shall be returned* in the sand.

I rowed hard against the choppy waves, peering over the portside. About fifty yards off the starboard bow, the bay pitched and boiled as an island of orcas erupted from below. I counted six top fins. It was the same group from a few days ago. I hoped to get behind the pod to see what they were doing.

I sat watching them whistle and click to one another in a bed of kelp and seaweed. Their blowholes puffed and yowled like the pipes of a great church organ. One orca stood upside down using her fluke like a sail to push herself along. Another breached out of the water, spinning through the air as if he were a Spanish dancer.

"I bet that donah of yours finally said yes, didn't she?" I shouted, standing up.

They tried to coax me into the water with top fins waving and flukes slapping the waves. Derain quietly glided up to my gunwales. I rubbed her head and felt the hypnotic pull of that tranquil eye again. I plunged in the water, grabbing her fluke for a quick spin around the bay. I let go of her tail in the middle of the circling orcas.

Above us, the comet shone brighter than ever. It didn't take long for one of the orcas to come straight up next to me. He nudged my stomach with his head, and I grabbed hold of it in an embracing hug. Spyhopping out of the water, we twirled about as he swayed back and forth in a water waltz. I slid down to his flippers and he released me to my next partner. All the time I kept an eye out for Jungay.

He was nowhere near.

I stood on Matong's nose with my arms outstretched as he froze above the waves. We slid into the water and I hung on to him while we rolled our way back to the surface. I danced with Yindi and her sisters, going from flipper to flipper as if we were at an autumn bush dance. I jumped to my rambunctious Kayle and we bobbed up and down doing a wild sailor's jig, tossing from one side to another. Her movements and mannerisms reminded me of myself. Suddenly, she slipped from my arms and they were all gone.

I floated alone in the cold water. A distant call broke the quietness of the lapping waves.

"You, off the starboard bow, present yourself!" he shouted. "Do you need assistance?"

I could recognize Abe's deep nasal voice anywhere as the shad's bright white jib cut across the blue sky.

"It's me, Savannah!" I yelled, waving my arms.

Abe glared overboard and tossed a heaving line my way. He lugged me along in the water without stopping, even though he had to luff the sails at any moment.

"I ought to put ya in that dinghy bouncing over the waves," he said, gripping my elbow and forearm as he pulled me onboard. "You shouldn't be out here alone."

Abe threw his peacoat over my shoulders. We stopped to rope in my borrowed dinghy and headed to the inlet. Abe had to go to the bunks to talk with the crew. I was welcome to come when I got properly dressed, he said. I returned the skiff, got my garb back, and wiped my note out of the sand.

Abe sat the crew down and gave us the bad news. The syndicate wouldn't front any money for a boat until we had whale oil for collateral, but McMahon and Hopkins had pledged their support. Abe telegrammed Papa, who said we should sit tight until he returned. Three boats meant that six of us would be looking for something else to do.

Suddenly, finding Jungay was the least of my problems. As the youngest there, Figgie and I were prime candidates to be left off the roster.

"What d'ya think they'll do?" I asked him, leaving the bunks.

"Draw lots based on service time, I imagine," he answered glumly.

"I'll lose on both counts," I said. "What can we do?"

"Find a whaleboat," he said laughing.

"That's it!" I exclaimed, snapping my fingers. "There's stoved whaleboats all over this bay."

"Where are they and in what condition?" Figgie asked.

"Old Charlie Brennan knows."

With Abe all tied up in paperwork, it was easy enough to clear the shad off its moorings without anyone noticing. The sailing lessons McMahon gave us on his hoy had come in handy.

We were on our way to the Pelican House.

The right and proper name was the Old Whalers & Seafarers Home, but everyone called it the Pelican House because the birds roosted in its three chimneys and walked about inside wherever they pleased. It had once been the biggest and most beautiful beachfront home in Paradise, with rooms for twenty men, a live-in cook, and a maid. Now there were only five boarders left, not counting the pelicans. After I was born, a storm wiped out the sandbar protecting the cove and surrounded the house with water. At high tide, the codgers row in and out, entering through a door on the third floor. Despite this inconvenience, none of them would live anywhere else.

We continued our fine seamanship by lowering the sails to pull alongside the Pelican House. The entire structure sagged to the portside like a cake on a slanted pedestal. A four-story saltbox of a building, most of its white shingles were weathered to clamshell gray, its walls lashed with seaweed and algae stains marking the tides, the front porch obliterated by wind and waves. What was left of the gabled roof belonged to the pelicans who gathered there in splendid white and black tuxedo feathers as if they were yacht club dinner guests. Henry "No Legs" Morrison twirled about in an old gamming chair, hanging from the yardarms of a wooden T-beam off his third floor window. He lowered himself on a pulley, trying to grab our mainmast.

"Ahoy! Ahoy!" he shouted, with a toothless grin.

"Careful or you'll shish kebab yourself," I warned.

No Legs lassoed our main mast, then swung himself back onto the windowsill to his room. Giddily he shouted, "Down below, down below!" and dropped a rope ladder to us. The ladder must have been made for high tide, or was caught on something, because we couldn't reach it despite No Legs egging us on: "There you go! Oh, just missed it. Try again!"

Figgie grabbed a long gidgee fish spear and wrapped the

point around the rope ladder. We tugged and pulled until it dislodged from under No Legs, sending him flying back out on his T-beam and us on our duffs. We clambered up the ladder, careful not to get our fingers caught between the rope and the wall. At first I thought it was rain I was hearing, only to realize it was the clack of beaks and the sound of pelican guano hitting the roof shingles—and hopefully not us. I counted twelve rungs to Henry's window. With each step I was afraid we'd drop in the drink between the shad and this creaking house.

Figgie easily slipped on and off the sill, while I barely fit through the window and dumped myself unceremoniously onto the sticky hardwood floor. Inside, two small pelicans sat perched on Henry's nightstands like table lamps. They eyed us suspiciously before flying out his front windows. I stuck my head out to see where they were going. Most houses have a candle in every window. This one had a pelican. Scrimshawed whale's teeth were strewn on every bureau, desk, and table in Henry's room, along with his carving tools. Most of the scrimshaw represented clipper ships or landscapes, but a few depicted mermaids in nature's dress bearing the faces of women in town that I knew. As we turned to walk toward the stairs, we heard Henry laughing on his swing. The hallway smelled like our barn only more birdy. The hay thrown about did little to disguise the offensive odors of dung, cigar smoke, and sweat. Two larger pelicans waddled out of rooms to escort us. I warned them not to peck us, which made Figgie laugh.

"These birds do what they want," he said. "Pelicans are sacred, you know. A mother will sacrifice her own lifeblood to save her dying young."

Figgie's village saw them as black warriors who painted themselves half-white to frighten their enemies. In one room, the oldest man in Paradise snored away as a pelican watched over him from the headboard. Reaching the stairs, I could hear Brennan talking up a storm. I don't ever call him crazy the way most people do because I don't think he is. That was my other reason for wanting to visit him. Brennan talked to whales. He understood them. He could help me find Jungay. As Abe said, Brennan sees the world differently than the rest of us. Papa always reminded me that Brennan had taught him whaling and was the best boatsteerer that ever there was. He and Pop Alex used to go out in a rowboat and ten whales would beach themselves, just to avoid a hunt.

Brennan sat at the parlor table playing Patience. Four pelicans perched on chair backs intently watching his every move. He'd once told me that these fifty-two cards were the only thing that could turn the virtue of Patience into a vice. His flowing white hair and beard made him look like the father of the Federation Henry Parkes whose photo hung on the wall behind us. A bucket of mulies sat on the table next to Brennan. Between slapping the cards down, he randomly tossed the mulies into the air for the birds to snatch.

"G'day, Mr. Charlie," said Figgie with a wave.

"Always a good omen when a Dawson comes to visit, especially when they bring along a young prince," Brennan said to the pelicans, who clacked their beaks in response.

"How goes my cook's helper?" Brennan asked, looking at his cards.

"I ain't cook no more," I said, wagging my collar at him. "Tub oarsman in Papa's boat."

"Well, say ya don't say," said Brennan, dropping his cards and grabbing my hand. "What do you think of all this, Calagun?"

"She can more than hold her own on the open water," he said proudly. "She rode an orca on her first hunt."

"Not surprised, not surprised at all," Brennan said, with pride in his voice.

"Not just any orca. Jungay."

"Jungay," said Brennan, looking up from his cards. "Most folks think him just a legend."

"I want to see him again," I said, leaning over the back of Brennan's chair. "How can I find him?"

"You don't," he said. "Calagun here likely told you that. Many people claim to see Jungay. None of it ever holds."

"We are certain," said Figgie. "It *is* him; I feel it."

"He'll find ya if need be," said Brennan, cutting the deck as his pelicans stared.

"I'm the one that needs it," I said.

Brennan ignored me as he lined up his cards in columns. "We like to play cards," he said, "because it brings order to an unordered world."

"I don't know how to play games," I admitted.

"Patience needs a good foundation," Brennan said, holding up an ace. "It requires unveiling yer cards at the right time and keeping yer options open."

"In a way, that's why we're here," I said. "We need a whaleboat—stoved even—if its condition is good."

"That's all?" said Brennan turning over his cards. "A whaleboat I can get ya, a spirit orca is another thing."

Brennan smelled of mildew and whiskey as he told us that just before the storm, a party of city knaves capsized a renter in ten feet of water about thirty feet off the rocky sandbar in Horse Head Harbor.

"There used to be a pier we dove off as kids near the palm grove. It's sunk now but you can see the pilings at low tide. Follow that line straight through the camel's eye and you'll see it," he added. "But it's damned near impossible to pull her up."

We figured to go mark the spot and return with Abe and the crew. While Figgie went to ready the shad, I stayed to give a final "Hooroo" to Brennan. When I turned around, the look on his face had changed. His eyes were wild with a piercing blue glow. His hair and beard were storm-tossed and his voice quivered with uncertainty. I could tell his mind was galloping ahead of the words he was trying to say.

"The lads come to me on the beach dressed in white

linen with the waves lapping at them," he muttered, furtively looking around, as if afraid someone might hear. "Their eyes were out and their hands clawed at me. Eli and Asa begged for revenge, but I had none to—"

"I had the same dream," I blurted out.

Brennan slumped back into his large leather chair, as if the very effort of thinking had drained his strength. I seized his hands, and it felt as though I pulled on the branches of a great cedar. I poured him a glass of water and he took three desperate gulps.

"Tell me who I must take revenge upon," I demanded, seizing his shoulders. A surge of energy flowed through me. All the old anger surfaced again like some ancient ocean rising up to meet the wind.

A look of terror froze Brennan's face.

"Tell me," I asked again. "Who did it?"

"The sea is not to be trifled with, child," he said, looking away. "It swallows everything and returns nothing."

He laughed and kicked his feet out in the little jig he often did while sitting in the chair. Furious, I began to walk away, but he pulled on my wrist with the force of an iron shackle. "A black wave come over them, a black wave…" he whispered mournfully.

"I have to go," I said, breaking his grip.

"Darkness is descending upon the world," he yelled, as I ran back up the stairs.

A cluster of pelicans crowded the hallway. As I pushed past them, they snapped at me with their long pink beaks and burning yellow eyes. No Legs sat on his bed, laughing and waving goodbye while I made my escape down the rope ladder. The pelican jabs stung and bruised my already battered body.

Figgie let out the sails. It was still low tide, as I turned the wheel toward Horse Head Harbor. What was the black wave Brennan kept mumbling about? How was it we had had the same dream? Kayle swam up beside us, shadowing our route. She had two oblong cuts on her broad head. I yelled at her for playing too close to boat propellers.

The water spray hit my face. I felt spit upon by the bay. Are you a friend or an enemy? I asked it, but I received no answer.

19

It wasn't so much Horse Head Harbor that Brennan had described, as it was the rocky outcrop known as Camel Spit. They'd called it that because the Prommies had dumped a bunch of humped mules there fifty years ago. Although no one had ever seen a camel this side of Adelaide, I imagined a few had ended up in a bushman's pot or two.

The granite boulders and swirling backwaters of the spit made it the perfect trap for Sunday lubbers out for a joy ride.

"This won't be easy," said Figgie, dropping anchor. "These rip currents could have us halfway to Tasmania before we know it."

We took turns searching for the boat, tying a rope around our waists in case the current got us. I was afraid to jump, thinking my brothers might be coming for me. But we needed that boat so I dove. On my sixth dive, with Kayle nudging me to play, I spotted the white tip of a boat bow. Even at low tide we couldn't get horses close enough to drag it out.

"We might have to pass on this," said Figgie.

"Let me take one more look," I said, grabbing some rope.

If I could find the hawser used to tie off the boat, we might be able to connect our rope to it. I was happy to see Kayle still sniffing around. At least I didn't have to worry about any intruders. She pawed under the seats with her snout as I surfaced for air. When I returned, she held the heavy rope in her mouth. She tugged on it to no avail and swam off clicking. That whalie seemed as upset as I.

"You're right," I said, breathlessly, "we can't get to it."

Figgie wasn't paying attention to me. He pointed in the

distance. "What is it?" I asked, turning to see two top fins descending upon us. It was Matong and Towrang. Figgie jumped in the water, and we both watched Matong pull the hawser while Towrang dug her head under the boat and began lifting. The two orcas flipped the craft with their flukes, nearly emptying it of water. It sat bobbing on the surface.

"See, just like I said," I added, in hushed awe. "If that ain't ridgy-didge, I don't know what is."

The orcas circled us twice and left.

Once we finished bailing out the whaleboat and got it back to the station, all we had to do was check the lost ship's registry in the *Hook & Harpoon*. If the insurance had paid out, we were free to own her right and proper. We left the whaleboat tied off with the rest. Later that afternoon, when the crew discovered the boat, I explained to Abe how we had watched the orcas un-stove it. I left out the middling details, but Abe was never one to look a gift horse in the mouth. He kicked his boots against the piling, his arms folded across his chest, and reminded me that Papa would be back in two days.

❧

That night all I could hear was that school clock ticking in my head. Once that bell rang, I'd be a weekend whaler.

Figgie watched the orcas. They were acting peculiar, territorial, and aggressive in a way that made him fearful of going near them. I wondered if that danged comet was making them nervous or if they were angry for dredging a boat with no whale tongue to pay for it. Abe was busy going through Papa's ledgers.

I took that to mean Figgie and I were on our own.

We jumped into his canoe and began searching for the orcas. It took only a few minutes for Kayle to find us. She impishly splashed and breached, hoping we'd follow her. We paddled as fast as we could, trying to keep up. Kayle stopped and spyhopped out of the water as if saying, *Wait here.*

We sat for a while, floating in the calm bay. Figgie started talking about my school situation when we saw the oddest thing. Eight of the orcas emerged, swimming back and forth in single file. Their top fins looked akin to teeth on a rapidly cutting saw. Burnum and Yindi began slapping the water with their side fins. Soon the other orcas were surrounding them in wide looping circles. They snorted and called out in bellowed tones. Towrang, Matong, Kayle, and others all joined in. We didn't dare move closer as this whirlpool spun faster and faster.

"Something's going on down there, and I aim to find out what," I said, unlacing my boots.

Figgie already had his shirt off and we both slid into the water. While our eyes adjusted to the underwater light, I saw Derain moving listlessly in the distance. She shook hard as the glimmer of a tiny wagging tail appeared under her belly.

"She's having her baby!" I cried out, emptying my lungs into air bubbles.

We surfaced and descended again. Derain moved with a determined zeal as more of the calf protruded. With one final shake, the baby orca emerged in a cloud of diffused blood. It lay motionless as an enormous shadow appeared.

Finally, the big fella.

Jungay gently carried the baby on the top of his snout, bringing her to the surface. He held her aloft in the warm sun as she took her first breath. She lay across his brow, yelping and wiggling her tiny tail as the rest of the orcas drew into a close circle around them. I felt their joyous chatter bounce off me as the orcas slapped their tails and porpoised around the two. As the baby darted about, each orca took turns rolling the poddy off their backs. The nipper wasn't much bigger than me. Towrang and Yindi flanked the infant as they led her back to Derain for her first meal.

"They are Derain's sisters and will help raise Miah as their own," said Figgie as we swam back to the canoe. "Uncle will be thrilled we were allowed to witness this event."

"Miah?" I asked.

"Yes," said Figgie, holding on to the side of the canoe. "Uncle named her after the moon because your mother's knowledge brought light to our village and the bounty of the tides followed her."

"That's how you learned the King's English, ain't it?" I said, fitting the pieces together.

"I was very young, but your mother was an excellent teacher."

Before I could digest that, Jungay breached into the air and fell back into the bay with a thunderous wave that washed us into Figgie's canoe. By the time we righted ourselves, all the orcas were gone.

"That was as strewth as strewth gets, mate!" I yelled, jumping to my feet.

"Bonzer!" shouted Figgie, pulling me into a hug, the canoe rocking beneath us.

It was the unprompted joy that happens during a cricket match or after finding someone thought lost. The longer it lasted, the more it felt like an embrace—at least what I figured one ought to feel like. I drew Figgie closer, and we intertwined the way plants do when growing closely together. We stayed there, tightening our grips on something I knew was already losing its hold. Kayle bumped the canoe, sending us toppling backward on our rumps. She wagged her head up and down gleefully as we laughed.

"Here ya go," I giggled, tossing Figgie a paddle. "Time for us to make some waves."

As our laughter died down, the silence between us gave me time to think about what had happened between all of us. These orcas are a democratic lot. The females are the pod leaders and get to choose their mates—*fancy that!* Both males and females work together as equals to make sure the entire pod is healthy. As Figgie said, all the orcas will help raise Miah. In a way, Papa had raised me that way too. Yet

I'm supposed to fit into a mold made by people I don't know, living in places I've never been. It's as if we're all buckets of meat poured into sausage casings someone else has chosen, only now it seems that maybe there's another way to see things.

"You're so quiet, Savannah. What are you thinking about?" asked Figgie.

"That I don't like bangers half as much as I used to," I answered.

By the time our feet hit the quay, it was late afternoon. The sun was still high overhead, but the comet demanded our attention. It looked as if it was about to swallow the hills, spotted with early autumn color. We headed toward the cricket glen at the top of the ridge overlooking Loch Bultarra and our tiny inlet. Lying there, we stared up at this beautiful yet terrifying spectacle that hung over the world.

Why was everything immense also so scary? I wondered. I rolled over on my side to face Figgie, who lay beside me with his eyes closed. I snapped off a long stem of grass bursting with seeds and lightly touched his face with it. He shooed it away without opening his eyes.

I waited for a moment, holding my grass blade in the cooling air like a wand. The comet continued to give off the light of a false sun keeping the long damp shadows of dusk from appearing. I noticed for the first time that the contours of Figgie's lips, nose, and forehead matched the silhouette of the mountain in front of us.

As I leaned on one elbow, touching his nose with the stem, those dark mischievous eyes opened.

"What's being grown up gonna be like?" I asked, lying flat again.

"I don't know," said Figgie as we looked at the sky.

"Will it be fun like this?"

"Maybe, if we're lucky," he said. "We'll stay who we are."

"I don't know who I am yet," I said, glancing at Figgie and then at the mountain.

"Your Dreaming will help guide you," he added with confidence.

Right there, I wanted to kiss that boy as much as I wanted to do anything. I remembered our unintended embrace just a few hours earlier. Moments like that should last forever, hang there like the comet to observe and ponder, but they don't. Instead, they streak across the sky and are here and gone, just as a meteor in the depths of space might do.

I did—he did—nothing.

Not out of fear or shyness, but out of knowing how much we had to lose. We'd be beholden to one another like two fish caught on the same hook. And I'd be wondering if it was me or the hook that kept us together. I could tell from his eyes that Figgie felt the same way. Neither of us wanted to risk our friendship for a union as vaporous or dangerous as the comet above.

A sharp breeze pulled the seedlings from the grass stem. I sat up while he brushed the seeds from his long flowing hair with that smile of his glowing.

"Ah, stick heck in a handbag," I exclaimed.

I pushed his shoulders down and planted my lips on his. I held them there until I was sure there was no mistaking what we did. I sat up and pulled my knees to my chest.

Figgie got up on his elbows, shaking his head like a sailor who'd been hit by a loose block and tackle. "I—" he sighed.

"Don't," I snapped. "Don't be ruining it with one of your Figgie stories that will take me three days to figure out. Just let it linger between us."

I slipped that moment into my memory the way you gently press a summer flower into the fold of a book for safekeeping.

We sat there, the two of us looking at the rust-colored mountain. Perfect.

❧

After Figgie left, I felt rudderless, drifting between Loch

Bultarra, Abe's cottage, and the bunks. I roamed over to the float dock and gazed across the bay at Paradise as the last streaks of orange drained from the sky. Turning to leave, I heard a low-pitched heaving.

"I knew you'd come," I said, without turning around.

I heard the water roll off Jungay as he came closer. I timed my dive as he pulled away from the dock. My hands rode over his saddle spot and grasped the base of his top fin. We'd ventured far into the bay when he dove below the surface, pulling me under with him. We paced off the way Spanish dancers do. Jungay's clicking sounds reminded me of the Flamenco dancers who came with Frieda's relatives on visits. He blew a shimmering water bubble toward me. It looped through the comet-lit water like a silver amulet. As it approached I pushed a wave at it in mock anger and sucked deeper into my lungs to hold my breath. Jungay lowered his head and shot another, another, and another, until a crown of bubbles landed on my head. Sensing my need to breathe, he launched me to the surface in a foaming phosphorescent gown as we sliced across the bay.

Jungay turned back to the inlet as if our future lay with the past. I sat wedged behind his top fin as he took a deep dive before torpedoing to the surface. Time froze as we hung suspended above the bay. At the apex of Jungay's leap, I stretched both my arms upward and let out a tumultuous roar. Our splashdown brought a trawler's spotlight to bear. As we plunged, I realized Jungay was bringing me home, whether I wanted to go or not.

"Just one more time," I begged.

Jungay would have none of it. He steered toward the float dock and let out a burst of steam from his blowhole to lower himself to the wooden boards. I rubbed his snout.

"I'll look for you every day," I whispered, waving as I ascended the stairs to the quay.

Approaching the final step, a just lighted lantern blinded me.

"I told you not to mess with those killers while I was gone," came a growl from the shadows.

20

Papa?" I asked, my knees buckling.

"Who were ya expecting? Abe, Frieda, someone else?" he said, lighting a cheroot.

"No, it's just that—"

"I'm not supposed to be back until tomorrow afternoon, yet here I am."

"Here you are…" I said, looking at the quay.

"What about the killers?" he asked, taking a long draw that made his cigar glow.

"I got friendly with them," I said, feeling the impact of my words.

"I can see that," he said.

"It—it wasn't out of disrespect of my pledge to you. I just had to. I can't explain it, but if I didn't go to them, I might as well have ripped my skin off and jumped in a salt bin."

"Odd behavior from someone who couldn't stand looking at a killer a week ago," he said, glancing out at the bay.

"I know," I said. "I fought it as long as I could."

"But the killers kept calling you," he said, grinding the neck of his cigar into the wood until it didn't breathe anymore.

"How did you know?"

"That's the way it was with me when I was your age."

"Papa?" I said, as baffled as I had ever been.

We sat on the edge of the quay, our legs dangling off the end, his arm around my waist, my head on his shoulder, holding on as if we were afraid one of us might fall.

"The killers came calling just as Prince Jimmy told me

they would," Papa said. "He said me and that big fella had some sort of destiny together, but I denied that part of me."

"Why?"

"I couldn't share…what it wanted. I needed to be a master whaler, a man of business," he added. "When Jungay appeared, I stood on the beach throwing rocks at him until he left."

"I'm sure he knew you meant no harm."

"Last week with you was the first I've seen him since. A day doesn't go by that I don't regret pushing him away. A day doesn't go by that I don't wonder if he might have saved my sons."

There was nothing for me to say as we sat there. Though I had felt its effects often, for the first time I understood what pain meant. Not the kind you feel from a hammer, or when a boy doesn't like you. A deep abiding pain that rips through you the way a boning knife does through a fish.

The lamps inside Loch Bultarra were glowing and Papa was home after flirting with his past. A past neither of us could escape. Yet Miah was born and Figgie and I had an understanding of things, and Jungay…he had his bay again.

"Now what's this I hear about a whaleboat?" Papa finally asked.

It took a few more days to figure out we could hold on to the stoved whaleboat. By then time had run out on our summer. The six of us marched onto the shad like prisoners off to Botany Bay. I was none too happy with the fancy collar on the dress Papa bought me. I'm to blame for not picking my own poison at Dilly's when I had the chance. At least this one covered Asa's moleskin breeches I wore underneath to protect my dignity while climbing.

Even with that lanced boil of a comet blotting the sky, it was too fine a day for tethering us to a classroom. With his bum leg healing, Aiden was the only one bouncing about the boat aching to enter Paradise. Ned loved spending his day off in Smithson's Billiards. He didn't want to hear a word about ditching off. That left me, the two Hobsons, the blacksmith's daughter, and Ryan to stew in our juices.

To everyone's delight, Kayle trailed along beside the boat, but she lost interest when we didn't stop and play. For the last indignity of the trip, I watched Figgie and his mates fishing off the barrier. They held their catch in the air and waved from their canoes. All I could muster was a weak hand gesture as we sped to our doom.

Although Etta Hobson found an empty bottle of spirits stuck in the bushes, the old Charyn House seemed no worse from its extended hours of weekend venery. I took the bottle and flung it off the property. The boys gathered in a remote part of the yard while we nestled near the doors. Both camps were too busy eyeing their own pack to show much interest in their foreign counterparts. It reminded me of the way the orca pod had its leaders and its followers.

I stood off from the rest of the girls with my Hobsons. Etta was four years younger than me and Benjamin was a year less than she. The three of us looked as out of place as whaleboats in the desert. With the wind picking up, I flipped Eli's cap around as I had done during the hunt. As the yard filled, everyone else seemed to know one another. Etta had her arms wrapped around a lunch pail that contained all three of our noontimes.

There was a flutter of whispers in the huddle of chirping chickens before one girl left the flock and inched her way toward us.

"Are you the American girl?" she sheepishly asked.

"No, I ain't," I said, arms folded across my chest. "We're from Dawson Station across the bay."

"Oh," said the girl, uncertainly. "Would you like to join us?"

"Good onya," I said, pulling my Hobsons along with me through a steady breeze.

I was about to introduce us when a horse's whinny turned everybody around. A white gig pulled up. The mare strained and bucked as it came to a halt.

The driver jumped down.

"Hello, everyone," she said, with a dimpled smile. "I hope I'm not late."

A blast of cold wind yanked the straw bonnet off her head and lifted it into the trees. Laughter rattled through the yard as the young woman stomped her foot.

"You there, tall one in the boots," she snapped, "fetch my hat."

"Fetch it yourself," I said, spitting on the ground.

The group of girls moved away from me like sheep from a wolf.

"Do fetch it immediately," she demanded again. "Please, you can reach it easily."

The matron began ringing a hand bell and showed the Hobsons to her door. The girl stared indignantly up at the branches, hands on her hips as the rest of us filed into a large parlor. A movable blackboard stood in front of the room directly under the smirking portrait of Captain Mordecai Charyn. The stories I heard about him won't reach the ears in any classroom.

All the others knew the routine. They pulled their desks away from the walls and arranged them in rows. Since there were more than twenty of us, we had to double up at desks. I sought out the girl who'd invited us into their group.

"G'day to you. I'm Annabelle," she said. "That's with two Ls and one bell."

"Well, bonzer to you, mate," I said, grabbing her hand for a good shake.

"There will be no complaining about desks or seating," a male voice declared from the back of the room. "In my day, we stood during lessons and were better for it. I dare say the empire is better for it."

Mr. Xavier Willis Davenport was a thin man with a sharp pointed moustache and round spectacles. He liked to walk in and out of our rows, tapping a long wooden pointing stick on the tops of our desks. He used it deftly to skim the cap off my head. It twirled on the point and fell in my lap as he announced it was improper to wear any haberdashery inside. Every boy whipped a cap from his brow and stuffed it in his back pocket. He took attendance. There were Andersons, Albrights, and Browns, but I shot up in my seat when he said, "Miss Arizona Bittermen."

The Yank sat by herself with no desk but announced a new one was coming.

I looked outside through the open window where everyone piled apples and snacks on the sill. Bittermen. I wondered if she had been the one in the red carriage that nearly killed me at the cricket match. My blood boiled listening to Mr. Davenport drone on about English kings. When my dunny time came, I laughed walking past the bonnet up in the tree.

It gave me an idea.

We practiced elocution by reading famous lines from Shakespeare, trying to keep our minds off lunch. Ryan rose with a hungry look in his eyes.

"My horse, my horse," he cried in anguish, "my kingdom—"

"It's a horse!" shouted Annabelle with two *L*s jumping up and pointing wildly.

The gig's mare poked her head in the window, wearing the most adorable straw bonnet. She proceeded to devour all the apples and food lining the windowsill. Half the class screamed. The other half laughed. The horse stuck its head inside and whinnied, showing its teeth. Miss Bittermen near fainted from the humiliation.

Mr. Davenport snapped his pointing stick in two trying to restore order. In the next room the youngsters rushed out the double front doors to see what was happening. That allowed the mare to step inside. Desks toppled, books fell, the blackboard collapsed. The horse looked more at ease in front of the class than our teacher did.

Everyone pinched up against the walls as Mr. Davenport demanded to know who owned that animal. Ever the Englishman, he enlisted three boys to help subdue the bonneted beast. Perhaps suffering from stage fright, the poor confused animal simply let all her inhibitions go. The result was quite a hefty deposit upon pages once dedicated to the bloodlines of kings. As the stench reached us, everyone ran from the building. The kindly old woman from the other room threw her apron over her head and led the race out.

With classes called for the day, we headed to the village square to eat our noonday.

"That was the most fun ever," cried an excited Benjamin Hobson. "I love going to school."

All over town we ran into scattered classmates. Word spread that Mr. Davenport was roaming the streets of Paradise with his broken stick looking for one of the boys to blame. One lad said Mr. Davenport planned to make a public exhibition of the culprit.

I ought to march right up to Mr. Davenport, I thought, and tell him that a girl can cause just as much trouble as a boy and do a better job of it. Served some lad right to take the blame along with all the misplaced glory. They wouldn't be the first innocents hung out to dry in this territory and they wouldn't be the last. Besides, fessing up only serves the curious onlookers. In *The Getting of Wisdom*, Laura tells a few lies and everything worked out for her so far.

A wide placard in the middle of the square drew a large crowd. Together again, Aiden and Benjamin dragged me to see it.

"Look, Savannah," urged Benjamin pulling me along, "it's a jumps race right here in Paradise."

So, it was. Anyone with a horse could enter if they hit their kick for £15. A first-place purse of £65 is what got the crowd buzzing. Whoever sketched the horse on the placard didn't do a very good job of it. The body was too thick, the legs too short and thin.

"That's good oil, you lads," I said, grabbing both their chins with a wink.

We couldn't get any closer to the sign so I took my three musketeers and headed to the pond. They ran onto the foot-bridge to watch the model sailboats. I decided to check in with Mr. Brown about my latest bridge drawings when the white gig galloped by.

The carriage overflowed with girls from class, including Anna one bell. Look what the bunyip dragged in, I thought. As the carriage pulled to a stop, I approached with my hands clasped behind my back.

"I'm sorry, there doesn't appear to be any room in here for you," said Arizona, holding the reins as she leaned out toward me.

Her dark hair shimmered like midnight waves and her eyes were as blue as Antarctic ice. She already had that cleft mark in her chin that certain women yearn for.

"I'm not going in the same direction you are," I said, start-ing for the pond.

"Pity. Mr. Davenport is so headstrong on finding the per-petrator of that mischief," said Arizona, gripping the reins tighter. "I told him not to worry, the hat was expensive but meaningless; perhaps it should have only been worn by a horse. I couldn't think of a single student who would dare allow a horse to disrupt a classroom with such antics. Can you, Miss Dawson?"

"I never pay no mind to yesterday's heavy weather," I said, petting the mare's long nose. "I just deal with what is."

"Well, I hope we meet on more equal footing the next time," said Arizona, leaning out to offer her hand.

"We're more equal than you think," I said, jumping up on a broken carriage step.

We stared at one another face to face. Her dark eyebrows cracked up and down like circus whips. "And I thought this school might be boring," Arizona said, snapping the reins before I had a chance to jump off.

"Try a size nine hat. It'll fit the mare better," I whispered in her ear as I leapt off.

The gig bucked and roiled as it bolted away to screams and laughter. I stood on the foot walk, searching for Aiden and my Hobsons. The pond bridge was empty and the toy boats were gone. Maybe I'd bitten off more than I could chew. I didn't think the horse would eat all those lunches or break into our classroom to do his business. On the other hand, I heard one of the gents on the bridge say it was a prank worthy of Ned Kelly.

Waiting on the shad for Ned, we six students decided to keep the day's events to ourselves. It was ours to cherish; besides, adults never understood these sorts of things. As we left the harbor, I looked for that roaming horse again. Instead I spotted a girl in a white gig at the end of Wharf Row watching our every move. This Arizona was every bit the predator as any shark, eel, or ray I'd ever run into. I asked Ned, "What's the best way to get a ship through an unexpected squall?"

"Why, ya luff," he said, surprised I asked. "Flatten yer sails, get before the wind, and slice through it. You ride out a storm. If you head into it, you'll be swept under every time. You ought to know that."

Deep down I did, but I let the day get the better of me. There were many ways to manage a storm; bluster and attacking headwinds wasn't among them.

21

The comet still gnawed at us from above, picking upon frayed nerves. It gave us a good excuse for anything that went unexplained. I waited around a corner and socked one of the lads in the kisser for making fun of Aiden, even though his limp was almost gone. The boy never knew what hit him. I locked Annabelle with two *L*s in the dunny for, well, having that extra *L*.

The explanations always led back to the comet.

Arizona and I went at it at least twice a day. Every little tick or personality quirk we discovered gave us a chance to torment each other. It was a sporting game. Mr. Davenport continued his inquiries about the horse incident. Sooner or later someone was going to point the bone at me. I wondered why Arizona didn't just give me up. Best as I could figure, she didn't want me to know how much the whole horse and hat ordeal got to her.

It got to me.

At first I hesitated to light all three candles in the widow's walk, worried this wasn't a downright calamity. One person's catastrophe can be another's routine day. With all the events swirling around me, Figgie knew I was like a marionette in the wind. He was as good as anyone at helping me straighten the strings. Yet hard as I tried, I always ended up in the same jumbled place.

I didn't have to wait long before I saw him in the yard. I scampered downstairs with Humphrey, Scud, and Quilp in tow. If people were more like cats or orcas, my life would have been a lot simpler. I worried too that not seeing Figgie as much these days might have changed things between us. They didn't. He was the same bloke.

Fair dinkum all the way.

He sat with his legs crossed and his eyebrows furrowed, listening to my school tales.

"What is the point of this classroom?" he asked. "When it was my time to hunt, I didn't sit in a hut talking about it. I joined Warrain and the others."

"Well," I said, "it ain't my job to defend Western Civilization. I figure you learn a bunch of things so it gives you something to talk about when you're a grown-up and there's no fun to be had anymore."

Figgie laughed and clapped his hands. Once again he held up a mirror for me to look at myself. And once again, I realized how seriously I was taking everything.

"Okay, Savannah," he said, touching my arm. "Why don't you tell me what's really on your mind."

I spilled on Arizona Bittermen, the goody-two-shoes who had everyone fooled. She was a sugar-sweet she-devil with an acid tongue and a shark's smile who always got her way with Mr. Davenport.

"Every morning she buys fresh-baked cookies for the whole class," I said, pacing about, "and she leaves me the biggest one."

"I can see how that would be upsetting," said Figgie sincerely as he rubbed Humphrey's belly.

"When she gives me the cookie she whispers, 'You need this more than the others,'" I exclaimed.

"Oh," said Figgie, petting two cats.

"Don't you see," I said, slapping hands on my hips. "I'm the waif, the ugly skinny girl who needs fattening up."

That was only half of it. In just a few days, she had Ryan and the rest of the boys eating out of her hand. They took turns watching her gig, helping her out of the carriage, and carrying her books. Annabelle did Arizona's homework while all the other girls just begged to be near her.

Figgie looked confused, as if he'd just turned down the wrong path in the woods.

"Uncle warned me that girls can become complicated at this age," he said, petting the cats before he left.

"We were *always* complicated, you just never noticed!" I shouted, as he disappeared into the woods.

The next morning before school, Papa handed me a small ivory envelope with a red seal. "I picked this up from the post the other day in Paradise," he said. "Looks like a note from one of your cobbers."

"What friends?" I said, opening it. "Those schoolgirls are the last ones I'd expect to…Oh no, it can't be."

"What's wrong?" asked Papa, sitting up straight.

"Bittermen wants to have us for dinner," I cried.

Papa took the note from my hand, glared at it, and muttered a few phrases in Gaelic that would have made Captain Charyn blush.

"Can't we say we're busy?" I said.

"He'd find another date," said Papa, slapping the note in his hand, "and like a herd dog he'll sense our fear and know he's on top."

"You mean—"

"Always meet a bully head on," Papa said, "or you'll be dealing with him your whole life."

I dreaded having to go back to school, knowing I had to face that viper Arizona with a we're-so-delighted-you're-coming smile.

Papa ran off to Abe's with the note so fast his cap flew off. "Find something fancy that'll put that outfit you wore to the cricket match to shame!" he shouted.

Less planning went into the Siege of Khartoum.

The Bittermen Wars had begun.

Knowing what was at stake, I fessed up to Papa about the hat and the horse. This was the second time I ever saw him belly laugh at something.

The dinner table would be our battlefield.

Momma-girl dyed one of Papa's worn-out linen suits black so it looked near brand new. He borrowed a four-in-hand tie from Warrain, who liked to fancy it up more than we realized. Papa painted his scuffed-up brown boots black to look shiny.

I imagined it was back to Dilly's for me, but Papa had another idea. One that had more to do with finance than fashion, I suspected.

In the village square, the shopkeepers and storefronts seemed different from our last visit. The owners waved less and their shelves were sparser. The baker, who'd given us free cookies just two weeks earlier, chased me from the sweet aromas of his window. The trawlers were empty and the pubs were full. No fish, no food, no barter, no money. Some jawed that prices were too high and the new government money was no good. Others pointed at the comet, claiming it was to blame for their woes.

We visited an old friend of Papa's on the waterfront. She wore a glittery dress and ran a hotel for young women. She had plenty of dresses left behind by lodgers that would suit me fine.

Well, she took one look at me and after a big hug said she had just the right outfit. It was a green and white drapey thing with an open back. I tried it on and glanced at myself in the full-length mirror.

It made me feel like those Greek statues in those fancy magazine ads. All I needed was a harp.

"Saints alive," Papa said when I walked into the waiting room. He jumped out of his chair, wringing his hat in his hands.

If it was good enough for Papa, it was good enough for me.

❧

On the day before our big dinner, I told the Hobsons to wait for me at the shad. I stayed as the classroom emptied out. The longer this intrigue about the horse in the school hung out on the line, the more power Arizona had over me.

I approached Mr. Davenport busy at his desk where the scent of horse still lingered. The slightest inhale made my overture even more precarious.

"Mr. Davenport," I said in a steady flat voice, "there is something you ought to know."

He went from pensive folded hands to twirling the ends of his mustache by the time my story ended. Mr. Davenport sat back with his arms folded across his chest.

"Admitting this is either very brave or a rather bad blunder on your part," he said.

"It's not a deed I lay claim to lightly, sir," I said, casting my eyes downward, "and I accept the consequences for my actions wherever they lead."

"You mean it, Dawson, don't you? I find that rather refreshing," he said. "You don't mind if I call that do you? The female salutation seems somewhat ill-fitting in your case."

I heartily agreed, and as I came to learn, we agreed on many other matters of substance as well.

"These geographical sketches you made," he said, pulling out my maps of Australia assignments, "are far superior to any student work I've ever seen."

"Thank you, sir. That's very kind," I said, blushing.

"Kindness has nothing to do with it," he snapped, sitting up straight. "If you have talent, it's my job to cultivate it."

I thanked him again for his generous compliments, but my joy was short-lived. He stood up, grabbing his new pointer. Punishment must be exacted for every infraction, he said, tapping the long stick on his desk; I gulped hard.

"I want you to…" he began, flexing the pointer between his hands, "sketch repentance, whatever that means to you. When you feel you've expressed yourself properly, bring it to me. That will be all."

With a sigh of relief, I headed for the door.

"Dawson," he said, stopping me in my tracks, "What is it you 'strines say, Hooroo?"

"Hooroo to you, sir," I said, waving from the door.

I should've spent the afternoon fixing my hair and practicing my finishing school manners. Instead, I used my time to draw. Mr. Davenport had let me off easy and I wanted to show him his faith in me wasn't unwarranted. Effortlessly, I sketched three scenes. One of a girl with her hands clasped in prayer, another of a child offering a basket of fruit to the viewer with her head bowed, the third of a girl gratefully accepted back into a group.

I was so proud of myself. At dusk I lit a candle in the widow's walk to show off my work to Figgie. I waited for his eyes to light up and those fancy words of his to start flowing about my artwork.

But they didn't.

He was quiet during most of the visit. He moved about my room as if he were in a place he didn't belong. He picked up things, put them down, and stood with hands in his pockets as if he were cold. Figgie never sat down or leaned in to say any of the words I expected.

"They are photographic renderings of the highest caliber," he said, while slipping out my window, "but, Savannah, they aren't art the way my people understand it."

Insulted by his comments, I decided he was unable to grasp the finer points of our culture. I couldn't sleep with this germ of his festering in my mind. I was angry with Figgie for not recognizing what I had accomplished. Hours passed. I got up and looked at the drawings again. Tore them to pieces and threw them out the porthole.

Perhaps Mr. Davenport gave me this assignment expecting me to fail so I'd realize my place in life. I regretted not spending my time more propping myself up in front of the mirror. I stared at the blank paper, unable to lift a pencil, rest, or sift through my feelings. Those old demons were howling in my head again.

I slipped down my window tree into the moonlight and meandered down to the float dock. I waited for Jungay, but I never sensed he was coming. I worried that somehow, I had offended my new orca friends by abandoning them for school. The water slapped at my knees as I sat on the float dock watching the empty bay. Although the water was still at its warmest, the air was cool. Soon I wouldn't be able to swim with the pod, and they would leave to follow their food.

Sickles of moonlight bobbed on the waves and sliced through my memories. They welled up as the disembodied faces of my classmates, Arizona, the crew, and townspeople. What did these apparitions want from me, why did they linger in my dreams? The serenity I had felt for the last week was shattered. Now I faced the full dread of responsibility. It was too easy to hide behind my obligation to attend school and not think of anything else.

I got my drawing things and returned to the safety of the tool room to be with my wall orcas. I lined up my pencils, pens, and paper and got to work. I stayed up into the wee hours sketching through my troubles on paper. I drew pictures of Laura and the other characters from *The Getting of Wisdom*. I imagined the situations they put themselves in and drew them as if they belonged on the comics pages of *Vumps* for boys. Only this comic was about things we cared about, even if most of the girls I knew didn't care much for what I cared for. These characters depicted more than a passing resemblance to my own classmates, though I left myself out of the drawings. Trying to sketch *Repentance* still lingered in the back of my mind, but Figgie's voice and disappointed eyes blocked every image I wanted to draw.

I took the rough sketches of each orca I had made at the float dock and transferred them to the back wall where Derain's image ruled. I thought of Figgie while I worked, which was both agitating and exhilarating. He had a way of distracting me when I needed to concentrate. Any image that came into my mind bled away. At the same time, his stories about the orcas and his reverence for them spurred me to try harder to capture what I wanted to draw.

Although he wasn't there, his presence was.

After a few hours, Scud came darting in with his tail raised. Soon the rest of the cats followed.

"What's the matter," I asked, picking up as many of them as I could, "you fellas miss me?"

They meowed and pawed at my arms and neck, curious about what I was doing. I put tiny Emma on my shoulder like a parrot to keep her from knocking everything over. I continued feverishly drawing. My fingers tore at the wood and I worked my pencils down to nubs. When I finally closed the door, the first streak of the sun stretched across the sky.

I didn't know if I was ready for that first glint of silverware later that afternoon or not, but I figured proper etiquette and war go hand in hand as long as the generals are fighting.

Once they leave the table, it's cats in a tinderbox.

22

"Let me say, it's a tragedy that it has taken so long for our two distinguished families to rendezvous," announced Jacob Bittermen, standing and extending his glass in the air. "To the Dawson clan."

"... and to the Bittermen family tree. May ya keep climbing up it," said Papa, as he carefully lifted his long-stemmed flute, trying not to snap it in two. "Hope you weren't too deigned inviting us over."

I put down my fork, jumped to my feet, and raised my cup. I was standing there admiring all the fancy crystal when I realized that I was the only one standing. Well, I dropped to my seat faster than an anchor in Port Phillip harbor. Arizona covered her mouth with a napkin, but I knew she was giggling underneath it. I figured by Monday everyone in New South Wales would know too.

If that wasn't enough to make me sweat, the glass roof above us magnified the sun. Its pale twin, the comet, hovered low as if listening to every word. We sat at a table about the size of our cricket field. Papa needed his spectacles to see Bittermen's face, but his pride prevented him from doing so. It was good that Arizona was more than an arm's length away. It helped keep things civil between us.

Jacob Bittermen appeared the same as he did at the Dodd's Cup match. A squat, low-browed man, his red stalks of prairie-grass hair looked best when covered by his wide-brimmed gaucho hat. His dark eyes revealed no secrets and his wispy goatee gave him an appearance of impatience. Wearing a bolo tie, snakeskin jacket, and boots to match, he reminded me of a swagman ready for a Saturday night dance.

"Now, Savannah," Bittermen said, as if he had heard my thoughts, "I understand from reliable sources that you are a whaler?"

I glanced over at Papa for a signal on how to answer. He nodded for me to go-ahead.

"Papa let me go out with the crew once," I mumbled, playing with my fork, "but we didn't catch anything."

Bittermen tugged on his goatee and slumped back in his chair, as if someone had shot him. "You are the embodiment of Diana the Huntress," he said, in his twanged accent. "I find that extraordinary, don't you, Arizona?"

"Extra, extra ordinary," Arizona said, chewing on a prawn.

"I do hope her participation wasn't out of necessity," chirped Bittermen. "My resources are always at your disposal."

"Thanks," said Papa, "but we're holding our own."

"That must have been a frightening experience," said Bittermen, motioning for a refill of his and Papa's glasses, "especially with those—"

"Orcas," I said, interrupting him.

"—killer whales," Bittermen continued, ignoring me, "around eating everything in my bay. They're very destructive creatures."

I stood up and defended the orcas. I told him how they live in family units, mate for life, and care for their babies for years. The orcas communicate like the rest of us, only through a series of clicks and whistles, I told him. They are sad and happy, like us, and they can camouflage themselves during a hunt. Most importantly, they take from the bay only what they need.

The forcefulness of my argument caught even me by surprise. Papa just winked my way. He said the killers haven't caused any problems in sixty years and weren't about to start. Bittermen clapped his hands and the main course rushed out. Arizona fanned herself, casting a slight smirk in her father's direction.

When the food wasn't ready, Bittermen suggested Arizona show me the house while he and Papa talked business. Before we left to go upstairs, he swung open the double doors to the library. Though uninvited, Bittermen's sweeping arm motions dragged me and Arizona in with the dust balls and cigar ash, revealing a gigantic portrait of a man in gray uniform on the back wall. The face glaring down at us reminded me of the comet. High on the walls, heads of a rhino, elephant, water buffalo, and lion stared frozen at attention, as if awaiting his orders.

"Who might that be?" I asked.

"Why, that's my father, Colonel Josiah Cornwallis Bittermen," Bittermen said in mock admiration while holding up his glass.

I asked if the colonel was part of the royal dragoons. Bittermen seemed agitated by my question. He said his family was part of the Confederacy done in by political blackguards. The colonel, Bittermen added, believed in attacking first and attacking last while giving no quarter in-between no matter how puny the enemy. I recalled hearing Papa and the crew mentioning that Bittermen was from the American South.

"I was born into the tyranny of an uneasy peace," Bittermen stated grandly for all to hear.

As Papa followed us into the great room, the paint on his boots peeled off in little black flecks across the white carpet. I didn't know what Bittermen's words meant, but they irritated Papa so I kept quiet. The heavy doors closed with a tumbler's click. Our fathers' silence swept us back out of the library toward the upstairs niceties of Arizona's abode. If the two of us had one thing in common, it was that we both wanted to hear the goings-on behind those locked doors. Neither of us trusted the other enough to admit this so we began an uneasy climb up the spiral staircase.

"Daddy thinks I'm so much like grandpappy I'll end up leading an army someday," said Arizona, walking two steps ahead of me so we could see eye-to-eye. "I must say you pulled that off brilliantly."

"Pulled what?" I asked.

"Tell me you and your father didn't rehearse that whole whale story, knowing it would get my dear daddy's goat," she said, putting hands on her hips.

"It's true, we're whalers. That's what we do," I said, the salt riled in me.

"Fine," said Arizona, starting up the stairs again. "I'll let you play this hand for now, but I'm on to you."

"I'm not playing anything," I said, pulling her back by the elbow.

I squeezed her forearm hard. Figgie told me I shouldn't beat the world to a pulp until it liked me. Even though I was still angry with him for blaspheming my drawings, I let her arm go.

"I wish I had your strength," said Arizona, rubbing her forearm, "and those high cheekbones."

I wanted to return the compliment, but there wasn't anything about her I could aspire to. Arizona was showing interest in me the way that shark did when our boat was smashed. I still didn't trust her, but her compliments were greasing the skids. Her bedroom seemed the size of Loch Bultarra with twice the furniture.

"This is hard for me to admit," she said, placing her hand on my arm as we sat, "but I've misjudged you and I'm sorry for that."

I tried to make the same stone face Brennan did when he drew a good hand. I sat there and said nothing. "Do you miss your mother?" Arizona asked. "I understand she died a long time ago."

"How do you know that?"

"Small towns talk," she said, "I've been a victim myself."

Arizona told me her mother was a socialite. One day she discovered her having "amorous intentions with another." She confided what had happened to her mother's best friend. Her parent's marital obligations ended up on hiatus as she put it.

"I've been banished to live with Father because of my honesty and trust," she said, while showing me her dressing room, "imagine that?"

Arizona's glum look after the revelation made me feel a kinship with her. I wanted to be charitable in my thoughts the way Figgie was.

"Sometimes I feel close to my mum, and at others, I feel motherless," I said.

"Let's start over, shall we?" she said. "We motherless ones should stick together."

We lay on her twin fainting couches watching a couple of wagtails singing in a tree overhanging her balcony. When called back to the adult world, we fell into our familiar roles as obstinate girls. We giggled, fanned ourselves, and hid behind napkins. Something had changed during that past hour. It was more than a friendly conversation between classmates. There was an acceptance, a lowering of swords.

Why, I didn't understand.

The table that appeared so sparse sparkled with silver and gold domed chafers. Oysters, turtle soup, filets of kingfish, saddle of lamb, and mushrooms on toast were just a few of the items I could remember. A butler stood next to each of us ready to serve.

The abundance of food upset Papa, though he tried not to show it. He often said the need for excess drives men to attempt foolish things. Without causing a scene, he served himself and I followed suit. Bittermen ignored our manners as he tucked a long napkin into his collar and told stories about the Virginia Commonwealth.

We were into mealtime small talk. At least our fathers were.

We sat playing with our food, shared eye rolls, and answered the few questions lobbed our way. To liven things up, all of us played a game. We each wrote down our favorite word and everyone had to guess it. For Papa, the table guessed *whale*, but he said it was *thanks*. Mine was *g-day* though Arizona suggested it was *water*. She was hard to guess; we went several rounds before Arizona admitted it was *trust*.

Bittermen didn't give us a chance to guess his.

"*More*," he announced as the desserts arrived, "because that's what I want. More of everything, more wealth, more land, more good friends."

As we finished our fancy ice cream and assorted cakes, Bittermen lit cigars for him and Papa. After we finished, he had one final room he wanted us to see. We followed Bittermen down a short hallway. At the end was a large carriage door on rollers.

"I'm an ambitious man," he said, pulling the sliding door open, "but I generously embrace others to join my dreams."

The dim glow of oil lamps slowly illuminated the room as if the sun were rising. As my eyes adjusted to the light, I saw the strangest collection of contraptions and inventions. There were glass flasks filled with colorful chemicals and jars packed with all types of animal parts – monkey hearts, cow brains, and squid tentacles. Miniature engine-powered carriages, winged trains, and cigar-shaped boats dotted the shelves or hung from the ceiling.

"Are you opening a museum with all this, Jacob?" asked Papa.

"No, no, this isn't about the past," he said, grabbing my chin. "It's the future. Imagine what the world will be like in five years, or even thirty, for that matter."

"What's that got to do with us whaling?" I questioned.

"I'll show you," said Bittermen.

He removed his shiny snakeskin jacket, as if he were molting into another creature. He snapped the white sheet off a large table in the center of the room. A gaunt, worried look came over Papa's face. Bittermen revealed a scale model of Paradise, Reflect Bay, and Doddstown, right down to the boulders on the beaches. The thing was it looked more like London or Paris than our little town. Tall buildings and long piers on both sides of the bay replaced most everything I recognized.

"What are all those pipes connecting the buildings?" I asked.

"Pneumatics, compressed air, the power of the future," said Bittermen, his eyes growing wide.

This mystery power had us transfixed. The pipes delivered mail right inside someone's home. Large tunnels would use forced air to propel omnibus canisters filled with people under the bay and to move elevators in tall buildings.

"You see these towers," continued Bittermen. "I've invested with a consortium that will bring wireless telegraphic transmissions here. Sound with no wires."

Bittermen could have used Mr. Davenport's pointer as he was flicking his cigar at the Snowy Mountains, covering them with ash. From there, he explained, the rushing water from ten dams would provide hydroelectric power to New South Wales and Paradise. Everything would run on electricity.

"The mountain water will be used to irrigate the deserts to grow cotton and tobacco," he said proudly.

"Lot of that is sacred land," I said, touching the gritty surface of his model desert.

"There's nothing sacred about sand, sweetheart," he said, patting my shoulder.

"Where's the whaling station?" Papa asked, looking at me concerned.

"This is the beauty of it," said Bittermen, directing us to a big brick box with smokestacks. "Notice how clean and efficient it is."

"Nothing clean about whaling," growled Papa, folding his arms across his chest. "It's a dirty business all around."

"Precisely. This is the twentieth century, the age of auto-mation," Bittermen replied. "Machines will do our bidding."

"Machines can't tell you when enough is enough," Papa said. "The Law of the Bay isn't to be trifled with."

"Law of the Bay?" sneered Bittermen from his gormless maw. "There's only one law—supply and demand. An efficient modern factory could process thirty whales a month all year long compared to, what, your eight for an entire season?"

"We take enough to feed our people, pay our crew, and meet our obligations," said Papa.

"You rely too much on those lazy scavengers to find your prey," Bittermen said, pointing at Papa. "Those killers scare away thousands of whales and fish from my bay."

"It ain't your bay, and you might want to think twice about who you're pointing at," Papa said, in a tone that sent chills down my spine.

Bittermen leaned over his Lilliputian model on both hands like a tired Gulliver. He apologized to Papa and me for badgering his guests.

"I know how hard you work; I hate to see you pass up a golden opportunity," he said, putting both hands on Papa's shoulders. "Germany needs high-quality whale oils for its military equipment, which means the Brits, French, and maybe even the Americans need it too. Every country has an army today."

Papa shook his head no faster than a tub line leaving a whaleboat.

"Let's not make any *hasty* decisions," Bittermen said, backing off. "Maybe I need to further evaluate the situation."

Everyone relaxed for a moment. Arizona slipped her arm through Bittermen's.

"Please, Mr. Dawson, father means well, he truly does," she said. "Do forgive our American improprieties."

"It would do me good to learn more about your bay," said Bittermen, nodding. "Let me make amends. We need good people like you to be part of the town's future. Savannah, you seem to know an awful lot about those—"

"I know everything about the orcas," I said, jumping in. "I've drawn their pictures and see them all the time."

"How would you like to share what you know at an exhibit during next week's Harvest Festival?" asked Bittermen excitedly. "We'll call it 'Life of the Orcas.'"

I was so thrilled; I didn't pay much attention to the rest of Papa's conversation with Bittermen. They talked about the Jumps Race. The next thing I knew Papa was making a wager with Bittermen. Double the £65-pound purse if Papa ran that white town horse against his. Even I gulped at that bet. The town horse can barely walk without tipping over. Some folks even shot at him for eating their apples and grass.

When we walked out that front door, I was relieved to hear the aches and pains of the village again. I told Papa I felt like a python had just swallowed me whole and I had come out the other end. He laughed loudly, which wasn't so remarkable anymore, and rubbed my neck. He felt a bit squeezed too, he said.

"You look pretty in that gown," he said. "We ought to buy more things like it."

"Not if it means leaving Loch Bultarra for that factory place," I said. "Is that what he wants you to do? I don't think I could ever use silverware again."

"Sure, I could be president of something or other," said Papa, digging his hands into his dyed trousers. "Get rid of the killers and the villagers—they could only work and live on those cotton ranches of his, you know."

"Papa, you wouldn't. What about Figgie and all our friends?" I said, alarmed. "You don't have to listen to him, do you?"

"Last I looked, I'm still a free man," Papa said, pulling on his jacket lapels. "He's not the first to challenge us. Pop Alex dealt with some grizzly ones too."

I was never happier to leave a place. I was grateful for the late afternoon breeze taking us back, even if it wasn't compressed air. Arizona was still a shark, but they only bother you when hungry. After Arizona was done gnawing on me, I wondered when she would feed next. Whatever came of this, I had a chance to explain the orcas and that made it a risk worth taking.

Streaks of orange covered the sky as I stood on the bow, feeling the cool freshness of early fall. I turned and looked out at the ocean. "What's that off the port side?" I yelled to Papa, pointing.

He swung the shad to the east so we could get a closer look. Two of our whaleboats were on a hunt. Lon was leading the crew in one boat, Abe in the other. Lon shouted they were down two men. Papa readied to drop anchor as we made our way to the boats.

"I need an oarsman," said Lon. "We can't keep up with them. There are three heading due north ready to rise in ten minutes."

"The orcas aren't with us!" shouted Abe, "but they'll show." I lifted my gown high enough to step into the whaleboat, exposing more calf than I intended. Lon wiped his forehead with a kerchief as I passed to hoots and catcalls.

I locked my oar in place.

And settled into my seat like any other member of the crew.

23

L on gave the order for both boats to "toss oars." All twelve of our sculls stood upright at attention. We looked like a floating forest. Papa passed across our boat to Abe's, and Abe came back to us. Now we had Ned and Papa in one boat and Abe and Lon working in ours. I was the only one out of place, in more ways than one. Scanning both crafts, I didn't see Figgie among any of the crew. Papa lobbed his jacket to me, rolled up his sleeves, and wrapped his necktie around his head like a bandanna.

"Boss, that's my lucky kissing tie!" bellowed Warrain.

"Not anymore it ain't," said Papa, to belly laughs all around.

"Oars fall," shouted Lon, still laughing, "and give way together!"

I couldn't have been farther from the Bittermen place on Cornwallis Street if I'd been standing on Granite Beach in Tasmania. More than anything, I needed not to be thinking but doing.

"Pick up the stroke on the starboard side and ground those oars if we're gonna have a fair go at catching this carpenter fish," yelled Lon, with no trace of humor in his voice.

It was my side of the boat he earbashed. I forgot to roll my wrists after pulling my blade from the water. With the flat spoon of the oar against the wind, it slowed us down and made it harder for me to row. As much as I hated to admit it, Lon was right and I had to listen to him. I picked up my pace.

"Put yer backs into it," shouted Lon, hands cupped around his mouth. "Needs must when the devil drives."

"Ol' Lucifer might be forcing us to row, but he'll not be getting a pinch of my share," one of the crew called out.

"He got all my money Friday night," shouted another crewman to more laughter.

"Pull harder, mates," screeched another voice behind me. "We can't let that boat full of old men beat us to the spot."

I was taking shorter, quicker strokes when I looked up at Lon, standing tall and holding the steering rudder with a firm grip. Our eyes met unexpectedly. Usually, I glanced away whenever that happened. This time I gazed back. His hair, the color of rust wheat, blew across those hard-gray eyes softening that glare. His square jaw quivered as if he was about to say a few words. I waited for him to say something awkward, but no words were forthcoming. Lon pulled hard on the rudder and pointed two hundred yards, due east off the horizon.

"There's our mark," he said, pointing so we all could see. "They're heading into the deep water for the night."

We glided like butter across a skillet and went into silent mode. Abe ran a sharpening stone over the tip of his iron for good luck. We were two good pulls away from laying into the whale when my oar hit something hard. I pulled up as all the others did.

"Mother of mercy," Lon mumbled.

Dozens of leatherback turtle shells popped to the surface. They looked like bottles floating up from the bottom of the sea. A few of the crew grumbled that the comet's vapors were seeping into the atmosphere, causing this odd behavior.

Lon ordered, "Stand by oars," so we stacked them inside the gunwales for safe keeping. Mindful of our floating status, the crews of both crafts leaned over carefully to watch as the flotilla of hundreds of turtles passed below us. If they had a mind to, the whole lot of them could have done away with us. But they kept to their gentle task. Wasn't a soul on board either boat who didn't understand the grandeur we witnessed. Off in the distance, three water spouts shot into the air right on queue just where Lonny said.

"Sperm whales, for sure," shouted Abe to Papa.

"Aye, about fifty or more barrels apiece judging body length to flukes," Papa shouted back.

The last leatherback paraded past us. It was the largest turtle I had ever seen. Abe said it looked well over a hundred years old. That meant Pop and Nana might have seen it on the bay, too.

"All right, ya bottom feeders, back to your stations," growled Abe in mock anger.

There was no giving up a hunt on sperm whales, so I spit into my hands and grabbed my oar again. To stay clear of the leatherbacks, we looped out of the bay and headed for the neck past the Doddspoint Lighthouse. Any whale leaving the bay needed to get by us first. I pulled harder on that oar than I did anything in my life. Soon we were in the current leading out, and we put up sails to save our strength for the chase. We were out farther than the time Figgie and I had first met the orcas in his canoe. As we drew near the spot Lon had picked, Ned spied four top fins. There was none for the finding.

"They'll be surfacing again soon," said Abe, "then all get-up will break loose."

Sure enough, the massive head pitched up and we were off after it. Abe and Warrain didn't waste any time. I stole a look. They were still too far away for their irons to catch skin.

"Put yer backs into it," bellowed Papa for all to hear. "A dead whale or a stove boat!"

A roar echoed from each crew as we laid into it. Abe stood, getting his footing and balancing the iron in his hands. He heaved it in a long arcing spiral as the whale swam underneath. Warrain threw a dart skimming along the wave crests. Both lines of rope whistled into the whale with a snap. Abe's harpoon descended into the creature's long head while

Warrain's iron lodged in its tailstock. The crews whooped and cheered at the lucky hits.

I wet the line as it danced from the tub like a cobra leaping from an open basket. The whaleboat thumped across the tops of the waves. As we launched on a sleigh ride, the clips Frieda had put in my hair flew out and the men's beards bristled straight behind them like tails from running foxes. The boat hit a deep shallow that nearly flipped it over. On another bounce, my pidgin full of water sprang up and smacked me in the chin. The jolt knocked me to my knees. Dazed, I staggered.

"I've got you," Lon said, gripping me firmly.

I wanted to thank him, but the line finally strung out full, humming down the center of the boat. Lon carried his lance toward the bow like Caesar passing before his legions as he and Abe switched places. About a quarter mile off, the bow of Papa's boat pitched into the waves as he hunkered down, ready with his lance.

The boats pulled along this way until the sun lowered to the mountains. We slowed to the point where the lads hauled the line back in, drawing us closer to the struggling behemoth. I re-coiled the rope in the tub, nervous it might spring back to life at any moment.

We were close enough to see the battle scars on the whale's briny skin. I took a moment to absorb the magnificent beauty of this creature. From the small ridges on its back funneling to a tapered torso that flowered into the perfectly symmetrical curves of its wide flukes, the whale was bursting with life. Its rhythmic diving danced to the song of the sea, its rich dark skin alive, even as death was about to call.

It occurred to me that I had never seen a live sperm whale this close before. I had only viewed them in dissected sections, compartmentalized and de-whaled.

We came upon the frantic and exhausted beast bearing no mercy. Lance after lance pierced the defenseless creature.

The crew stabbed and stabbed again, missing their mark, as if the whale were giving us a chance at redemption if only we stopped. Finally, an anonymous lance hit its spot, stabbing the beast through the heart. Choking on its own blood, the confused whale rolled on its side, curling into a near circle as it thrashed about pounding its tail and bobbing its massive head gasping for air. Its eye rolled up at me and seemed to ask why it had befallen such a fate. It had caused no man or creature harm or quarrel.

"Chimney afire," the men cried out.

Suddenly, a spout of blood rained down upon us from its blowhole. Covered with a stinging mix of hot blood and stomach acids, both crews held their oars overhead and howled in primal guttural shrieks I had never heard before. They leapt up and down in triumph like apes in a zoo as blood doused us. We all looked the same covered in red. I stood alone in the aft of the whaleboat, my arms stretched upward, my hair, face, and dress soaked in blood.

Tears streamed down my face, and I asked myself, *What have we done?*

The whale swam in smaller and smaller circles in a ballet with death known as the flurry. Abe and Lon yelled, "Stern all, Stern all!" as we backed the boats away from the thrashing whale, which snapped bitterly at the air as it gasped for breath. It slapped its thunderous tail on the water, as if alerting the entire bay to its demise. Then, finally, it made several loud clicking noises, then lay motionless, its side fin hanging limply in the breeze.

"Fin up," one of the men croaked, wheezing with exhaustion.

While we rowed toward the floating corpse, Abe stood next to me and put his hand on my shoulder. I looked up at him, the blood from my busted lip mixing with that from the whale.

"The killing is hard," he said, in a hoarse and weary voice, "but you get used to it."

With this haul, I heard some of the crew say I wasn't such a bad luck Jonah after all. We pulled alongside the lifeless husk, poling our way down the sixty-foot-long body with our oars. Its dry skin reminded me of the Arve Big Tree in Tasmania.

Now the two forests have met, and the battle had been won.

I stared down at the poor creature's eye, hoping it could give me some inkling about its life. Like a snuffed candle, it gave no light or hint of what had led it there.

Papa and Lon took cutting spades to each of the whale's flukes and ran the lines through them to the boats. It would take hours to haul the dead carcass to Dawson Station. I overheard one of the mates proclaim that we'd landed a cow carrying a calf—a few more barrels of unborn oil. My thoughts went immediately to Miah.

To pass the time, Abe took punts on how many full barrels we were dragging back. Then he asked each of us what we planned to do with our share. Warrain was spending every cent. Ned was sending his take to his mum and two half-crowns to me for saving his arm, which drew foot stomps and huzzahs from the crew again. Before I could say anything, they had me down for a new fancy dress. The men drew lots to see who would retrieve the anchored shad. We tried racing the other boat but Papa said we should save our strength for the coming days. The lads, happy with their late day's work, broke out in raucous whaling songs, trading verses between boats. When I was sure no one was watching, I retched over the aft gunwales.

I purged myself of the rich man's food, but not the guilt I carried within me.

24

We rowed the carcass back to the tryworks where the grizzly work of flensing took place. Despite their absence, the orcas claimed their fair share of the catch. Overnight, they feasted on the whale's tongue and lips as the corpse lay on the bay floor. Derain received vital nutrients for Miah's milk, while other bay life thrived on the dead animal, too.

That Monday, Papa piloted the shad to Paradise to take me to school. He looked worn out from the hunt and allowed Figgie to steer while I did homework. After we'd left for class, the two of them planned to search for the town horse. Knowing Figgie's way with animals, Papa recruited him to help train the white beastie for the Jumps Race. He wanted Figgie to jockey that animal if it could stay upright. I would never ask, but I think Papa regretted making such an outlandish bet.

Even with a fast and steady wind to our backs, I was still nervous about getting to class before everyone else. Not because I worried about other kids gawking at my fat lip and bruised chin, but because I preferred to be alone while Mr. Davenport reviewed my artwork.

I kept my illustration rolled tight with my tucker. I showed it to no one, especially Figgie. I didn't need any more advice on what to draw, or how to do something better. Papa and Figgie left to go horse hunting while the younger ones played tag in the schoolyard. I slipped into the building as Mr. Davenport was busy at his desk.

"Oh, Savannah. G'day," he said, pulling on his vest. "You're here early."

"We had a strong tailwind," I said, rummaging through my tucker, "and I got this."

"*Have* this," he corrected, clearing away his desk. "Excellent. You've finished the assignment."

Mr. Davenport carefully unrolled the paper. If he noticed my bruised face, he said nothing about it. He leaned over his desk, staring down at my drawing with his hands on his thighs. Then he rose, took off his glasses, and stared at it again.

"I gave you this assignment for the purpose of reflection," he said, finally. "I half expected a sketch of a child praying or some sort of church scenes. Instead, Dawson, you give me this—"

The door swung open followed by giggling voices.

"Do not disturb us!" Mr. Davenport shouted, pounding his fist on the desk.

The sound of feet shuffling back into the yard echoed into silence. Mr. Davenport looked at me blankly, as adults often do when they lose their thoughts. I wanted to blurt out that I had tried all those things, but they just didn't work. They just weren't true.

I had used every piece of paper I possessed. I had taken a canister of Diamine ink powder and mixed it with water till it ran as red as blood. I hadn't slept in the two days since the hunt, and I still....

"Dawson, you're wasting time here. You realize that, don't you?" he said, biting on an earpiece to his glasses.

"I wouldn't say—" I mumbled.

"This transcends any work a student has ever produced for me in fifteen years of teaching," he continued. "The depth of feeling it evokes shakes me to my core."

Other than offering a weak "thank you," I didn't know what else to say. Mr. Davenport said I belonged at a fine arts school. They were expensive, he said, but he would make sure that I got into one. A chum of his from Eton knew the

administrator of an art institute in Sydney. He was planning
to see him when we were in recess during the Harvest Festival later in the week.

"My God, Dawson, you're exceptional," he exclaimed.

It was hard for me to look at my drawing with him looking too. From this distance, the screaming girl standing alone
in the open boat, arms outstretched, her gown and tortured
face covered in blood, looked small, insignificant. Up close,
the horror on my face still frightened me.

The rest of the day passed like shoreline fog. Images and
moments came into focus only to disappear again. Arizona
tended to my lip and chin cuts with a bottle of colloidal silver
she kept in her purse. No one asked how my injuries had
happened, but I imagined each had misguided ideas about
them.

All the while, I kept thinking that if Figgie hadn't been
honest with me about my drawings, all that praise would
have been out the window. My thoughts turned to leaving
for boarding school and Laura's troubles in *The Getting of
Wisdom*.

Being away from Papa, Abe, and the orcas…How could
I live without my nightly ventures with Jungay? What about
Figgie?

Figgie wanted to see where I spent my days, so I asked him
to meet me after class in the back schoolyard. I waited by the
tree where all the ruckus had started last week, with no sign
of Figgie. I looked about anxiously when I heard a horse
whinny. Looking up into the colorful leaves, I spotted those
dancing almond eyes.

"Thought I heard a horse. What are you doing up there?"
I asked.

"So, this is school," he said, jumping down.

"And who do we have here?" said Arizona, plowing down
the steps.

"He's a friend," I stammered.

"I am Calagun," Figgie said, offering his hand to Arizona.

"Calagun, what an interesting name," Arizona swooned, dropping her handkerchief. "Would you like a ride in my new carriage? Father felt I deserved it for all my hard work."

"Thanks," I said, stonily, "but we're meeting Papa at the shipyard."

"Do say hello to him for me. Father and I so enjoyed the meal we shared on Saturday," cooed Arizona, snapping the reins.

Figgie picked up the handkerchief and put it in his pocket.

"Is that your—?" he began.

"Don't pay her no mind," I said. "Did you find him?"

Figgie gave me the lowdown as we walked over to McMahon's shipyard. The expedition hadn't gone easy. Papa snuck up on the Town Horse in the Widow Nesbitt's yard, only to have him charge through her hung laundry. Chasing a stallion with a lopsided gait wearing old ladies' undergarments into a wedding party was front-page news for the *Hook & Harpoon*. Papa and Figgie knocked over a painter's ladder and chased the Town Horse to Cooper's Brewery, where they secured the Town Horse to a building railing and reposed to McMahon's to recover.

The group soon gathered there as well.

"Calagun here knows his horses," said Papa, rubbing the bridge of the animal's nose, "and I'm betting on him being right."

"Right about what?" I asked.

"The horse's diet," added Figgie, patting the stallion's belly.

"He figures moldy hay is what got this big fella listing sideways," said Papa.

"How do you cure that?" I asked.

"What goes in must come out," said Figgie, sounding like a doctor.

We watched as he put together a concoction of herbs, barks, and grains that Papa had brought to straighten out the animal's innards. The horse wouldn't eat it, so Figgie picked up two jugs from Cooper's Brewery and poured several quarts of flat Victoria Bitter and Cooper's Stout into the mixture. The horse suspiciously sniffed the bucket, whinnied once, and dove in face first. As Papa held the feedbag, a thunderous rumble echoed off the walls.

"What was that?" asked Aiden innocently.

"Sounds like Gabriel's horn to me, son," said Papa, laughing.

The rest of us held our noses as we rushed out for fresh air. Whatever the horse had eaten from neighborhood yards, he deposited back ten-fold on his way to the shad. Figgie pulled the bloated horse by the bridle, guiding him down to the docks. The heavy clumping of iron shoes on wood announced our presence just as much as the trumpeting from the horse's other end. Crews on the trawlers, tugs, and bay craft took notice while our group paraded down the quay. Foghorns, ship whistles, and hooting seamen joined our cacophony of wind.

When we reached the ramp to the lower dock, the harbormaster waited with two armed constables and a shovel. His right eye rolled about on us like a cue ball after a billiards break. He wanted to know by what authority we were removing this horse from Paradise. Papa said he was declaring unclaimed wildlife as his own, since no one had hitherto proclaimed ownership of the steed.

The three of them scratched their heads and gammed. While we waited, Aiden and Benjamin began pulling strips of peeling green paint off a trawler lifeboat. I paid them no mind until I saw the paint underneath. It was white, blue, and yellow—Dawson Station colors.

I elbowed Papa and he nodded at me with a side glance. Figgie's horse meal continued to work its charms until the three magistrates finally caved to their sense of smell.

A horse on a sailboat is a peculiar sight indeed. One col-
icky kick could send us all to the bottom of the bay. But
this horse was more interested in Figgie's concoction of beer
meal than his surroundings. I stood upwind with Papa at the
wheel and asked him about our stolen whaleboat from the
previous season.

"I suspected the trawlers had something to do with it,"
he said.

"Make them give it back," I said, the hair bristling on the
back of my neck.

Papa pointed out that we held all the cards now. "We're
better off not laying them all on the table until we've upped
the ante a bit," he said.

Papa asked Figgie to trim the mainsail while I pulled the
jib leeward.

As the shad docked at Loch Bultarra, the whale, filled
with deadly gases, had arisen to live again as oil for our
lamps, lubricants for our machines, and bones for our cor-
sets. Gamming with Papa and the others, Abe figured double
shifts through the week should finish the flensing before the
Harvest Festival started.

That began the night of long knives.

I heard the singing sound of steel on bone and the groans
of those "cutting in" to take blankets of blubber for the
pots. The next morning billowing black smoke laid a shroud
over the inlet. The stench of burning blood, blubber, and
grease etched its way into every crevice of the station. With
each slab of blubber dropped in the caldrons, the image of
that stillborn calf would not leave my mind. I begged for
forgiveness; none was forthcoming. I had to live with my
actions.

My sole consolation during those long hours of boiling
was to see Miah's tiny top fin playfully darting about in the
bay.

Every day the stacks of oil barrels grew larger and my
bruises grew lighter.

The horse improved too. He ran with strength and grace, the moldy hay problems now behind him in more ways than one.

"He's feeling his oats," Papa said.

Figgie rode him every day—first bareback, then with a saddle and blinders. He took a page from my book, setting up a mini-course using fences, hedges, and walls to jump, just as I had done with my cats and the tub line. The big fella moved with grace and readily took to the terrain. Figgie said he was a bit of a swooper, which meant that he liked to challenge the pack from the back. He would wait for the other horses to tire out before running hard.

With all the barrels sealed and delivered and the carcass towed away, Dawson Station closed for the festival. Everyone headed to Paradise for the big race the next day. School let out at noon, and we skipped over to the old General Gordon Arms Hotel where half the crew was bedding down on Papa's veteran discount.

Dinner there was as fancy as could be. There were red-checkered tablecloths in the dining room, and we all ordered pie floaters with tommy sauce. The young ones liked dropping the meat pie into the pea soup. After dinner the men lit their cigars and slowly made their way to the music room. I corralled all the poddies into our second-floor room where yours truly was in charge. I told the six of them to play quietly until I got back.

I went to visit Figgie in the paddock.

"You hungry, mate?" I asked, tossing him a meat pie wrapped in a napkin.

He devoured it and I felt bad that no one else had given him food. Figgie said he missed Uncle's turtle dinners. I did, too. I asked him about the track conditions and the field he was facing. Twenty horses were entered in the race, he told me. Two came from as far away as Sydney. Figgie picked up a horseshoe nail and began outlining the track in the dirt. The Town Horse leaned his large head over us, as if he, too, were listening.

The track was three miles long with twenty-four obstacles: fifteen log fences, or brushes called sticks; three streams; four hedges; and two stone walls. The more Figgie described the course, the more dangerous it seemed. He told me Bittermen had constructed a fifty-foot-high tower for the race callers to shout out the action. This wasn't kid's fun; it was an adult extravaganza with Figgie in the middle of it.

"Are you worried about the race?" I asked.

"We have a good horse," he said, finishing the pie. "We should do well."

"Papa has so much riding on this, it scares me a bit," I added.

"Look at this big fella, he's a born chaser if there ever was one," said Figgie, slapping the horse's flanks. "If he gets near a track with other horses, he'll be on his toes."

"What does that mean?" I asked.

"He loves feeding off the crowd," said Figgie. "He'd rather die than disappoint and now he has a name."

Figgie explained that Papa wanted to keep calling him The Horse, but the racing stewards wouldn't allow it. Finally, Papa settled on Crack the Wind.

"I almost forgot," I said, startling myself.

I removed the chock pin from my blouse and fixed it to his jockey shirt that hung from a hook.

"For good luck," I added.

"I will honor it and your family," Figgie said with that smile.

We sat on boxes, kicking our legs. I thought of our kiss in the glen, but I didn't want to ignite his dash-fire before such an important event. I gave him a hearty hug and ran up to my room, availing myself of the fancy indoor loo in the hall on the way. Pulling the overhead chain, I was afraid the rusty water closet might douse me instead. Snuggling down with all those warm little bodies I was watching over reminded me how much I missed my cats, wee Kayle, and my home. Every flea room, bed, and open space in Paradise was booked that night.

This tub of humanity was simmering toward a boil. As any failed cook knows, if you don't let the steam out, the pot will boil over. Things figured to get a lot more heated before they cooled off.

25

To see all the action, the next morning I took my spyglass and trudged up to the rooftop of Hooks, Lines & Sinks while Papa attended to the horse and Figgie. Overnight, the warm bay air had climbed ashore and cooled to fog over the crisp fall landscape. We were at the highest point in Paradise waiting for the gloaming to clear from the hills and rooftops. Bittermen paced the streets in his white suit, as if every minute's delay might cost him an extra minute of glory.

Fists filled with money changed hands as old ladies with penny purses played the neddies. The scuttlebutt had us as a roughie, or longshot, meaning the punt paid well if we won. At eighteen hands, they said Crack the Wind was too tall and our rider too short. Other bookies wouldn't place bets on us because Figgie was riding. They called him a darkie and said only true blues ought to race. Well, there's no one truer to this land than Figgie in my book.

The sun came on strong, drying the fields and stone paths. As the sky cleared, we beheld a sight that sent murmurs through the crowd. The comet appeared bigger than ever. It looked about ready to burst through the blue sky and swallow us whole. I got nervous every time I glanced up. The comet clamor gave way to another punting frenzy that reached a fever pitch as the trumpets blared, "Call to the post!"

The horses strolled out of the paddock and paraded through the cheering crowd. Using a giant megaphone, the race caller announced each jockey and horse passing Bittermen and the city officials at the reviewing stand. Johnny

Reb—the big red Bay that Bittermen owned that had won the Virginia Gold Cup—strutted past, shaking his mane. Comet Rider and Arch Duke Ferdinand from Sydney followed him. Sir Lancelot and Blind Ambition were a couple of Novice horses. Victoria and Shambhala, owned by a few jackaroos, were the only mares in the race. When Figgie rode our horse sidestep in front of the stage, they introduced him as "Collin at eight stones riding Wind."

After the procession, Bittermen rose to address the crowd.

"Good people of Paradise," he shouted into a mega-phone, waving his Panama hat in the air. "Our city has en-dured many calamities over the years and we have always risen to the occasion. Today is a celebration of our good will and sportsmanship. Welcome to the first Annual City of Paradise National Chase."

During the applause, I tried to find Arizona in the grand-stand but she wasn't there. The two race callers perched themselves up in Bittermen's crow's nest. I always looked forward to Papa taking us to Bega for the Cup races. I loved watching the lazy way the horses sauntered onto the track as the tapes rose. It's a quiet moment before the eruption of straining muscle became the swishing of hooves atop spruce boughs and the thumping of heavy iron shoes upon the earthen track.

I got my spyglass out and had a good view of the starting point from where we stood on the roof of Hooks, Lines & Sinks. Figgie was easy to follow because he was riding the only white horse. Papa was by his side, leading our steed behind the tapes. Abe and Sam were too worried to watch and paced about, shouting out questions to me. Papa gave Figgie a gentle grasp about the neck, the way I imagined he had often done with Asa and Eli. I watched Bittermen give a slight sneer in Figgie's direction when he assumed no one was watching. Bittermen held the starting gun aloft and fired. The sound echoed across the bay, followed by a constant dull crowd roar that reminded me of a beehive.

"And they're off!" shouted the first race caller into the megaphone with attached binoculars. "The first annual Paradise National Chase, a three-mile open race at no set weights is underway with a high sky and good visibility. Blind Ambition and Comet Rider are a bit behind the others as they go through the first set of sticks. Johnny Reb is moving up on the outside as Sir Lancelot, Victoria, and Arch Duke Ferdinand bunch toward the center. Neptune's Daughter is the first faller."

I yelled to Abe that the fallen horse looked fine as the rest made it through the hurdle. Three more horses fell before reaching the fifth fence. Abe kept asking where Figgie was in the pack, but I couldn't see him in the rush of horseflesh.

"Johnny Reb is in the lead," the caller cried.

By the time I found Figgie, Abe had already heard the announcer. "Crack the Wind is slowing to the back of the pack and looking stone motherless. As they make their way through the first quarter, the leaders go streaming onto Brunson's pasture."

As the other race caller picked up the action, I could see that Johnny Reb was well ahead, leaping over the first stone wall.

"After a hard right, the leaders jump the stream on Dover's meadow. Crack the Wind, still in the back of the field, lingers behind Sir Lancelot, Comet Rider, and Victoria. Johnny Reb, shadowed by Great Sandy and Blind Ambition, holds the lead and dictates the chase.

"Turning toward the outside, Crack the Wind is in the ninth slot as they chase through the Umbara Orchard. The field thins taking the turn toward Amesly Road as Blind Ambition pulls up short. Crack the Wind narrowly avoids a dust-up at the tenth fence with Arch Duke Ferdinand, who is the fifth faller of the chase. At the halfway point, Comet Rider, Shambhala, and Sir Lancelot are bunching at the center as Crack the Wind continues to lag on the inside, forty lengths off the leader. Johnny Reb clears another hurdle thirty lengths ahead of his closest pursuer, Sir Lancelot. No horse has ever had a midpoint lead this large on the jumps circuit."

The field was so spread out it was hard for me to relay positions to Abe. I didn't have the heart to tell him and Sam that our horse looked even slower than the caller said. Poor Figgie was so much smaller than the other jockeys.

"The rest of the pack has fallen off, with Shambhala and a distant Crack the Wind the only pursuers of Johnny Reb. There are two more fences to jump and the lead for Johnny Reb looks insurmountable. Twelve stone and six on the back of Johnny Reb, eight stone on the back of Crack the Wind, and eleven stone on Shambhala.

"Near the three-quarter mark, Johnny Reb has cleared the final fence as he gallops the straightaway to victory," the first caller said, jumping back into the fray. "Crack the Wind is seventeen lengths back and Shambhala at ten lengths turning onto Studsberry Street. Two hundred and fifty yards to go and the celebrations have begun for Johnny Reb. At two hundred yards, Crack the Wind is charging up the middle, but it may be too little, too late. Crack the Wind keeps coming as Sir Lancelot and Comet Rider pull up before the turn.

"Johnny Reb is ten lengths ahead of Shambhala, and just making the jump is Crack the Wind fifteen lengths behind," blasted the second caller taking the megaphone.

"One hundred and fifty yards to the finish line, it's Shambhala making a move on Johnny Reb, with Crack the Wind still ten lengths behind!" the announcer shouted, pulling the megaphone off its stand, his face puffed red and full as a circus balloon.

"Shambhala is gaining on Johnny Reb as Crack the Wind is coming hard on the outside and closing fast. It's…Shambhala and Crack the Wind bearing down on Johnny Reb. Shambhala is a length off as Crack the Wind is catching them both."

"Give him the whip!" someone shouted below us.

"Don't," barked Abe, coming onto the roof as they passed, "let the horse take over."

"It's Crack the Wind and Shambhala neck and neck," the announcer screeched, "as Johnny Reb falls back. It's Shambhala. It's Crack the Wind as they come thundering toward the chair. It's Shambhala and Crack the Wind in a head-bobbing, heart-pounding, pulsating dead heat too close to call!"

The crowd went mad as it swallowed up Figgie and the other jockey. Papa shook Figgie's hand so hard it looked like it might fall off. The three judges conferred in earnest, using their bowlers to block public view of their discussion. Everyone was milling about waiting for the decision as a boy carried a piece of paper up to the crow's nest.

"Ladies and Gentlemen," the race caller blasted, "the judges have reached a decision. After careful deliberation and review, the judges have declared a tie. The owners of Crack the Wind and Shambhala share all the winnings for their equal finish. On the official race card, Crack the Wind and Shambhala place first at 12:36, Johnny Reb second at 13:06 and Sir Lancelot third at 14:46."

The crowd sang "God Save the Queen" followed by the "Death of Alec Roberson" as Figgie and our horse made their way to the winner's circle along with Shambhala. The two jockeys held the silver trophy aloft between them.

"You're a regular Tommy Corrigan, mate!" someone in the crowd yelled at Figgie, who was all smiles.

When I finally caught his eye, Figgie pulled on his shirt collar and gave the chock pin a slight jingle. I hugged Papa in the winner's circle and couldn't wait to tell him my news about art school as he spoke to the reporters.

"We might have gotten more, but I'm thankful for what we won," Papa told the reporter from the *Hook & Harpoon*. "I plan to use the winnings to pay off our debts and investors, with enough left for a good tin of tobacco."

I stopped in my tracks as the rest of them headed back to the Gordon Arms. How could we win so much and I still end up losing? With no extra money, I couldn't afford art school even with a scholarship. Papa turned down an invitation from Bittermen for a victory dinner. He said we had a whaleboat to paint. As we gathered at the paddock for some fancy dancing, Papa asked me what I wanted to talk about.

"It was nothing, Papa," I said, kissing his cheek.

The leaf band from the village serenaded us with old whaler's ditties. Much later, I asked Papa what he had seen in our horse. He laughed, motioned me and Figgie over to where Wind was resting.

"See that," Papa said, pushing back the mane on his forehead. We both looked at the black diamond with bewilderment.

"Ever hear of a horse called Briggen?" he asked.

"Have I ever," said Figgie his eyes lighting up. "He was one of the best steeplechasers ever, but he was lost at sea two summers ago."

"Aye," said Papa with a grin, "meet himself."

"Briggen?" said Figgie.

"Papa, a ringer?" I added dumbfounded.

"Now, now, I only suspected he was Briggen," Papa said. "My wager with Bittermen was worded…Let's say I took advantage of his over-eagerness to make a whaler look like a fool."

"I can't believe I rode Briggen," exclaimed Figgie, raising his arms over his head.

Papa put his fingers to his lips and turned them like a key in a lock as he gave us both a wink. Before the night ended, I waltzed with Figgie to the "Blue Bells of Scotland," our heels clicking on the red gum-planked floor. Abe and Frieda danced too, as did the whole crew. The barn echoed as we all sang the last verse together.

"Oh, where, and oh, where is my highland laddie gone,

He's gone to fight the French, for King George upon the throne,

And it's oh in my heart I wish him safe at home

For it's, oh, my heart would break if my Highland lad were slain…"

The next morning several out-of-town businessmen offered to buy our horse and enroll Figgie in jockey school. Papa made his mind up; he filed papers with the constables' office, freeing Briggen. Figgie turned down riding school. He said he loved horses too much to trot for money.

Later that day, Papa took the bridle off Briggen and slapped him once on the hindquarters. The horse bolted into a cloud of dust. When it settled, he was gone.

26

The world went mad the day the Town Horse left.
Instead of uniting everyone, the steeplechase served to divide and embitter the townspeople. Neighbor turned on neighbor for perceived slights. Bittermen awakened the lust for wealth that he knew lay dormant within us like a virus from some plague.

More than anything, I wanted to get back to Loch Bultarra to be with my orcas, cats, and Figgie as it had been just a few days ago. In order for that to happen, I needed to show people that another way existed, and the orcas were the best example I could think of. People needed to understand the Law of the Bay.

The orcas were part of that law, and with the help of Figgie, Aiden, and the others, I put together a sample of the drawings. My pictures depicted the pod members, their behaviors, and their family life. We found some old restaurant placards and mounted my drawings on the back of them. I broke off the end of an old fishing pole to use it as a pointer, just the way Mr. Davenport did in class.

Papa, Abe, and Warrain helped me carry all my materials to the opera house. Along the foot path, scuffles between street toughs and villagers broke out. Those who had cheered Figgie the day before were now blaming him for not winning the race outright. Every corner had a cabbage crate podium occupied by some galah or dag grizzling about our state of affairs.

The stage flickered with a ghostly hue as the Drummond lights lining the floor came up full glare. I set my artwork up on chairs for all to see. I heard Figgie and Aiden hawking my lecture outside as the room filled with people.

"Learn all about the life of the orcas. Secrets of killer whales, our ocean friends," they shouted, handing flyers to passersby.

Bittermen introduced me as the city's resident expert on killer whales. If I had stopped to think about it, I would have realized that I was nervous being in front of so many strangers. But I was so anxious to share what I'd learned that I forgot where I was. As I made a point about their size, colors, and distinctive markings, I saw Arizona and a few of our classmates slip into seats in the center of the hall. I was happy to see some kids my own age. One man was particularly interested in why we used aboriginal instead of biblical names for the orcas. I told him they already had names that meant a lot more than anything I could think up.

"These are extraordinary perceptions for a youngster," Bittermen said, applauding. "Do tell us more."

Blushing with confidence, I showed drawings of how I had taught the pod to eat out of my hand and to come when I called. I spoke about how orcas used sound to disorient and catch fish. I explained how underwater noises could damage an orca's ears and drive them to beach themselves. I felt proud when I was able to answer all of Bittermen's questions about that to more applause. Orcas lived in family units, I told the audience. If you separated a calf from the pod, the whole group chased after it, no matter the danger. Next I showed a sketch I'd made of everyone rescuing Derain. I declared that orcas were the most loyal animals on the planet and would never hurt a person.

"You're leaving out how you use dark powers to control them!" a man shouted from the shadows.

At first, I didn't recognize the voice, and the hot glow from the lights prevented me from seeing his face.

"I don't know what you're talking about," I said.

"Oh, I think you do," the gravelly voice said, hanging back in the darkness.

"That's my daughter you're speaking to," said Papa angrily, standing up.

"Here, here," said Bittermen standing in protest. "This young lady is a guest in our city; her character should not be attacked."

"An unwanted guest," said the man, moving closer, "for I've seen her perform ungodly acts on our waters."

"I have not," I shouted, stamping my foot.

"That's enough," said Papa, moving toward the man.

Men in the audience sprang up and restrained Papa, Abe, and the rest of the crew.

"This is outrageous," said Bittermen. "If you're making accusations, show yourself, man."

My stomach began to turn as I realized who was stepping out of the gloom—the captain of the fishing trawler, the same man who had dumped chum on me and Figgie.

"She's the one I saw from my trawler that night dancing around with those devilfish," said the captain, moving toward the front of the stage. "She was alone on the water with the little dark fella, and they were casting spells, too."

Gasps echoed through the room as Bittermen called for quiet. I tried to speak but couldn't. I felt as if a python were squeezing the breath out of me.

"Oh, it's worse than that!" bellowed the captain. "You desecrated the Lord's likeness with depictions of native idolatry and pagan images!"

He held up the dinner scene I'd drawn of Uncle and the villagers.

"How did you get that?" I shouted.

The audience clamor mimicked lyrebirds shuffling through the brush. "This is an outrage," said one. "Disgusting," yelled a woman. "How could this happen here?" said others as rows of people got up to leave.

"See, I always knew those whales were nothing but trouble," said another.

"Funny, how a whaler wins a race with a lopsided horse and a jockey who doesn't even belong here."

"None of them were affected by the comet because they bought all the medicine with money took from our bay."

"And our schools, what are we paying for? To have our kids taught this!" shouted a man, picking up my dinner scene and tossing it at the stage. The tip of the wood frame hit the Drummond stage light. The loud pop and flaring flame caused everyone to panic and push toward the exits. Some stumbled and fell, women screamed, men smashed chairs and tables. Figgie and Aiden battled up through the crowd until they reached me on stage.

"No, please don't leave," I begged the crowd weakly from my knees. "The orcas help the bay; they don't harm it!"

As the men let go of Papa and Abe, they rushed to me on the stage. The heat from the lights lashed at my skin. I covered my face with my hands. I wanted to cry, but I wasn't going to let anyone get the better of me. Bittermen looked stunned. He smoothed the brim of his hat and left.

Arizona stood alone, staring at the stage and wiping tears from her cheeks. Our eyes caught as she left a piece of paper on a chair.

Papa hugged me as I assured him Figgie was just a good friend and our canoe trips were about the orcas. It didn't matter to him. He said the whole kit and caboodle of us would leave tonight if I wanted to, but I'd have none of it. I wanted us to stay and enjoy our victory. As we left the opera house, I picked up the slip of paper Arizona had left on the chair. *I think I can help*, she wrote, *meet me by the cannon tomorrow at six p.m.*

৵

When we got to the hotel, the door to the boatsteerer's room was open. I glanced inside. There were two Murphy beds against the front wall and four canvas cots strewn about. Warrain sat facing us, leaning on the spindles of a straight-backed chair, his arms dangling like octopus tentacles in an open-air market.

"He was yabbing it up at Smithson's Billiards," said Warrain, waving us in.

The both of us looked at each other and said, "Who was yabbing?"

"Him," said Warrain, pointing behind himself with his thumb.

I waved for the rest of the youngsters to go on to our room while I joined Warrain. The back window of the boat-steerer's room had been flung open. I could smell the seaweed and lapping briny water of the rising tide against the building. A bedsheet was tied to an iron waste pipe that ran down the back wall next to the window and through the hotel room floor. The sheet intermittently jerked slack and taut, as if a large fish were caught on the end. We rushed to the window to look out. A gagged figure hung upside down, flailing against the brick wall like bait jumping around on a hook.

"He talked too much, and then he didn't talk at all," Warrain boomed. "Now maybe he will talk some more."

Warrain told us that he and Ned had overheard the man bragging about a plan to rid the bay of all its problems. When he boasted about pinching a girl's sketch of a village banquet, Warrain made up his mind to grab him in the alleyway.

"Meet Noah Brown who likes to hang around town," laughed Warrain, pulling up the sheet hand over fist. "Let's see if he remembers better now who is behind all this hub-bub."

"Are you ready to talk?" Warrain asked in a friendly tone, patting the man's jowls.

The daggy fella violently shook his head *yes*. "See, more blood to the brain helps a person think," said Warrain, removing the gag.

Breathing heavily, Brown asked for a glass of water. Between sips, he admitted to spying on Loch Bultarra and stealing my drawing. I soon realized that he was the figure I had seen circling the family graves some weeks ago.

"I want you to know, I feel bad about doing this," Brown said to me apologetically, "but when you can't fish no more you got to do something to earn your keep."

"Weak men are good at feeling bad, less so at making amends," said Warrain, grabbing him by the collar.

"Okay, okay," the man muttered, staring down at the water. "You got to understand, this comet has made people crazy…do things they'd never dreamed of doing before."

Warrain untied the man's hands and feet. He took hold of his collar with both hands again and leaned the man back out the window.

"Feel bad faster," Warrain said.

"They're gonna kill off them black whales that follow you around," he whimpered as he hung halfway out the window.

"Who?" demanded Figgie angrily. "Who?" he repeated, shoving the man in the chest.

The man tumbled out the window, cursing like the sailor he used to be, before hitting the water with a wail.

"Bye now," said Warrain, closing the window shutters to his cussing. "Everyone's tired. No one will hurt our blackfish tonight."

Figgie bunked with Warrain and the rest of the harpooners. I perched on our window ledge, listening to the soft clang of harbor buoys. There was a cedar downspout out the window as close to me as the tree branches at Loch Bultarra were from my porthole. I waited until all the kids fell asleep, then leaped for the downspout as if it were my tree back home. My weight pulled it away from the roof gutter. As the downspout sank deeper into the tidal mud, it lowered me toward the water. When I was close enough, I dove. The air was cool, but the water was still summer warm. My nightshirt billowed around me in jellyfish fashion as I swam toward the clanging in the distance.

I climbed onto the big red harbor buoy gently bobbing to and fro.

Jungay had never had to find me beyond the whaling station so I waited patiently. Somehow, I needed to warn him about the fishermen's plans. Yet what was I warning him about and how would he understand? I had no answers to these questions. I wasn't even sure they were the right questions to ask.

The last sliver of moon cast the bay in enough shadow light for me to see the forest and mountains surrounding our home miles away. So often I had longed to be here, among the lights of Paradise, only to now ache for our darkness again. I fell asleep to the heartbeat ding of the small buoy bell. I was half asleep when Jungay's jagged top fin tweaked my nose.

Silently I stood behind his top fin as I always did. This was our sixth journey together. We set out methodically pacing ourselves for a long dance neither of us wanted to end. His mournful song told me he understood the warning I bore. The high-pitched cries that followed echoed deep into oceans I'd never dreamed of and touched consciousness I'd never imagined existed.

We were, in our own ways, lamenting a planet that had lost its Dreaming.

We stopped for a moment, drifting on the waves and waiting for a reply that never came. Jungay's clicks and melodies acted as lassos of sound roping in the heavens and pulling the southern lights toward us in massive curtains of green and gold.

An ocean of stars.

For a long time my head lay on his saddle patch by his topsail like a pillow as I gazed at the abundance of life in the universe. This time I wasn't afraid of the immenseness.

Its energy flowed through us. No words could harm me; no memories could come between us.

Afterward, I found myself standing on the beach, watching his defiant black sail fade into the morning fog. I opened my lips to call out, but there was no need for it.

27

After I got dressed, I joined Papa at the Gordon Arms Café for breakfast. I picked up the festival edition of the *Hook & Harpoon* in the lobby on the way.

"Listen to this," I said, reading from the paper. "'Famous author visits Paradise...Henry Handel Richardson and his wife, Ethel, will anchor in Reflect Bay this weekend as guests of Lady Alice Hawthorn aboard the SS *Galileo*.'"

"Who's that?" Papa asked.

"He wrote *The Getting of Wisdom*, the book Sam gave me. Maybe he can help us protect the orcas."

Bad as things were, Papa didn't like strangers getting involved in local business. The killers would be fine, he said. The more questions I asked, the itchier he got. Finally, he asked me along to deliver six barrels of Sam's oil to the lighthouse.

I didn't mind getting out of Paradise so we jumped on the shad. We laughed as we talked about Warrain's skills of persuasion questioning that poor old salt Noah Brown by hanging him out the hotel window to get the lowdown.

"Wasn't a full moon last night, but with all that raucousness and hullabaloo, it sure felt like it," Papa said. "The jail and the annex are full—after a total of seven fights, three fires, and two robberies. Now there's prosperity for you!"

Lon was one of the fighters who'd been jailed the night before, and the only one defending my honor. Papa rolled his eyes but felt obligated to post bail when we returned. I laughed again. Before long, Kayle was porpoising and breaching off our portside. I told Papa she would come to greet the shad every morning we left for school. Her fat little tongue hung playfully from a half-grinning mouth.

The shad glided up effortlessly to the rickety quay. The Doddspoint Lighthouse tower was seventy-five-feet high and made of stone, which is why it's lasted so long. It's white iron turret and lamp top made it look like a wedding cake during the day. At night, it was called the Beacon of Hope.

All the construction and equipment at the base of the tower caught us by surprise. The brick walkway was all dug up where a fat black snake of a cable was laid in a trench that led into the lighthouse. We dodged around the holes and made our way into the tower where a staircase spiraled up inside.

"Putting in a bigger wick, Martin?" Papa asked the lighthouse keeper.

"I wish," he said, pointing at the new equipment. "They're bringing the electric in soon. Didn't Sam tell you?"

"No, he skipped that part," Papa said, with a worried look.

Mr. Barrett lived alone in a fancy adobe house across from the tower. Papa threw down the rolling planks and slowly backed the barrels off the shad and stored them in the fuel house. I meandered over to the fog-signaling building and stared at the two giant horns attached to the roof.

"Seems the whole area will be getting wired before long, including you if you want," Barrett added, looking up. "Same fifteen lamps since she was built in 1817. Well, got to change with the times."

Barrett took us up the tower for a look-see of the new light by switching on a test bulb the size of the globe next to Mr. Davenport's desk. It gave off a pale illumination, making the room seem smaller and colder. Even our shadows seemed faded in the harsh glare of this phantom light. He paid Papa and shook his hand.

Papa usually liked to stay for a few rounds of draughts and stories. This time he stowed up all his barrel-moving equipment quickly. Before we knew it, we were heading back to the Gordon Arms. We didn't say much, but I could tell we were both thinking about the Law of the Bay.

If people had no need for whale oil, there was no reason for us to take it. Yet we still had to honor our pact with the orcas and our crew.

As we got closer to the harbor, Papa spotted the SS *Galileo*. A single-stack steamer, it was smaller than the newspaper had described and likely had room for only twenty or so people. That got me to thinking and took my mind off the bay. Maybe the best way to meet Mr. Richardson was to pop on to the boat. That way, we could keep an eye on those fishermen too.

Papa left for the jail to pay Lon's bail. I ran into our room and got my things. Figgie wasn't so sure that boarding another ship was the best way to meet a famous author. I assured him that the element of surprise had its virtues.

We paddled into an endless headwind before the *Galileo* appeared on the horizon. It looked like a floating wedding cake. As we came closer, Figgie guided us to the open loading doors. He managed to catch a rope knot between two steel hull plates and walked up the side of the ship. Figgie found a rope ladder, and we tied off his canoe as I boarded with my drawings.

The ship was as empty as a bushwhacker's kick. Figgie heard the cooks talking about how many people went ashore to the festival. He handed me a warm scone.

"Your man's off shooting billiards in Smithson's or signing books," he said, laughing.

"Anyone who wrote that book isn't playing pool," I added, looking on the cabin doors.

"Can I help you, miss?"

I turned around and saw a man in a blue naval uniform.

"Oh, I'm looking for my mother, but I've lost my way," I

said demurely. "We're staying next to the Richardsons' cabin."

"They're around the corner on the left," he said, tipping his cap before walking away.

"Of course, how silly of me," I said apologetically.

Figgie jumped down from the steel crossbeam as I approached the door by the corner. What had seemed such a great idea just a short while ago suddenly felt nerve-wracking. I knocked on the door.

"Maybe he's in the loo," Figgie said, "or taking a bath."

"Why do you always—"

"If you're from the tabloids, please go away," came a stern female voice, "or I shall call the captain and have you removed."

Figgie backed away from the door and my mouth turned to gravel.

"My name's Savannah. I'm almost thirteen, and I loved Mr. Richardson's book and I just had to tell him so," I blurted out.

We stood motionless for a moment before the door popped open with a rusty creak. I peered into the dimly lighted room. A woman craned her neck from around the door. Her pursed lips looked ready to give us the once over.

"You really are thirteen, aren't you?" she said from behind the door.

"In just about two months," I stammered.

"Well then," she said, opening the door. "My name is Ethel. I handle all of Mr. Richardson's correspondence. You may enter to explain yourselves."

She wore her dark auburn hair in a short wavy bob like in the magazines. Her pointy nose seemed to run up into her high-arched eyebrows, over which her dark eyes gleamed with a penetrating stare. Suddenly, a smile broke out across her face like the sun breaking through the clouds.

"Please, tell me about yourselves," she said.

I was itching to talk so I introduced myself and Figgie

as we entered the room. She was interested in Figgie's real name and could say it better than I could. She didn't remember seeing us on board and asked how we got there. That's when Figgie jumped in and told her about the canoe and the climbing.

"A canoe?" she said, standing up. "You paddled all the way here to see Richardson? What on earth for?"

"Because anyone who can write a book like that knows this place and how people here think," I blurted out. "We need someone to tell the truth and save the bay before it's all gone…"

Seeing how worked up I was, Ethel asked us to sit down and offered us gooey finger cookies while we talked a long time about the Bittermens, the bay, whaling, school, and Figgie's village. She made us laugh and feel better about things as she wrote down some notes.

"What was it that made you admire Laura in Richardson's book so much? Her brashness?" she asked, cocking her head to the side.

"I can't say that I liked her," I said. "I wanted to be her but being like that got me in a mess of trouble."

"So I imagine you weren't rewarded for your own defiance the way she was."

"Well, come to think of it, maybe I was," I said. "But it wasn't so much my brashness that got rewarded as it was just finding room enough to be me."

I had scarcely time to say another word before Figgie jumped up to show her my drawings. We spread them out on the floor, and Ethel got down on her knees to look at them with us. Though Ethel is her name she said her friends all called her Ettie. I could tell by the way Ettie examined them that she was interested in my drawings. It wasn't until I pulled out the sketch of Laura deciding whether she would cheat on an exam that she gasped. Ettie stared at it for a long time until Figgie asked if Mr. Richardson was present.

"You see, dear," Ettie said, with a smile, "I am Henry Richardson. We are one and the same."

At first this didn't make any sense to me, but the more I thought about the orcas and the goings-on in the bay, I understood. Ettie caressed my cheek and asked if the scars were worrisome to me. Most people paid a lot of attention to my scars by ignoring them. I told her they didn't bother me at all, but then I confessed that I was ashamed of them and of the things people said about me.

"You needn't let that stop you," she said, rolling up her sleeve to reveal a dark purple birthmark that covered her entire arm. "Each one of us is scarred in some way or another."

A butler knocked on the door, announcing that tea was being served in the galley. Ettie invited us to stay, but it was getting late and we still had to patrol the bay. She asked for the name of my art school so she could write the headmaster about what a fine student I was.

"I don't have one," I said embarrassed. "Mr. Davenport is trying to get me a scholarship, but I still don't have enough money."

I could see Ettie felt bad about bringing up the subject. Figgie looked upset for not knowing about it. To change the topic, I gave her the Laura drawing as a gift for allowing all her readers to feel as if they were her collaborators—just as her dedication said.

Ettie walked us onto the open deck where we took in the panorama of the bay.

"I do love my Australia so," she said, with her arms around us. "Such innocence waiting to be lost. It must never be allowed to change. Figgie, I know you understand."

"I do, ma'am," he said gravely. "I shall always protect her."

Away from the harbor, the red sky boiled a good omen for tomorrow. We moved faster in the open water, yet not fast enough to outrun ourselves.

"I wanted to tell you about the art school, but it happened so fast," I yelled, trying to get Figgie's attention.

"You owe no explanation, nor do I expect one," he said, pulling his oar harder.

"If it wasn't for you, I'd still be drawing in the sand," I said.

"There's nothing wrong with sand art," said Figgie, "unless—"

The canoe hit something that pulled it upward like a whale rising underneath. Had Jungay found us? We bounced up and down, toppling onto a metallic surface. Water drained off the flat surface as we rose upward, revealing a sleek hull of riveted steel with a lone turret that jutted into the sky. Water rushed from its sides like some great sea monster surfacing.

Figgie grabbed my arm as we hid behind the canoe turned up on its side. I felt the vibration from a rumbling engine beneath us. A release of air sounded, reminding me of a lance piercing a whale's lung. We heard two voices.

"Übergeben *Sie sofort!*" one shouted.

I peeked around the canoe as a third man emerged from the metal box, clearly in command of the other two.

"Identify yourselves and your purpose," he said in English. "We are the Imperial German Navy. Our vessel has drifted into your waters."

I'd heard that the Germans were poking around the Australian coast, but I'd never paid the rumors much mind. The waves swelled over the deck and upended our canoe, exposing our crouched forms. Dripping wet, we rose to our feet, looking at the three men in dark uniforms, who laughed heartily at the sight of us. Figgie shoved the canoe off the iron vessel and leapt into the water after it. I followed, sliding down the side of the metal ship.

We clambered into the canoe and took up our oars. As we watched, the strange metal ship sank beneath the waves; it reminded me of Jungay drifting down into the shadows of the bay. I wondered what he would think of this metallic thing invading his realm.

The rest of our patrol was uneventful. While we were out searching for trouble, it was waiting for us in Paradise. Mobs roamed the waterfront looking for any excuse to exert their power. Carefully, we made our way through the chaos of the streets toward the Gordon Arms.

Two blocks from the hotel, we spotted the growling captain as he parked his fancy dark blue carriage behind shrubs. He was holding court in a back-alley square. His smooth words wooed the crowd. All their problems boiled down to two things he said—killer whales and villagers. With a shock I recalled our canoe bouncing against his trawler's black hull and the chum he had rained down upon our heads.

"For an expert seaman, he nearly hit us like a killer wave," I whispered to myself. "…a black wave!"

God love the wild mystics.

"It was his black trawler that killed my brothers!" I said to Figgie, pointing at the captain.

"Mind what you say in this crowd," said Figgie, pulling me to the side of a tree.

"Remember Brennan's black wave?" I cried. "It was *his* ship."

"I believe you," Figgie said, "but if you shout about the rants of a crazy man, we'll both end up in the gaol."

"I want a closer look at that carriage. There might be some clues about what he's up to in it."

We slipped behind the growing crowd. I jumped up on the first step and leaned inside while Figgie kept the horse quiet. It was as clean as the insides of momma-girl's kettles.

"Nothing here," I said, angrily stomping my foot.

The iron step below me broke loose. I stumbled against the carriage. As Figgie held the bucking horse at bay, I righted myself and began fixing the step.

"Look, your hands are blue," Figgie said.

Sure enough, smudges of wet paint covered my hands and dress. Underneath, the cab was white.

"That step was broken on Arizona's white gig, too," I said.

Figgie helped me fix the step and we managed to smooth out the paint without notice.

"I smell a dead fish," I said, "a big fat Seppo one at that."

"It may be her carriage but we don't know how the trawler captain got it."

"There's more Bittermens, boats, and bullies here than cats at a fish fry," I huffed. "First they stole one of our whaleboats so we couldn't hunt properly. Now they're trying to separate us from the orcas and break our pact with the bay. They'll do anything to put us out of business so they can have the bay to themselves."

Figgie urged temperance toward Arizona until more facts emerged. Under the circumstances, I thought it best if I didn't meet her at the cannon that night.

When we reached the Gordon Arms, Papa and Abe had already finished loading the shad. I didn't realize how dangerous things were until the harbormaster waved us out with no inspection or fees. We made our escape with Figgie's canoe in tow. After things settled down I made my way to Papa at the wheel. He let me steer, but I had other things on my mind.

"Papa," I said, turning the wheel, "I know what happened to Eli and Asa."

"Lass, we've been through this before," he said.

"It was a trawler that hit them. Brennan had a vision about a black wave. It all makes sense."

"We all shook hands with the superintendent of fisheries not to trawl or whale that week. No commercial ships were supposed to be on the bay," Papa said.

I laid my head on his shoulder.

"That's why the lads weren't keeping an eye out for any off the point," I said.

"I should've been smarter and paid more attention to

everyday things," he said. "All that help we got from the harbormaster was just a cover-up."

"Figgie says the only thing we can change about the past is how we feel about it," I said, putting my hand on Papa's shoulder. "We'll figure out how to deal with Captain Speedwell later."

Arriving at the village, we dropped off Figgie. The camp elders were worried about the violence and invited Papa and Abe to the Tjungu to gam about it. That left me free to walk about and look for my mates.

"Savannah, we were so afraid when we heard about you being among those wicked people," Ghera said.

"What do you want us to do now, Savannah?" Corowa asked, balling her hands into fists.

"What do you think we should do?" I asked.

"Are you not our lead cobber?"

"No, Corowa, you are," I said, hands on her shoulders. "It's always been you."

"I know nothing of leading."

"Caring and understanding is a good start," I said. "The rest will come."

"We shall fight for ourselves no matter what," she added, gathering her group.

As we left for Loch Bultarra, I stuck my hand in the dark water. The serenity I felt with Jungay was gone. Angry blood seemed to course over my fingers.

Inside the bay's currents, the spirit world howled around me.

28

After dawn, thunder woke me. It sounded far off but soon was upon us.

"They're killing the whole bloody bay!" Papa screamed from the porch.

I shot out of bed and nearly jumped down the entire flight of stairs. Hopping around on one foot as I put my boots on, I watched a motorized skiff leave a path of destruction.

"The orcas, Papa!" I yelled, pushing against the railing at my wondering spot.

"They'll be long gone by now," he said as the speedboat faded into the distance.

I ran back to get my spyglass. I saw four men hooting and laughing as they continued tossing sticks of dynamite into the bay.

"Kayle!" I cried, running to the float dock. "Don't play with—"

Papa shouted for me to come back and rang the storm-warning bell to get my attention. Abe and his crew were milling about and Figgie and Warren were gathering irons for the blacksmith's fire, but I didn't pay any of them no mind as I rushed to my boat. I rowed as fast as I could, to the spot where Kayle had popped out of the water to surprise me.

She wasn't there.

I continued sculling along the bar, making sure I wasn't snapped into the currents. Out further, I rowed through schools of upturned fish and sea turtles floating lifelessly. I took out my glass and scanned the horizon again. As I looked east toward Paradise, a line of slow-moving motor-boats came into focus. Though miles away, I saw long metal pipes hung off the boats, descending into the water as men rhythmically beat them. Thirty yards ahead of the boats a jumble of black top fins frantically zigzagged and collided.

"They're running an oikomiryou," I said, in disbelief.

The fishermen were carrying out a drive hunt, the very kind I had talked about on stage. Banging on pipes in the water created a wall of sound that disoriented the orcas. I rowed out farther to get a better view. They were herding the orcas toward Snuggler's Cove near the Cow Bight.

As fast as I had rowed out, I pulled the oars even harder going in. To save Kayle, Derain, Miah, and the others, we had to get back across the bay.

I spotted Kayle peeking out of the water. Relieved, I rowed toward her and braced for a splashing.

"You naughty whalie, I've been worrying about you," I said, giving her a gentle poke with my oar.

In the distance, I spied Abe and Figgie rowing toward me. Kayle slowly rolled to the left as I approached, revealing blood dripping from her mouth and earhole. The stiff line of her jaw retracted from her teeth.

"No, no, no!" I cried, jumping in the water to help her. You're just a poddy, it's not your time...Someone help me!"

I pulled up on Kayle's top fin to lift her snout from the water, hoping to revive her.

"Breathe, like you do when sticking your tongue out at me," I sobbed.

Though still a baby, she was too heavy for me to support, and her mass flipped me below her.

"Savannah, you'll be dragged under," I heard Figgie yell as he dove into the water.

"Faster, lads!" shouted Abe. "Put yer backs into it."

As Kayle began to drift downward, and I up, our faces passed. I wrapped my arms around her head and shook, hoping I might waken her. We surfaced again as she rolled over, and my eyes met her own. It was as if I were staring into a dark room. There was no glimmer, no spark of life in her eye, no effervescence to her skin. Her mouth curled in an unnatural smile, the dried grin of death.

But I couldn't let go.

I wrapped my arms around Kayle's midsection, kicking my legs as hard as I could to stay afloat. It felt as if the entire bay were pulling on the other end.

"Please, Savannah," said Figgie softly as he pulled up next to me. "It's time."

"I can't," I said, shaking my head as he moved behind me.

"It's the Law of the Bay," he said, trying to hold me up.

"I won't let go, I won't," I shouted.

But as hard as I tried to hold her, Kayle's smooth skin slipped from my fingers. I felt her tapered body and the smooth curvature of her fluke pass under my hands. Slowly, she sank into the darkening green water.

"KAYLE!" I cried, emptying my lungs of all air.

Figgie wrapped his left arm around my waist and paddled with his other to the whaleboat. The lads pulled me up over the gunwales as Abe hooked his hands under my arms and lifted me onto the hull. He held me to his shoulder, and we wept together until Papa arrived. On the way back to Loch Bultarra, the bay mocked me with the haunting images of all the souls it had swallowed. Papa and Abe spoke in hushed tones as I wrapped myself in a blanket.

"There's only one way to deal with a bully," Papa said. "Confront him head on."

"We ought to talk to the other stations," Abe suggested. "Yauncy and Bathers Bay will stand with us."

"This is our fight," said Papa. "We're standing for what Pop, Prince Jimmy, and your da believed in. Anyone who comes along is strictly a volunteer. I mean it, Abe."

"Everyone stands with ya," Abe said, "and will pay their own way if need be."

Later that morning, we took the shad to Yauncy Station to meet up with the others. The crew grew quiet except for the wind pulling on the ropes and sails. Each deckhand laid down his tasks and came to the aft where Papa held the wheel. Some were men who had skimmed oil or cheated Papa over the years. Others, like the bloke who'd made crew with me, barely knew him.

"Those whales are as much crew as we are," said one of the lads.

"We're with ya, Captain. The devil be damned!" shouted one of the sandgropers.

At Yauncy Station, we barely had a chance to sit before Brayden Yauncy himself stood up. A half-whale of a man, he kept running his fingers along the rim of his slouch hat waiting for the crowd to simmer down.

"We've known Caleb here all our lives," he blurted out. "And over the years we've had our barneys with Dawson Station. But the way I see it, if they can stuff up Caleb then who's to say we won't be next. We're with ya, mate."

"Stone the crows if we'll let some Seppo take over our town," added a few from Bathers Bay.

Suddenly, Figgie was among them shouting "huzzah" along with the rest. When the group quieted down, I dropped my blanket and stood too.

"That's right, Cap't," I said. "We're all in."

Papa said it was too dangerous for any children to return to Paradise. I reminded him that we were already involved. If we didn't learn to stand up for ourselves now, we'd live the rest of our lives afraid.

"It's settled then," Papa said. "We're crashing the gates of Paradise and it's damn napkins to anyone who tries to stop us."

༄

Our ragtag armada of patched sails, dinghies, and rafts must have looked quite amusing to the harbormaster. As we approached Paradise, I got my first glimpse of the holed-up orcas penned in Snuggler's Cove. A twenty-foot-high barbed-wire fence on one side and a ramshackle jetty on the other hemmed them in. Men with rifles guarded the water corral.

When we entered the Gordon Arms, a yellow poster hung from the front desk.

The headline, *Spectacle of the Beasts*, screamed across the top of the broadsheet. It listed all the atrocities the orcas had supposedly committed. Some crackpot scientist had called for the removal of the diseased animals, as if they had cattle plague. Bittermen, I saw with horror, had arranged a "cleansing event" for three o'clock that afternoon. Public autopsies for scientific observation had been scheduled, with all whale by-products going to the poor.

"Papa, you won't let them do it, will you?" I cried.

"Don't worry. We'll see about this," Papa replied grimly.

He sent for McMahon and huddled with Abe, Lon, and Figgie and I lugged everyone's biddle bags up to their rooms. When we came down, you'd have thought the king of England had died. All the men sat glumly staring at the table.

"What's the matter?" I asked, frightened of the answer.

"We been talking it through," Papa said gloomily, "and we cannot think of what can be done, short of getting ourselves shot too."

"With the orcas gone," Lon suggested, "we could put a man in the Doddspoint Lighthouse to spot whales. With faster motorboats and rifle harpoons, we could still hunt."

"The orcas are still here," I said. "Using those motor-powered boats makes us no better than Bittermen."

"I agree," Papa added. "There's got to be another way."

The fact that my talk had provided Bittermen with the tools to capture the orcas caused heavy weather in my soul. How could I have given away the secrets the orcas had protected for thousands of years? I took my spyglass and headed toward the water jail with Figgie. Looking down from the Cow Bright pasture, I could see the cove was more of a crater left over from an old volcano, the middle of which had rotted out and filled with water when the inlet was formed. The large rocks jutting up made it sufficiently secluded for risqué swimming—bathing suits optional.

From a patch of trees, we watched as workmen reassembled the grandstand used during the horse race at the cove. They hammered away at the platform where Bittermen's fancy wooden platform would overlook the cove known more for canoodling than killing. At the far end of the inlet, the corralled orcas' moods swung between listlessness and agitation. When the hammering and sawing stopped, their mournful screeches and sighs made Figgie cover his ears as if he felt their pain too. The black top fins stood out of the water like tombstones rather than sails. Jungay hung in the water, barely moving, as if asleep or dead. Some of the orcas tried to ram the barbed-wired posts, but as they did, guards in motorized skiffs banged on the metal pipes to create a wall of grating sound.

Increasingly agitated, the orcas fought amongst themselves in the tight confines of the prison. They were granted neither food nor rest. The guards—I overheard them talking—wanted to keep the orcas barely alive for a proper execution.

"Soon they will try and beach themselves, just as Derain did," said Figgie, pointing down at the cove. "They would rather die than live under such conditions."

Returning to the Gordon Arms, it was all-hands-on-deck. Four of the crew drew cards to see who had to go fetch Brennan while Abe was busy writing notes to other villages for help. Ned and Warrain were gamming with Bashir before he shooed them off to McMahon's to make arrangements. The action whirled about me on a carousel fly-by.

"Your father's looking for you," Abe told me. "He might have been a barrister, that one."

Papa was sitting at a table strewn with papers, his spectacles slipping off his nose. He waved for me.

"What's this, Papa," I asked.

"Our ace in the hole," Papa said, grabbing my arm. "I got an emergency hearing with the magistrate at three o'clock."

"About the orcas?" I asked excitedly.

"Our stolen whaleboat," he said, pointing to his forehead, "but that means Bittermen has to delay his antics for another day. We bought ourselves some time, at least."

Magistrate Shamus Wimbley liked to convene his court at the scene of the transgression, which made many a proceeding cannon fodder for newspaper grizzle.

Bittermen showed up at the dock with three lawyers and a reporter, all of whom the judge disliked. After an hour of his barrister's babbling, Bittermen denied any wrongdoing. He didn't help his cause any by not knowing the importance of the boat markings. The highlight of the hearing was the testimony of one Charles Horatio Ignatius Brennan—painter of the alleged stolen whaleboat. Old Charlie identified the family colors and the time-honored tradition of baymen returning lost vessels.

"That was the last whaleboat Alexander Dawson commanded!" shouted Brennan, shaking his hoary fist at Bittermen and the crowd. "By herrings, he died with a lance in his hand and the wind to his back. No man could ask for a better ending or deserved one more than he!"

"My client has no need of a whaleboat," said Bittermen's main barrister, snapping his suspenders against his shirt, "as he owns several yachts and a fishing fleet already."

Papa peeled a long strip of green paint off the whaleboat in question to reveal the Dawson colors and handed it to Bittermen, saying, "I reckon this is yours."

"Sir, this is beyond the pale," said Bittermen, removing his Panama hat and waving it at the crowd. "I am a man of honor, which prevents me from dignifying this accusation with a response."

"It also prevents the truth from coming out," someone shouted, to much laughter.

By the time Wimbley brought the court back to order, I noticed the audience also included a new black carriage and horse off in the distance. I watched as the female driver took off her cloak and climbed out. I recognized the dark red dress with the white ruffles as one from Arizona's immense closet. She began pacing about in the shadows, and that American swagger of hers all but gave her presence away. I felt like yelling, *why don't you come and join us!* but I knew she was hotter at me than a bushfire in the woop woop for missing our meeting.

Before he left for a lathered shave, Wimbley ordered Bittermen to pay a fine and restore the whaleboat to its former Scottish glory. To prevent further shenanigans, he also doubled all levies for trespassing and vandalism in the village through Samhain.

The few of us from our side cheered. I made my way toward Brennan while Ned proposed a toast over at Smithson's.

"Charlie!" I shouted, trying to get his attention. "I have something to tell you."

Brennan finally turned around, his eyes wild and his mouth open.

"We figured out the significance of the black wave," I said.

"Wave, what wave?" said Brennan.

"The one you warned me about," I said.

"I did?"

"It was a trawler that done my brothers in," I said. "I feel it, Charlie."

"What do the orcas say?" he asked. "They ain't talking much nowadays."

"They're holed up, Charlie. Papa's tending to it now," I added.

"That Captain Speedwell would sell his mother rotting fish for an extra quid."

"Can you talk to the orcas?" I pleaded. "Can you help us save them?"

"I lost the gift. There's too much sadness for the bay to hear anything," he said, dropping his chin to his chest. "Their fates are sealed, child."

Ned and Abe took Brennan with them while I waited outside the barbershop for Papa. He told me that Wimbley had ruled from the barber chair that the orcas were undeclared property, just as the Town Horse had been. With hot towels piled on his face, Wimbley muttered that Bittermen owned the orcas now and could do with them what he wanted. Papa telegraphed a couple of old army pals in Sydney with government pull, hoping to stay the executions.

"All we can do now is wait," Papa said, digging his hands into his pockets.

"Papa, why did the other station crews decide to come with us?"

"No one likes to get pushed around. If you find a bunch of folks who feel the same way, they stick together."

"But you didn't always trust these fellas. I've heard you and Abe say that."

"Well," Papa laughed, putting his arm on my shoulders, "trust is a lot like the tides. You count on them being the same every day. Even though you trust they'll be there, that doesn't mean you trust them to do right by you all the time."

We walked a bit in silence—me, as confused as if I were looking at a compass through fogged glass. Papa sensed my muddling so we stopped for a moment.

"You can only trust something to follow its nature," Papa said. "I trust my crew to be who they are, not who I think they ought to be."

"Does that go for me too, Papa?"

"It does now, lass, it does now," he said, giving me a hug.

At that moment, I knew that I owed Arizona a visit. We had to have a girl gam and hope the high tides of bluster didn't wash over us.

29

Finding Arizona's house wasn't hard; it took up all of Resurrection Hill. A week before, I'd sworn I'd never set foot in it again. Going through the front door meant sending a note, waiting for an invitation, or sitting on the leather couch in the foyer, like some tonic salesman. I wanted to do this on my own terms. I wrapped my belt around a wrought-iron fence post and hoisted myself over the granite wall. I climbed a tree near the balcony off Arizona's bedroom and dropped down onto it.

I was mighty proud of my ingenuity, except...

She wasn't there.

I double-checked. That new black gig of hers sat in front of the carriage house. I paced the balcony, looking for a way in. The lamps in her room put all her frilly things on display. I jiggled the handle and the door to her room popped open. I stepped gingerly onto the plush white carpet. She had more vials and dishes of creams than a Sydney apothecary. Cut-glass pufferfish-sized perfume bottles with rubber balls attached to them sat on their own table. I picked one up and squeezed, shooting myself in the eyes.

By the time I'd cussed the sting out, I saw a red specter wavering in front of me.

"Wipe your eyes," Arizona said, handing me a handkerchief. "Water's in a pitcher over there."

"Fancy seeing you here," I said, with a blurry half-smile.

"I'm surprised Father's hounds didn't get you," said Arizona, offering me a chair.

"I have a way with animals," I replied, not recalling any hounds.

"Yes, I'm well aware," she said, smoothing out her dress.

"That's what I came to talk about," I told her, pulling her note from my pocket.

"This whole situation is out of hand," she said. "Father is distraught over your treatment at the theater and the whale-boat thing; he had no idea that happened."

"I'm more interested in what *you* know," I said, "and freeing our orcas."

"Whatever do you mean?" she asked, with a cold glare. "Those men with the explosives have been apprehended. Father gathered up those beasts for their own protection."

"That spectacle he's planning isn't saving anything."

"Sadly, an ocean expert found all those orcas are diseased. They must be destroyed for our own safety, especially yours. It's all on the up and up."

"You have an answer for everything, don't you?"

"The facts speak for themselves," Arizona said stiffly, sitting up straight.

"Well, here's one that needs explaining," I said. "How did the good trawler captain end up with your old gig?"

"I wasn't aware he had it," she replied airily. "Perhaps Father sold it to a broker or Mr. Speedwell purchased it. We're constantly ridding ourselves of useless things."

"One of those useless things was Kayle, a little orca who loved to play by boats and trusted people," I said, moving toward the balcony. "Now she's gone."

"Trust is often misplaced," said Arizona.

"Trust isn't a place you can force people to go," I said. "It's letting the hurt of the world in so the scars it brings won't change you. That's how my mum saw it, my da, and me too."

"I fought my better nature to trust you, and look how you repaid me."

"Trust doesn't come from a bank," I said, brandishing her note. "Why'd you leave this?"

"Because I felt for you, alone on that stage," she said,

looking down. "It reminded me of the all the times Mother put me on display for suitors, like I was a pig at auction. I'm nearly sixteen, you know. My own window for freedom is rapidly closing."

"It doesn't have to," I said. "You can still be who you want."

"Don't nauseate me with your whale stories and how much they mean," said Arizona.

She threw open the balcony doors and walked out into the late afternoon air. Arizona leaned on the railing and shouted, like a captain degrading a crew.

"I came halfway around the world and nothing has changed," she yelled, staring at the empty yard. "I'm still the girl everyone wants to use but no one trusts. If that's the way it is, so be it. I don't need you. I don't need anyone."

"But you don't—"

"I'd appreciate it if you'd leave now, Savannah. You know the way."

I was ashamed of the thoughts that gathered in my mind, yet they lingered like funeral smoke. I was still unable to believe her. Trust wasn't there, but maybe something else was.

"I can't give you what no one else can," I said, taking a step closer to Arizona. "But what I can offer is acceptance. I've learned being accepted for who you are is a lot better than having someone trust you because they think you'll change."

Arizona turned away, trying to escape my words. A cold breeze blew the curtains across the room.

"What's done is done in my book," I said, opening the door to that long spiral staircase. "The past won't improve none for all the wishing we do on it."

I was nearly at the bottom of the stairs when the bedroom door slammed shut. I didn't know if it was the wind or Arizona's anger.

The reverberation echoed through the house and out into the empty street.

30

I had to see the orca pen again.

The early red sky gave way to a purplish then cobalt blue. There would be no sailor's warning this day. Figgie arrived at the café after brekkie so we could sneak over to the Cow Bight pasture that sloped down to Snuggler's Cove. The workers were busy moving rocks from the end of the jetty to the opening of the Bitter Ditch. I wanted to tell Figgie about my confrontation with Arizona, but I decided that matter was between her and me. I had tried to recruit her with forgiveness, without realizing that some people didn't want a pardon.

My failure had condemned the pod to their fate, I realized with a heavy heart.

Figgie and I considered swimming up to the fence and snipping the wires underwater, but the guards had taken care of that too. They'd poured animal blood and chunks of horsemeat around the perimeter, and the water was teaming with pointers and other sharks.

Papa was right, no one could go near the place.

"Think that's Bittermen's racehorse they're chumming?" I said to Figgie, poking his ribs.

We laughed with a sense of gloomy resignation. There was nothing more to do. We sat, sadly, watching a giant banner being erected over the completed grandstand. Some of the old salts sat down because their joints were hurting. "A storm is coming," they complained as we laughed again, squinting in the sun. Across the fluttering white banner, red letters proclaimed: *Man Conquers Nature.*

I looked up at the green sloping hill that lead to the pasture, then turned toward the town. The sky was an artic blue-green without a single cloud. I couldn't remember a time when it had looked more like Paradise. The comet was gone, but it had left a legacy of fear.

By afternoon tea this spectacle would be over. The orcas made high-pitched moaning sounds, like the ones I'd heard Jungay make the previous night. Miah swam frantically around her mother. I ran down the pasture toward the bight and stopped at the canal. No one would shoot a girl, and maybe, if I stayed with the orcas, I could find some way of saving them. Figgie grabbed my arm before I got too close.

"Think about what you're doing," he whispered, trying not to draw attention to us.

"The orcas will protect me and them," I said, pushing past Figgie.

"You'll never make it to the water without being snagged," he said, glancing at the guards.

"I need to do this," I said, twisting away from him.

"Just what are you trying to save, your pride or the orcas?" Figgie asked.

I folded my arms across my chest, saying nothing. I really hated it when Figgie knew me better than I did myself.

"What you need are more helpers so the guards can't focus on one person," Figgie said, drawing me over to the shade of a gum tree. "Others we can trust who are willing to go into the pen."

With our midday meal approaching, there was little time left to prepare. We started the long walk back to town. As we climbed up the pasture, talking through our plan, a passing drizzle began to fall. Along with the two of us, we figured Aiden had something to prove; Corowa and Ghera were fighters and good swimmers. We planned to jump into the pen right as the event began and not leave until the orcas were freed.

"Do we even have time to contact them?" I asked.

"I already have," said Figgie. "We are meeting at Mr. Brown's bridge construction site by the canal."

"Well, I'll be," I said, with a grin.

"A leader leads all people, someone once said," added Figgie.

"You're a good friend, mate," I said, punching Figgie in the arm. "I wish I was half the friend you are."

"Savannah," he said, his arms outstretched, "I've visited worlds with you that I would never have seen in ten lifetimes. It is I who should be thanking you."

"Really?" I said, moving closer.

"Keep your dirty hands off her, ya fizgig," a voice growled. Lon knocked Figgie to the ground and ripped the sacred copper medallion the villagers had given him from his neck. I could tell by the smell of him that Lon was already shaking a cloth in the wind.

"You're nothing in this country," Lon slurred, holding the necklace over his head.

"Don't do this, Lonny!" I shouted as he knocked me down too. "I'm not your donah, never was."

Figgie locked his legs around Lon's neck and pulled, choking him. It was raining steadily now, making it harder for me to pry them apart.

"Stop, both of you!" I yelled, slipping on the grass. "Give me the medal, Lon. Give it to me!"

"Did he tell you he started the round robin?" barked Figgie, scissoring his legs around Lon's neck like a vise.

Lon gasped for air but managed to toss the necklace into the ditch. Figgie might have killed him if I hadn't finally pried the two of them apart. The three of us lay on the muddy grass, winded and wet.

"Lonny, how could you?" I said.

"Doesn't matter," he wheezed, rolling over.

Lon said he was leaving Dawson Station and heading for

the backblocks of Gippsland to play for the East Melbourne Cricket Club. He staggered to his feet. No wife of his would ever work a whaleboat, he said, stumbling away. A heavy roll of thunder drowned out whatever else he had to say. As I looked to see if Figgie was all right, the others, who'd heard us from the bridge site, came running over. Corowa helped Figgie get back on his feet.

The sky was dark as iron-gall ink and the wind nearly knocked Aiden down. A light drizzle turned into a downpour as we searched the ditch for Figgie's medallion.

"Keep looking," I said, shielding my eyes from the rain. "It's down there in the muck somewhere."

With a storm coming, the bridge crew might return from tea to collect their things, so we called off the search and headed back to the cove to go over our plan. Aiden was scared by the thunder.

"This will all be over in a few minutes," I said, wiping the tears and water from his face. "I'll show you through my spyglass."

We stopped far down the pasture in the open space. Before checking the weather, I focused my spyglass on the orca pen. Heavy water drops fell faster and faster, pockmarking the cove until it was indistinguishable from the fog and gray sky. At the back of the pen, several black topsails were periodically illuminated by lightning, a reminder of why we had come.

I looked westward toward the ocean with my glass. The sky was green. Lowering the scope, I saw a fifty-foot-tall wall of brown water bearing down on us. It was as though the hand of god had descended, pushing all the water on earth our way.

The cyclone hurtled at us with the ferocity of wild beasts.

"Run!" I screamed, grabbing Aiden by his shirt.

There was no time to make it back to the Gordon Arms, so we sprinted up the hillside as the foaming wall came ever closer. I could feel the ground rumbling as if a band of brumbies were upon us. Aiden fell, twisting his ankle. Figgie tossed him over his shoulders. I grabbed Ghera's hand to pull her along. Bailed up, we needed a bolt-hole faster than Duffy needed a land map. At the crest of the hill was an abandoned lodge used by goat and boar hunters. The five of us crammed into its meat-hanging cellar. Figgie tied the doors shut as we held each other tight.

Time slowed as we waited for the inevitable. The cellar doors shuddered and rattled. We heard the windows smash one by one. Nails pulled out of the walls and floorboards. I felt the house rumble and shred to bits above us as the wind skirred through, devouring everything with savage claws. The doors to the root cellar jerked violently until Figgie couldn't hold them any longer and they burst up into the air. We screamed and pushed ourselves down as hard as we could into the belly of the earthen pit embracing us.

Though I was afraid, I lifted my eyes.

The angry face of a vengeful god mocked us.

"Leave us alone!" I screamed as sand, wood shards, and hailstones pelted our upturned faces and huddled bodies.

Several inches of water and floating debris had filled the cellar by the time we finally ventured out. The lodge had disappeared entirely, wiped from the hillside as if it had never existed. Bittermen's *Man Conquers Nature* banner lay flailing in the branches of downed trees by the shore.

When I looked toward the crater rim, hoping the orcas had escaped, I saw to my dismay that they remained imprisoned. The inlet was blocked with construction rubble and two abandoned half-sunk drifters with their fishing nets all in tangles.

The rest of Paradise was in a sorry state. The harbor wharves were submerged, and a sailboat had been deposited by the bank on Studsberry Street. Pleasure craft of the well-to-do, anchored in Purgatory Bay, lay smashed together on the shore. With blustery winds and high tide nearing, the waters wouldn't recede for hours yet. Ten- and twenty-foot waves still pounded the shore as we headed to where Water Street used to be.

Then, to our astonishment, a powerful gust of wind blew a rogue wave across the bay, holding the Pelican House on its crest, spinning like a top. Brennan sat on the roof, his arms wrapped around a chimney, a pelican on his shoulder. His white beard blew back as he rode the wave like a bronco-busting Father Christmas. Behind him, tied to the opposite chimney, was the trawler captain's blue carriage, skipping over the waves in dinghy-like fashion with the captain leaning out one window, screaming for mercy.

There was some justice in that, I thought, with satisfaction.

"Hooroo!" Brennan shouted, waving to us as he surged by. "I'm whaling again with no one ta stop me! Once ya got whale in your blood, yer can't get it out. I'd rather be a-whaling than king of the world. Give me an iron and a piece of bark, and I'll bring back a hundred barrel! A whaler I am, and a whaler I'll always be…"

Brennan, the blue gig, and the Pelican House disappeared into the surf foam and fog.

We stood stone silent, jaws dropped, unable to believe what we had just witnessed.

"Well, that's putting the house before the cart, isn't it?" Figgie said, as serious as can be. We all burst out laughing. Aiden, with his old limp back, couldn't stop talking about seeing the real Saint Nicholas.

"You told me I had to find Calagun's medal," he went on. "Will Father Christmas still visit me if I can't find it? The water in the ditch is too deep now."

"What's that, Aiden?" I asked, turning my attention to him.

"The water's really deep in the ditch," Aiden repeated.

"Yes, it is, isn't it," I cried, running toward the canal.

The water was lapping at the grass. I recalled the drawings I'd made for Mr. Brown's bridge. They showed that the canal had a width of thirty feet and a depth of twenty-five feet.

"That might be just enough room for seventeen orcas to file through," I said, excitedly. "If we can get them to swim in single file."

With the guards gone, we raced to the cove in our wet, muddy clothes. The pen was still intact and the orcas seemed none worse for wear. While the water level was much higher, it was still not high enough for them to jump out of such a confined space. Bittermen's grandstand lay in shambles at the opening to the canal. It looked like a schoolbook beaver dam, and it stood between the orcas and their freedom.

"Even Jungay cannot make that jump," said Figgie, pointing at the mound of wood.

Everyone just stared at the remnants of the grandstand with no idea of how we could move it. The fog was settling in so fast that I could barely see the barbed-wire fence. Wading to the pile of wood, I hauled out a two-by-four.

"Well, that's a start," I said, heaving it onto the shore.

The water line was beginning to dip, lowering to the top of the canal bricks. We only had a few hours before it would fall too low for the orcas to escape. Just as the others were about to join me, we heard a heavy series of thuds that grew louder and louder, until the white head and mane of the Town Horse—or Briggen, as we now knew him to be—appeared out of the fog.

"What are you doing here, old boy?" said Figgie, rubbing Briggen's forehead while the horse nuzzled him back. A moment later, a chestnut mare appeared. Briggen whinnied loudly, shaking his head. "You got yourself a girl, haven't you?" laughed Figgie as the others petted both horses.

"And we got ourselves some muscle to move that pile," I

said, recognizing the chestnut as Arizona's hat-wearing mare.

Corowa and Ghera went back to the bridge site to find rope, pulleys, and grappling hooks. I asked Aiden if he felt strong enough to walk back to the Gordon Arms to get Papa and the rest of the crew to help us.

"I can do it, Savannah," he said, limping proudly away.

When the girls returned, we set out to methodically dismantle the jabberwocky of timber, poles, and boards that blocked the canal opening. Although Bittermen's ditch had never floated a single paying barge, his failed feat of engineering offered us the best chance to save our orcas.

We tied two ropes from the horses to the grandstand stairs jammed at the center of the blockage. The mare matched Briggen's motion as Figgie coaxed the horses onward. Their hooves slipped on the wet grass and mud. Muscles strained, the horses brayed, but the stairs didn't move. The three of us got on top of the twenty-foot-high wreckage and pushed against the staircase with our legs. There were creaks and groans and a few stray planks of wood hit the water, but nothing more.

I found an iron rod and we climbed up on the pile. I wedged it as deep as I could behind the stairs and yanked on it. Corowa and Ghera pushed hard with their feet, as Figgie pulled on Briggen and the mare again.

We bucked, jumped, and pulled in unison.

I strained, driving myself against the rod.

"Ghera, leap like you're going to the stars!" I shouted, the metal rod near breaking.

Ghera catapulted into the air. Her powerful legs slammed on the wood as I threw my body against the rod with all my might.

The stairs snapped loose. As the wood structure collapsed around her, Ghera lost her footing and toppled over the embankment, toward the darkened water.

31

I froze, watching Ghera's arms and legs flail in slow motion, her mouth and eyes open in full scream with no sound coming out as she helplessly plunged underwater.

In seconds, Corowa dove in the water after her, followed by an avalanche of wood sliding toward the shore. The sound of snapping beams and cracking plywood drowned out my screams. Reflexively, I jumped on top of the grandstand platform where Bittermen had spewed his lies and rode it like a sleigh to the water's edge. When the pile settled, there was no sign of either girl.

Figgie dove into the churning water, knocking away broken beams and debris. I waded in to help, and we shoved aside fragments of the grandstand in search of the girls. Suddenly, Corowa burst through the chopping waves, gasping for air.

"Over here, help us!" Corowa cried, pulling Ghera's head out of the water. "She hurt her shoulder and can't swim."

Figgie raced over and they both slid Ghera onto a piece of plywood. She coughed and spit out water as Corowa slapped her back. Figgie pulled them in as I swam out to help them to shore. We stood in silence for a moment, admiring our cleanup job. Then Corowa and Ghera began jumping up and down, cheering. The opening to the canal was finally cleared.

"We did it!" I shouted, jumping up and down with the others.

Careful not to hurt Ghera's sore shoulder, the four of us hugged and clutched each other the way Papa and the lads did after winning a cricket match.

"You're free, go now!" we shouted at the orcas.

But they seemed strangely detached from our efforts to free them. They huddled in the far end of the pen without showing the least bit of curiosity about what we were doing. The water was already an inch lower on the canal brick by the time Corowa had finished making a sling for Ghera from Bittermen's canvas sign. Soon dusk would settle over the bay and we wouldn't be able to help them. I waded into the cove splashing water in their direction.

"Go on now, get," I yelled, pointing at the canal. "LEAVE!"

Figgie laughed at me, which grew more irritating by the second.

"Well, if you have a better idea, mate, let me in on it," I growled.

"They are afraid, hungry, and out of sorts," said Figgie. "We must gain their trust again."

How do you gain the trust of an animal twenty times your size? Figgie had that look on his face, as though he was holding something back.

I asked what was on his mind.

"I hope you understand they won't be back," he said, looking away from me.

"Of course, they will," I said, annoyed. "By this time next year, this will all be forgotten."

"They will not return," said Figgie. "Our pact with the orcas is broken."

"But we didn't do anything wrong. We're trying to save them," I pleaded.

Figgie stood silently with his shoulders slumped searching for the right words.

"Then I'm going to show them trust," I added, pulling my muddy dress over my head and diving into the surf in my camisole and Asa's breeches.

I swam toward the pod. Jungay was in the back of the pen by himself. Miah slid up close to her mother. I passed between Matong, Towrang, and Burnum. Yindi clicked as I approached, as if signaling I could enter the king's chamber. I darted underwater. Jungay's full profile made me realize just how large he was and how dangerous this journey would be for him.

I scissor-kicked around his head, but Jungay did nothing to acknowledge me. I took another deep breath and swam down to rub the top of his snout, as I was accustomed to doing, and hugged him with all my might.

My lungs were about to burst, but I would rather have died right there than let go. Finally, he opened his mouth and gave me a toothy grin. Then, Jungay ascended, holding me gently in those five-inch-long teeth as I gasped for air. He pivoted in a circle so I could see the whole pen from his view before slipping back into the water.

Figgie swam halfway to meet me.

"You were under for some time," he said.

"Jungay doesn't always recognize the needs of small lungs," I added, "but I have an idea about winning the pod's trust."

Back on shore, I explained how we could make friends with the orcas and save them too. My idea met with blank stares, even from Figgie. They questioned everything. It was getting too dark; the guards might return. Finally, Corowa just said what was on their minds.

"You want us to ride whales?" she questioned.

"It's easy. I do it all the time…" I said, my voice trailing into blank stares.

"Savannah, this isn't an easy thing to do," said Figgie.

"You just keep your feet steady," I said, "and hold the top fin like a wind sail. It's easier than it sounds. The orcas will only trust us is if we go with them, and if we don't lead them out, they will beach themselves tonight. You know they will."

"How do you know this, Savannah?" Corowa asked.

"I just know…" I said, pausing. "Jungay told me."

"Very well, we shall go," said Corowa, nodding approval.

"Yes, we shall and hope Caleb, Abe, and the rest of the crew come soon," added Figgie, as we looked out at the pod.

"No one else is coming," a female voice sounded behind us. "They're all lost in the fog."

Aiden and Arizona materialized out of the mist.

"She tricked me," cried Aiden.

"I followed him for a block and then gave him a ride here," Arizona said, waving her hand, "but let's not quibble."

"Are you going to tell on us," I asked.

"That depends on what you're doing," said Arizona, trying to make sense of the scene.

"We are riding whales to their freedom," said Corowa, hands on her hips.

Explaining the situation to Arizona was a hard yakka. I expected her to laugh at every word. Instead, she listened intently, studying the orcas and us.

"So, our captain was right," said Arizona. "He did see you riding a whale that night."

"Well, maybe a little," I said sheepishly, "but it was more like a carriage ride home."

"Why go through all this trouble…for little whales?" she asked.

"Because it's our duty to the bay," I said. "You might not feel it yet, but this place is part of you. If we ignore it, we'll be no better than the rest of this town. At least we have a chance to make a difference for ourselves and this orca family."

"Your whale friend, the one that died," asked Arizona, "was she part of this…family?"

"Yes, she was," I said, starting to wade back into the water.

"Can I still help?" asked Aiden meekly.

"Of course, mate," I said. "We could use another hand too."

Holding Aiden's chin but looking at Arizona, I added, "The great thing about families is they include anyone who wants to be part of them."

"People use each other," said Arizona, pacing the shore. "Trust exists only in poetry."

"Did your father teach you that?" I asked her. "We can free the orcas, but you're the only one who can free yourself."

Figgie and Corowa waded in with Aiden and me. We were all apprehensive about the sharp-angled orca top fins that waited for us fifty yards away.

"Hold on," yelled Arizona. "It'll take a minute to get this damn dress off."

Ghera helped her remove the voluminous cocoon and soon she was wading toward us in frilly neck-to-knee bloomers.

"Father gets awful belligerent when he gets his way all the time," Arizona said, pulling off her stockings. "Besides, we motherless ones need to stick together."

"We do at that," I said. "Can you swim?"

"In Virginia, I studied acrobatics and fencing without Father knowing," she said, joining us in the water. "I learned to swim when I was five."

Arizona was right about the fog. It was continuing to settle in over the jagged rocks that formed the crater rim of the cove and the back of the orcas' prison. She dove into the surf. Arizona's swimming form was as good as ours. I kept an eye on Aiden to make sure he could keep up as Corowa and Figgie led the way. Ghera waved from the shore with her good arm and yelled, "Hooroo!"

We swam to the midpoint of the cove where the barbed wire fencing was ripped away from the pen and waited for the pod.

The fog was rolling in but the sky was clearing.

The twilight-lit sky was empty of stars.

It was as though the comet had pulled them back with it. Yet I felt safe again in our own world as the orcas drifted toward us.

"They don't eat people, do they?" Arizona asked, treading water.

"They are pretty hungry," I said, with a grin, "but they can't stomach that rich American diet."

Jungay moved away from the others so I could meet him. Arizona's mouth hung open as I hopped onto his back and surveyed all the saw-toothed fins huddled together.

"Wait over here," I said, pointing to the back of the pen, "while we pop around and get things in order."

Figgie moved our reluctant riders away from the pod while Jungay maneuvered between the inert orcas. He shook suddenly, knocking me off his back, and then dove, cupping me under his right front flipper. All the other orcas plunged, too, and I was thrust into a world of darting, diving, clicking, thrashing creatures. I don't know which hurt more, my lungs or my ears from Jungay's piercing songs. Just as quickly, we surfaced and I lay on his stomach gasping for air.

"Savannah, are you all right?" yelled Corowa.

Arizona screamed as did Ghera from the shore. Aiden just cried.

"She's fine," said Figgie.

I sat up and waved but Jungay bobbed listlessly in the water. The other orcas touched him with their flippers and eyed me as they passed. I shouted for the others to come over and meet the orcas. They went with Figgie to each orca, rubbing the tops of their foreheads so they could sense our kindness toward them.

"They are as afraid of us as we are of them," I said, joining the group.

By the time we had petted each one, all of us relaxed, including the orcas, who clicked with delight. We went about picking a rider for every fourth orca. Figgie, behind me, would ride Burnum, his grandfather the great warrior. He hopped up on his back the way a gymnast would a balance beam. Corowa followed Figgie by sliding onto Towrang's saddle patch and grabbing her top sail.

"I am a shield like Towrang!" shouted Corowa, joyfully thrusting her fist high.

Aiden looked at Matong's grinning teeth sticking out of the water and floated back into me.

"I'm afraid," said Aiden, throwing his arms around my neck.

"No you're not," I said, helping him swim to the orca, "you're just like Matong. Quiet and powerful."

"But he doesn't like me," cried Aiden.

Matong sank below him and gently rose, sliding the boy past his blowhole to his dorsal fin. I showed Aiden how to hold it. He stood with wobbly legs but held on.

"I suppose you want me to get on the big one," said Arizona, as we swam toward Derain at the end of the pod.

"You'll be on top of the mountain," I said, slapping Derain's side. "Don't worry. She'll keep an eye on you."

We glided toward the canal opening, straightening out the long line of orcas as Ghera chased after us along the shore. A fleet of black sails in single file formed a four-hundred-foot-long caravan of orcas and riders. Jungay approached the opening slowly.

It was narrower than the rest of the canal.

"Stay low and hold on," I shouted back. "They'll dip low and then jump."

The orcas bucked and bobbed up and down, creating waves that crashed against the lowered jetty. Figgie slipped off Burnum but jumped right back on. As a large wave created by the other orcas crested, Jungay rode it into the canal, scraping his flanks on sharp jetty rocks. The larger orcas each took a mini dive and leapt into the canal as Jungay had done. When it was Derain's turn, she jumped in the air, causing Arizona to shriek.

Several dogs barked and ran to the edge of the steep gully that led down to the canal as lanterns lit in the distance.

There was no turning back. All the orcas in the canal were fleeing for freedom. If someone discovered us, the townspeople could converge on us with guns, harpoons, or worse—Bittermen. Our progress was silent and steady through the backyards and businesses of Old Town. We passed under an awning of flame trees that seemed to light our way. The sounds of neighbors helping each other clear the cyclone from their lives echoed to us. It was a peaceful floating parade punctuated by the rhythmic orca breathing. I didn't have to speak to Figgie or the others to know they felt the same serenity I did.

Three kelpies charged down the embankment, snarling and barking at our pilgrimage. Jungay stopped and lifted his head to show his teeth, sending the dogs off with a whimper. I signaled that everything was fine by waving to each rider, and they each returned my wave all the way back to Arizona, who was now standing upright like the rest of us.

As we reached the bridge construction, I knew we were halfway there. It made me think of what Figgie had said about the orcas not returning, which would end whaling at Dawson Station and might kill Papa. The Law of the Bay, Mum, Uncle, and all my cobbers filled my mind.

Figgie was right. The whales were no longer ours to hunt and share with the orcas. Our bond with them had been broken.

They will go on and survive as they have for millions of years and the bay will live on, too, if we let it. I also thought of the terrible price Asa and Eli paid and the rage that lived on after them. I wondered if somehow the bay would finally grant them peace.

We were at the final wide turn into Horse Head Bay. I didn't know if around the bend storm debris blocked our path, or if it opened a gateway to freedom. We traveled through the everyday lives of Paradise with no one suspecting our exodus. A hobo encamped on an outcrop struggled to his feet as we passed under his makeshift abode. He stared at us, then started to raise his hands to his mouth, as if to shout an alarm. Instead, in shabby attire, he stood at attention and saluted us as our procession passed his reviewing stand.

I saluted him back.

On the outskirts of town, a banjo from a boardinghouse balcony serenaded us with "Farewell to Greta" as we silently slipped away from Paradise under the cover of bottlebrush, wattle, and eucalyptus trees. The canal flowed effortlessly into the wide expanse of the channel. Beyond it was the Tasman Sea, the great South Pacific Ocean, and all the possibilities they contained. Jungay emptied into Horse Head Bay with a breaching jump that sent me airborne, except for a hand gripping his top fin.

All the orcas entered playfully.

Above, the emerald southern lights danced across the sky. We riders stood on our orcas not sure what to do, knowing that we didn't want our journey to end.

"Can't we stay like this forever?" begged Corowa.

"Do it again, do it again," shouted Aiden with glee.

Figgie just looked at me with that wide, impish grin that I'd first seen in the woods when I met him. Each of us shared a communal moment of contentment that can't be purchased, explained, or recreated. Even Arizona wiped a tear from her eye as she patted Derain's top fin.

One by one, our riders slid off the backs of their orcas and swam for the beach.

Figgie slid off Burnum and swam over, hopping up next to me on Jungay. The water was still as can be.

"It's time, Savannah," he said, placing his hand on my shoulder.

"I know," I said, tears welling in my eyes, "I know."

Figgie patted the scar on Jungay's top fin and uttered a few phrases in his native tongue before diving into the surf.

"Take me with you," I whispered to Jungay, lying down on his forehead.

As the orcas set out under magnetic ambient light, he slid me gently into the water with his answer. I gripped the base of his top fin with one hand and paddled to stay afloat with the other.

And held on.

There was still so much more to I wanted to say to him, Derain, and Miah, whom I hardly knew. Jungay rolled his head out of the water, and I looked in his eye one last time. The withdrawing waves pulled me toward Jungay's world and farther from the mundane worries of my own. Then Jungay pulled back, creating the slightest bit of space between us and I knew our time together had come to an end.

I released my grip. My fingers glided off Jungay into the choppy water. The savage rage I had sensed from the bay only a few days before was gone.

The bay and all it held were at peace.

I stood in the chest-high water and watched the glowing horizon. My heart pounded faster with each inch Jungay's black sail slipped below the waves. When the surface of the bay was empty of his presence, I felt my heart drop like an anchor cut loose from its chain.

I stumbled on the long walk toward the sandy berm when Figgie ran down to help me to my feet. Soon the others followed until the six of us huddled together, staring out at the future as if it should begin like a kinetoscope.

We hugged without words, trying to hold on to the moment as the waves lapped at our feet.

WEST WIND REDUX

I stood alone where we had once stood together, the waves still lapping at my feet. The bay is as pristine and fresh as I remembered, but my memories are not. And yet returning here, the stories have unfurled much the way my long white hair drifts and blows in this warm offshore breeze.

Removed from world events at art school, I received a photo of Figgie in uniform. While his head had been shorn of its gorgeous flowing locks, that impish smile and those mischievous almond eyes showed he was still my Figgie. He joined the Fifteenth Battalion of the Australian Imperial Force, his horsemen skills making him a valuable asset.

At Uncle's request, Warrain had gone with him. Figgie was protecting his ancestors' home, he said, from the Central Powers and those men in that strange underwater ship we had chanced upon in the bay. Figgie landed at Gallipoli and died on the beach that very same day, as did the invincible Warrain. Although new city ordinances would never allow the three of them to meet on the streets of Paradise again, Captain Davenport died only a few feet away from Figgie and Warrain, defending an indefensible beach in an indefensible war.

I knew then what I know now. That Figgie's spirit is still part of the mountain we gazed upon that summer evening when we asked what the future would bring. Back then, he said if we were lucky, we would remain true to our child-selves. That same mountain still graces the horizon, still holds our spirits from that time. I vowed to protect it from ever changing or forgetting us. Every year I purchased a

little more of it, and every year I planted a blue fig tree in
his memory. Now there is quite a grove of trees on Figgie's
Mountain for anyone to enjoy, a quiet grove that acknowl-
edges the sacrifices made by Aboriginal soldiers who fought
in the Great War.

After I lost Figgie, it seemed that everything from that
time in my life began to disappear. Abe's son Benjamin went
to college and became a manufacturing engineer in the new
German Republic. Abe moved his family to follow his son,
and we wrote faithfully until the horrors began, after which
I never heard from them again. Lon made the National
Team that won the Sheffield Shield several times and opened
a restaurant in Melbourne called Lon's that his family still
owns.

Corowa, Kabam, Merinda, Tathra, and Ghera were destined for domestic service, but I couldn't let that happen to
my cobbers. I helped place them with art school friends and
paid them not to be servants as best I could. None of them
lived past the age of forty. When Uncle heard that Figgie and
Warrain had died, he left his hut and became an orca, taking
all his beautiful stories with him. Aiden was the last of the
Dawson's Station people to go. His granddaughter wrote that
he was dying from bone cancer and wanted to speak to me.
I visited him instead. He was thin and small, much as I had
recalled him to be.

"Tell me that it's true," he said weakly from his hospital
bed. "Tell me we really rode those whales the way I remember."

I reassured him we did and that he had performed splen-
didly.

"I've done so much in my life," he rasped, "but that was
the most incredible, the greatest thing to ever happen to me,
yet no one knows but us."

Paradise never reached its pre-storm heights of commerce.
When the orcas were gone the next morning, Bittermen

was the laughingstock of New South Wales. His scheme to bring hydroelectric power from the Snowy Mountains only brought scandal and was as flawed as his canal. By the end of the Great War, he had sold all his holdings and moved back to the States. By leaving, Jungay and the other orcas had saved the bay. Unwanted and unproductive, the bay remained intact, left to its own laws to thrive and nurture the future. Capable of great kindness and great cruelty, Arizona pushed me to define who I was. She lived a long and wealthy life. After she passed, her executors found she gave generously to the study of orca and human behavior.

Loch Bultarra is abandoned now, waiting to be reclaimed by the bay. The graves are weathered and unkempt. Before leaving for first-year art school (which I discovered that Ettie Richardson had partially paid for as my anonymous benefactor), I asked Papa to take a walk with me. He knew where I was going and let me take his hand and lead him there. We visited the graveyard together.

We stopped at Pop Alex and Nana Effie's stones as we made our way to Mum's grave. I finally opened the letter in her brooch. I'd been afraid of it for so long. I read it aloud, ending with this short and beautiful phrase: "Always live with charity in your heart and in a place to absorb the suffering of the world." Then I asked Papa to pin Mum's brooch on me and we cried and grieved over her grave. We did the same for Asa, Eli, and all the others too.

With the orcas gone, Papa took what little money there was from Bittermen's settlement and sold the shad, whaleboats, and equipment to buy a small two-mast caravel. He figured now that people didn't need whale oil, they might be interested in watching these graceful creatures and hearing old stories of the hunt. Papa rented out the empty bunks, saying rich people would pay a lot of money to pretend they're poor so why not help them out.

Mama-girl stayed on to cook for the guests, and it got so

that by my later visits, she gave up her room and just stayed with Papa. Charlie Brennan, who had survived the collapse of Pelican House, came to live out his last days at Loch Bultarra. Mama-girl said he spent hours every day talking to my drawings on the tool room wall.

Now faded to near nothingness, the raw passion of those crude drawings still startles me. How could anyone ever be that in love with the objects they were conceiving? Seeing all the old names—Derain, Matong, Burnum, Yindi, and little Kayle—makes me yearn to be with them once again.

Papa lived long enough to see Elvis gyrate on the telly, but wished he hadn't. That summer he flew with me to Japan for one of my exhibits. When the pilot announced we were flying over the volcano Mount Ontake, he squeezed my hand and kissed it. He now rests next to Mum and his kin, as he'd always wanted.

Though the night still cups a last bit of moon, the tide is coming in. A warm breeze is blowing from the west that will grow in intensity as the day takes hold. For now, I dabble my feet in the cool sand as I walk along the bar toward the open bay. Above, the Southern Lights create a cathedral ceiling of vaulted waves extending into infinity. A handful of small meteors slash orange darts across the shimmering green sky. Figgie had often told me that these streaks of light were unborn children coming to earth from their mother's Dreaming to deliver their birth totems.

Shadows dance atop the surf, drawing me into the bay. The warmth of its waters feels like an old glove fitting my hand. I don't see Jungay until he's almost on top of me. Knowing I can't jump on his back as I used to, he dips his top fin to the water and tenderly lifts me onto his back.

"Show-off," I say, patting his familiar scar. "Took you long enough."

I check my collar for Pop Alex's chock pin as Jungay leaps westward toward the heart of an unknown bay that I face with fear and anticipation. A bay that contains the Dreaming of all our ancestors and delivers us to oneness.

We are leaving on a wondrous journey. Me and Jungay.

Abbreviations, Foreign words & Phrases

Australian Lingo
    Akama (whale)
    Bailed up (stuck, in a jam)
    Bangers (sausages)
    Barney (talk)
    Berko (bad fight, berserk)
    Billy tea (homemade tea)
    Kelpie (an Australian sheep dog)
    Bolt-hole (a hideout or getaway place)
    Bonzer (excellent, first-rate)
    Brekkie (breakfast)
    Bringing the lollies (sarcasm for delivering good news)
    Buckley's chance (escaped convict, given no chance)
    Bunyip (mythical monster inhabiting waterways)
    Canberra (capital city of Australia)
    Central Powers (empires that fought with Germany in World War I)
    Choof off (turn away, snub someone)
    Chowder headed (stupid, dumb)
    Cobber (friend, mate)
    Coolamon (a long shallow serving dish)
    Croweater (someone from southern Australia)
    Dag (ill-mannered person)
    Damper (homemade bread)
    Derecho (fast, severe storm)
    Dinky di (honest, fair)
    Donah (female, girlfriend or sweetheart)
    Draughts (checkers)
    Duffy needs a map (Charles Duffy mapped most of Australia)
    Dunny (bathroom)

Earbashed (scolding or lectured)
Fair dinkum (genuine, real person)
Fizgig (flirting young woman)
Galah (a fool, clown)
Good oil (gossip, intel)
Good onya (sarcastic or sincere, sure no problem)
Happy as a Larry (giddy)
Hard yakka (a tough problem)
Hessian bag (burlap sandbag)
Hit your kick (pay for something)
Hooroo (fond goodbye)
In damned napkins (in trouble, a bind)
Jackaroos (sheep or cattle herders)
Jaw me down (overbearing person)
Larrikin (a big mouth or maverick)
Lubber (awkward fellow)
Lucky dip bag (similar a grab bag)
Nipper (little one)
Oakum (fiber from untwisting old rope)
Oikomiryou (drive hunt, creates a wall of underwater sound)
Pie floater (a meat pie in a bowl of pea soup)
Ridgy-didge (genuine, not false or pretentious)
Rippa (quite a story)
Salties (salt-water crocodiles)
Samhain (Gallic Halloween)
Sandgropers (workers from Western Australia also called "westies")
Scuttlebutt (gossip)
Seppo (slang for American)
Shebeen (an unlicensed public house or bar)
Starve the flaming lizards (disbelief)
Stockman's hobble (a leather strap used to keep animals in place)
Stone the crows (surprise, shock)

Strewth (shocked)

Strewth (surprise, or God's truth)

Stuff up (cause someone trouble)

Swaggies (laborers)

Tommy sauce (ketchup or tomato sauce)

Tucker (food, lunch pail)

Up a gum tree (in trouble)

Yobbo (a big mouth)

Nautical/Whaling Terms

A gam (talk or meeting)

Bible leaves (slices of blubber for the trypots)

Boat in the slings (wet the wood to stop leaks)

Bore tide (incoming and outgoing tide clashes causing a wave, very dangerous)

Caravel (agile two-masted ship)

Carpenter fish (sperm whale)

Catching crabs (poor rowing mechanics)

Chimney's afire (blood in a whale's spout, death was near)

Chock pin (kept harpoon rope from jumping out of its bow rut, worn as a trophy)

Cracklings (fried slices of blubber burned like wood)

Crying Bones (whale bones seeping oil)

Drift whale (dead whale)

Drifter (long fishing ship uses a drift net)

Duff (dough boiled in a bag)

Fetch (distance by wind or waves)

Fishy to the backbone (good leader)

Flensing (stripping the blubber from the whale carcass)

Hoy (small sloop-rigged ship)

In irons (or shackles, tied up, stopped)

Irons (harpoons)

Jack Nasty Face (cook's assistant)

Kid (a big stew pot)

Lay down oars (give up, submit to a higher authority)

Lee scuppers (plugs opened in a deck to let water run off)

Luff the sails (steer a sailboat closer to the wind)

Luffing through a squall (getting through a storm)

Needs must when the devil drives (you must fulfill your duty, job)

Oarsmen back water (slow the boat)

Point the bone (blame someone)

Refastening (getting ready for the season)

Sculls (oars)

Shad (a traditional fishing vessel with three masts)

Shaking a cloth in the wind (tipsy)

Stand by oars (stop rowing and lay your oar flat)

Swell your boats (get ready for whale season)

Toss oars (lift the oars from their locks and hold them straight up)

Tug hawser's cast (a heavy rope used to tie a ship dockside)

Unstayed mast (free spirit)

Whips and jingles (feeling queasy or hungover)

Yield palm (to concede)

Cultural Expressions

Anzac Day (Armistice Day, Jan 25)

Brumbies (wild horses found in Australia)

Chica bonita (a nice young girl)

Dash-fire (vigor, manliness)

Drags (kelp hooks, forks with handles)

Fluc (or top fluc is the bet that will pay out the most)

Game as Ned Kelly (willing try anything)

Kinetoscope (early motion-picture viewed through a peephole)

Kippah (Hebrew skullcap)

Longer than the Federation Drought (takes forever)

Neddies (horses)

Punt (a bet)

Quid (amount $1.25 US today)

Steeplechase (or jump's race, where horses leap hurdles)

Stone motherless (dead last)

Test team (major leagues for cricket)
The morbs (feeling depressed)
Time to pig down (find a place to stay)
Tommy Corrigan (famous nineteenth-cetury Australian jockey)
Übergeben Sie sofort (German, surrender at once)
Woop-woop (middle of nowhere)

ACKNOWLEDGEMENTS

To everyone I met at the Highlights Foundation, especially my mentor Amanda Jenkins who convinced me I belonged, I toss my oars in a fond and admiring salute. To all my workshop friends at A Public Space in Brooklyn, NY, keep sailing into the wind. For my magnanimous readers, the Wine Box Crew—Christine Alderman, Samika Swift, and Yolanda Ridge, a whaleboat of thanks to each of you. To my agent and fellow oarsperson Emily Williamson, you're as fair dinkum as they come, mate. And to Jaynie Royal, who kept a firm but gentle editor's hand on the wheel, and all those who work the deck at Regal House Publishing, my sincerest thanks and gratitude.